Elite: Wanted

Also by Gavin Deas from Gollancz:

Empires: Extraction
Empires: Infiltration

Also by Gavin Smith from Gollancz:

Veteran
War in Heaven

The Age of Scorpio
Quantum Mythology

Crysis: Escalation

Also by Stephen Deas from Gollancz:

The Adamantine Palace
King of the Crags
The Order of the Scales

The Black Mausoleum

The Thief-Taker's Apprentice
The Warlock's Shadow
The King's Assassin

Dragon Queen
The Splintered Gods
The Silver Kings

Writing as Nathan Hawke:

Gallow: The Crimson Shield
Gallow: Cold Redemption
Gallow: The Last Bastion

Elite: Wanted

GAVIN DEAS

GOLLANCZ

LONDON

First published in Great Britain in 2014 by Gollancz
An imprint of the Orion Publishing Group
Orion House, 5 Upper St Martin's Lane,
London WC2H 9EA
An Hachette UK Company

A CIP catalogue record for this book
is available from the British Library.

ISBN (Cased) 978 1 4732 0128 6

1 3 5 7 9 10 8 6 4 2

Typeset by GroupFMG within BookCloud

Printed in Great Britain by Clays Ltd, St Ives plc

The Orion Publishing Group's policy is to use papers
that are natural, renewable and recyclable products and
made from wood grown in sustainable forests. The logging
and manufacturing processes are expected to conform to
the environmental regulations of the country of origin.

www.stephendeas.com
www.gavingsmith.com
www.orionbooks.co.uk
www.gollancz.co.uk

In memory of the
three thousand and seventeen Cobras
we crashed

Chapter One

'Have you ever killed before?' The voice was little more than a low rumble. Ravindra stopped short as the massive fellow con − barrel-chested, red-bearded − stepped in front of her. He stood a little under six foot eight inches in his stained, white prison uniform. He reached down to touch the side of her face, her soft light brown skin. His hand was large and calloused.

Ravindra held his stare, looking up into hate-filled green eyes partially concealed under a heavy brow and thick red eyebrows. It was a stupid question. You didn't get sentenced to hard labour in the high security section of Warren Prison Mine on Ross 128 unless you'd done something really bad.

His name was Red and he was the daddy in cell block 214. She was new. She was weary to the point of exhaustion from the first few days of mining. Her muscles were agony, she was still shaking from the cold that had seeped through her flesh and into her very bones, or so it seemed, and her hands, despite the gloves, were little more than a bloodied mess of burst blisters. Ravindra and Red were standing in a mile-long tunnel, one of the abandoned mine shafts originally cut by huge robot mining vehicles. The tunnel had been turned into a cell block.

She didn't take her eyes off Red. She felt, rather than saw, people turn from her. Other prisoners. Some would be too frightened, others just deciding that it wasn't their business. It was the guards turning away that bothered her the most, though she wasn't all that surprised.

'I think you have,' Red rumbled.

Good call, Ravindra thought but remained quiet, seemingly impassive. She didn't want to give anything away.

1

'But I think you did it the easy way.' He gripped her face. The strength in his fingers suggested he could easily crush her skull if he wanted. 'I think you killed them from far away. The lazy way. I think there's no strength in you.' He tightened his grasp and pulled her up onto her tiptoes. It wouldn't have been difficult for him to lift her up but maybe he didn't want to bruise her skin. 'Do you want to do this the easy way as well? Or the hard?'

She let him see fear. It wasn't all faked.

'Easy,' she pleaded. 'Where?'

'Here,' he said letting her down onto the soles of her feet. 'So everyone knows what you are. Who you belong to.'

She looked around, apparently terrified.

'Please …' she begged.

'There is no—'

She palmed the flint-analogue-tipped shank and jammed it into his wrist, then she pushed it all the way up his arm to his arm pit. His eyes widened. He didn't scream. It was at this point that Ravindra knew this prison-cooked-steroid hulk was less than human; he was a monster. He shifted his grip. Massive, thick fingers wrapped nearly all the way around her throat. He lifted her a full two feet off the ground. Her vision filled with stars whilst simultaneously going dark as he cut off the blood and oxygen to her brain. She saw the vein bulging on his neck from pain and fury. At least she had a target. She jammed the shank into the vein. He didn't stop squeezing. Everything was going dark. She tore the shank out. The vein fountained red. The monster staggered back from her, clutching at the wound. Trying to stem the gush with his hand. Ravindra fell to the ground, nursing her near-crushed throat. She forced herself onto her feet despite her flickering vision, despite the light-headedness, despite a desperate wish to pass out. She tried to say something. It just came out a choking rattle. Red was still on his feet, staring at her as his life leaked through his fingers.

'Listen!' she finally managed. Red collapsed to the ground. Guards were sprinting towards them. 'Decide how many of you have to die

2

before I get left in peace!' Then the guards reached her. They beat her so hard with stun batons that she soiled herself.

'Mum!'

No! You can't be here! Ravindra thought. A moment of maternal panic as the confused boundaries between waking consciousness and dreaming memory merged. It was enough to make her sit bolt upright in her bed, drenched in sweat.

'What?' she asked blearily. She glanced out of the port-hole. They called them portholes. They were actually just transparent parts of the hull. They were still small because they cost more than non-transparent parts of the hull. She'd paid through the nose for a cabin with a porthole. She could see the stratified blues and whites of Motherlode below them. From their position in the upper atmosphere she was looking at the planetary horizon. Reddot was living up to its name. The red dwarf star was little more than a small ball of red light far in the distance. It always made her feel cold, looking at it. Even high in the mountains, Quince had seemed warmer, more immediate.

Whit's Station wasn't a space station, though everyone treated it as such until they were faced with the maintenance bills for the strain that multiple atmospheric re-entry put on a hull. It was the control centre of an automated hydrogen mining operation. Robots built to withstand the incredible pressures in the lower atmospheres harvested the hydrogen and delivered it back to the station. The station itself was, in fact, a huge mushroom-shaped aerostat.

So far out on the Frontier and close, in relative terms, to a number of resource-rich systems, Whit's Station would have been an easy target for pirates, claim jumpers and corporate raiders. So George Whit, entrepreneur and

3

founder of the station, had turned it into a Freeport. He'd supplied hydrogen to the pirates, the claim jumpers and the corporate raiders. He'd provided port and fuel to legitimate ships as well: explorers, surveyors and prospectors.

On a number of occasions during its hundred and fifty year history, corporate interests had tried to take Whit's Station over. Each time, there had been a loyal clientele prepared to fight them off. On one occasion, ships loyal to Whit's Station had even fought off a squadron of ships backed by the Empire. Ravindra had fought in that battle. It was during that fracas they had captured the *Song of Stone*. Yes, the Whit family had been clever. They'd ensured it was easier to work *with* them than to try to take over Whit's Station. And Ravindra had been given more reason than many to ensure that the Empire did not gain control.

The door to her cabin slid open and Ji looked down at his dishevelled mum. Ravindra had left the Warren Prison Mine pregnant. Everyone said that the seventeen-year-old Ji looked like a male version of her. There was nothing of his father in him. She had carried the stronger genes. Her owners and the gene clinics in Simpson Town on New America had made sure of that. He was tall, athletically slender, with dark hair that, at shoulder length, he kept much shorter than hers. They shared the same big brown eyes and high cheekbones that could make him appear either genuinely beautiful or very, very cruel, depending on the expression on his face. This morning the expression on his face was guarded. Seventeen years of maternal experience told Ravindra that this meant that Ji wanted something, something that she wasn't going to like.

But he just nodded at the comms light. 'Harlan's trying to reach you.'

4

She cursed herself. She'd cut off the comms link so she wouldn't be disturbed. She'd been up most of the night doing maintenance on the ship's only military-grade laser. Without an Imperial naval shipyard, and the proper parts, it was a struggle to keep the powerful weapon functional.

'All right,' she acknowledged. Ji didn't move. 'I'm going to need to take this privately.' Ji still didn't move. He looked as if he was trying to find a way to say something. 'You're much more likely to get what you want when I haven't just woken up with an important call waiting.'

He nodded and left the room.

'Privacy check,' she ordered. The cabin's expert system assured her that the call was fully security screened. 'Open call.' Part of the wall became a screen. A blinking red light in the corner of the screen told her that the call had the highest privacy and security rating possible.

Harlan Whit, great-grandson of George Whit, appeared on the screen. He wore a spotless white linen suit and was sitting behind a large wooden desk that he'd paid a fortune to import from Earth itself. Behind the desk was a very large porthole looking down on Motherlode.

Whit was a plump, balding man in his early fifties. His appearance was deceptive. He looked the epitome of softness, particularly out here where he was surrounded by hard frontiersmen and women. There was intelligence in his blue eyes, however, and Ravindra knew that he was perfectly capable of looking after himself with his fists, with knives and with firearms, and that he could make utterly ruthless decisions.

The Whit family made sure that their children grew up hard. They also instilled in them the value of loyalty and fair play – if for no other reason than out in the Frontier you *had* to be able to trust who you were dealing with, to a certain extent. If you crossed a Whit, however, it would end badly for you.

'You look like shit, young lady,' Harlan told her, grinning.

'Not so young anymore,' she said, smiling back. She knew that her hair was a mess, her eyes were still full of sleep and her sleeveless Jjagged Bbanner T-shirt was soaked in sweat.

'Bad night?'

She shrugged.

'Newman's in port.'

Ravindra cursed silently.

'You sure you want to get in bed with these people?'

'I'm sure I don't …'

'Look, I know I set this up, but you know who Newman works for. I can't protect you from them.'

She nodded. She knew the risks involved. 'Their reputation is for being harsh but fair.'

'No, their reputation is for going to any lengths to do exactly what they said they'd do. That's different.'

Ravindra sighed. She knew he was right. 'It's a big score, Harlan.'

'Enough to stop being an outlaw?' he asked smiling. It was what everyone talked about out here and nobody ever quite managed to do.

'Living the dream,' she said, smiling again. Then, more seriously, 'It's maybe enough for Ji …'

Harlan nodded. 'There's something else.'

'Yeah?' Ravindra asked wearily. She was pretty sure she wasn't going to like what was coming.

'Ji's been hanging around the *Magician*.'

Ravindra absorbed that for a moment before responding. 'Just so you know, I'm going to have a falling out with Captain Merkel,' she said.

6

Harlan nodded. 'Ain't none of my concern, man's a son-of-a-bitch as far as I'm concerned. I'll speak to you when you get back, okay?'

Ravindra nodded. The screen went blank.

Shit, she cursed. *They're here today*, and she had an argument with Ji to look forward to as well.

Ravindra had sent orders for the crew to assemble. She hadn't sent anything to Newman. She'd go and find him when she was ready. She'd showered, changed and put in her lenses.

Reddot was nominally in Alliance space – or rather, they had declared for the Alliance in a bid to avoid Imperial and Federation interference. The system wasn't quite resource rich enough, and the locals were just a little more trouble than they were worth, for either of the two big powers to make anything more than a token effort to try to control it. Being in Alliance space meant that her news feed mainly came from Frontier News. She had searches up for certain items from the main Imperial and Federation news organisations but the news could be anything from two days to more than a week old.

She walked into the kitchen, where the processor already had her concentrated-coffee-from-concentrate-beverage ready for her. It tasted foul but it was manufacturer-guaranteed to help her wake up. Ji was sitting at the breakfast bar, backlit by Motherlode through the kitchen porthole. His jaw was set, a look of defiance on his face. Ravindra pretended to ignore him as she searched the news feed playing on her contact lenses for anything of interest.

'Stay away from the *Magician*,' she said without looking at him. Trying to make it sound unimportant. Knowing that it wouldn't work.

'Okay,' Ji said. This surprised her so much that she looked over at him. 'Take me out with you. I know Newman's back.'

Her heart sank. It worried her that he even knew they were working together. She wondered who else knew who shouldn't.

'Don't be ridiculous …' she started.

'*You* were working when you were sixteen—' he began.

Her anger was like a flash-fire. She prided herself on rationality but it often went out the window in the face of her only child.

'And I was in prison at eighteen! I didn't have any choice!' she shouted at him. 'You're not coming out with me. Worrying about you could get me and the rest of the crew killed!'

'Captain Merkel—' Ji started.

'Merkel is a glory boy idiot who's going to be dead soon! He's an amateur, a wannabe! He doesn't have the slightest idea of what he's doing!'

'If you won't—'

She was across the small kitchen and had grabbed him out of the chair and slammed him against the external bulkhead next to the porthole before she even knew she was doing it. 'Stay away from Merkel!' she screamed at him. He tried to push her away but she'd locked him down tight.

'Let go of me! It's good enough for you … Why isn't it good enough for me?' He was struggling, trying to escape her armbar.

'Because I want something better for you!'

'As a station rat?' He stopped struggling as the anger drained from his face. Ravindra found herself looking at the face of a cold and distant stranger. 'We had a chance at another life. We could have been far away from here a long time ago. Why didn't you sell the *Song* when you took her?'

8

Because she's my ship, Ravindra thought. She let go of him. He pushed past her.

'You can't stop me doing what I want to do!' he screamed at her on his way out of the kitchen.

Good parenting, she told herself angrily, as she heard the door to the two-bedroom cabin slide shut. She was never going to be able to get across just how frightened she was for him – and all the time.

'Merkel.' It was rude enough to walk uninvited into the berth of another ship. It was even ruder to not address another captain or pilot by his title. But if Merkel was offended he didn't let it show.

Merkel was a handsome man, a little younger than her. His short, spiky blond hair was styled by the only saloon on the station. His deep blue eyes and his smile, full of white ivory, were very disarming and had gone a long way to make him extremely popular among certain men and women. He was wearing the closest thing to up-to-date fashion that the Frontier could offer. Probably the results of his last sloppy score, Ravindra thought.

'Captain Khanguire,' Merkel said, smiling, his hands open in welcome as he came out from under the shadow of the *Magician,* a heavily modified Cobra Mk. III.

The rest of Merkel's crew seemed a little more suspicious of Ravindra's presence in their docking berth. Ravindra didn't break step as she punched Merkel in the stomach with her right fist; as he started to double over, she brought her left fist up into his chin and then followed that up with her elbow in one swift action. He staggered back. She drew the burst pistol on her left hip and hit him in the face with it twice. His nose broke and blood squirted onto his face. He went sprawling over a packing crate.

9

The two men on Merkel's crew started towards the pair of them while the the third, a woman, reached for a shotgun. Ravindra drew her right hand burst pistol and pointed it in their direction. A crosshair appeared on her lenses showing where the bullets would hit if she started firing.

'You might get me in a rush, but he'll die.' She put the barrel of the left hand burst pistol against Merkel's lips. 'And I reckon I kill two of you before you get me.' The *Magician*'s crew stopped moving. She pushed the burst pistol hard, chipping several of Merkel's teeth, until she had forced half the barrel into his mouth. 'Convince me that you're going to have nothing more to do with my son.'

When Ravindra quit the *Magician*'s docking berth she was breathing hard. It hadn't been the imminence of gunplay that bothered her – she was furious with Merkel. She had wanted to hurt him, maybe even kill him. She was walking the curving corridor that ran around the station connecting the docking berths when she saw four figures approaching her.

This is just what I need, Ravindra thought. She recognised the lead figure, a nondescript man with a goatee, and salt and pepper hair. His name was McCauley and he captained the *Scalpel*. They were a professional crew who took down big, dangerous scores, and were the only crew reputed to be colder and more ruthless than the *Song of Stone*'s. Ravindra had always had the feeling that McCauley disliked her, though she had never been able to work out why.

McCauley's glare as he went by made Ravindra's hands move instinctively closer to her pistols. When the four man crew of the *Scalpel* had passed she glanced back at them. McCauley was looking over his shoulder at her, still glaring.

* * *

10

Ravindra was sitting in a 'coffee' bar stripping down and cleaning blood and saliva off one of her burst pistols when Newman found her. He had the compact, powerful but not massive frame that she had come to expect from ex-military types. His hair was cut short, close to the scalp, and he was attractive in an average sort of way. Ravindra wasn't quite sure how old he was, though she suspected he was close to her age. He was dressed conservatively but his dark coloured, utilitarian, multi-pocket trousers, his jacket and his boots all screamed ex-military. She couldn't make out where he was concealing weaponry, but she was sure he was. So far he'd been courteous and very professional and he would be doing the most difficult part of the job. All of this appealed to Ravindra. But something about Newman's strangely colourless eyes felt wrong.

Ravindra didn't know a great deal about his background. There were stories that he was either ex-Federation special forces, or one of the Emperor's own elite, genetically enhanced, clone soldiers. Now, however, he worked for very different masters.

Newman glanced down at the burst pistol, his expression devoid of emotion.

'Everything okay, Captain Khanguire?' he enquired.

'Fine,' she told him, looking up as she rapidly reassembled the burst pistol. 'Now?'

He nodded.

'I'd prefer more time.'

'We've done enough sims. It'll be fine, though I respect your commitment to preparation.'

She held up her right fist. Her personal computer took the form of a simple steel band around her middle finger. She bumped fists with Newman, touching his own ring computer. The final details of the plan were transferred to her securely. She saw the file appear in her lenses as a blinking icon in the lower right side of her vision.

'You're clear on the plan?' Newman asked.

'Yes,' Ravindra said. Part of her was irritated and part was gratified at the question.

'And your crew?'

She nodded. Newman turned to leave.

'Captain Newman?'

He stopped and looked back.

'I am aware of your background. I want this nice and smooth. No unnecessary grief.' Ravindra spoke calmly.

Newman smiled. The smile didn't quite make it to his eyes.

'Don't worry, Captain, we've done this before.' Then he left. Ravindra noticed another man and a woman, similarly dressed, fall in behind him.

Ravindra walked into the docking berth. The sleek form of the *Song of Stone* still took her breath away. The smooth, rounded lines added to her stealth signature. The nacelles gave her an edge in both speed and manoeuvrability. The *Song* had started life as a Cutter in the service of the Empire. It had been one of the ships that had come to claim the Reddot system. At the time Ravindra had been piloting an old Cobra Mk. II. The cutter was the faster, more manoeuvrable ship and had carried a lot more firepower but Ravindra had out-flown the Empire's pilot. Of course she had – the *Song*'s original pilot hadn't been genetically modified to be the best slave pilot the genetechs in Simpson Town could create by manipulating an unborn foetus. The other benefit of using an Imperial Cutter was that anything they did tended to be blamed on Imperial privateers.

They had renamed the ship the *Song of Stone*. It was named

for the think-tank that she had joined in the Warren Prison Complex. The think-tank had consisted of her current crew and had been run by Marvin Dane. Marvin had been captain of the *Song* before Ravindra, taking it over after the battle. He had been killed on a station in the Tiolce system by a bounty hunter. Ravindra still missed him.

The think-tank had been put together for two reasons only. They wanted to use their skill sets to become rich; and they were never, ever, going back to Ross 128. That was why, even though the bounty hunter had had the drop on Marvin, he hadn't surrendered.

Ravindra walked up the ramp and into the ship. Like anything Imperial the inside was comfortable, bordering on the plush, though it looked a little worn now. She walked down the corridor towards the bridge. The data from the ship's last diagnostic ran down her vision in a cascade. Everything was running well within parameters but she wanted to see more systems, particularly manoeuvring and weapons, running at optimum. She had decided a long time ago that this was what made the difference between this ship and her crew, and wannabe disasters-waiting-to-happen like Merkel.

She walked onto the bridge. The other four were waiting for her.

'Harnack?' she asked instead of saying good morning. Harnack was one half of the weapons team. He was responsible for the military laser. He was a small wiry man with a goatee. Ravindra knew that he seemed very serious unless you knew him well. He had served with the Gurkhas, a well-respected ground-force regiment within the Federation, a regiment with a very long history.

'I've simmed it. The cyclic rate seems good and it's holding power fine according to the diagnostics …'

'But?'

'I'd like to test it.'

'I suspect that Harlan would be less than pleased if we blew a hole in the side of his station,' Jenny said. Jennifer Storrow, on first glance, had looked an even more obvious victim than Ravindra in the Warren Prison Mine. But unlike Ravindra, the small thin woman – with short hair that changed colour every time they docked – had avoided bad things happening to her by being fast, quick-witted, funny and *very* useful. 'Besides, *I* did the upgrades. When has something that I've done not worked?' She was the *Song*'s engineer. As far as Ravindra could tell, Jenny had grown up on various tramp freighters throughout the Frontier. If she had a family she never spoke of it, though she seemed to know someone on every station they had ever visited.

'Your long string of unhappy relationships?' Jonty Davis suggested. He was the other half of the weapons crew and Harnack's lover. That the pair thought the rest of the crew didn't know about this was a little naïve, in Ravindra's opinion. She knew she was going to have to do something about it, as relationships between the crewmembers broke Dane's Law. On the other hand, she had been telling herself that she had to do something about it for eighteen months, ever since Marvin had died.

Jonty was tall and slender, which wasn't ideal for some of the gees they pulled in manoeuvres, but he survived. His hair was long and silver in colour, and even Ravindra had to admit that he was very, very pretty. His beauty was enhanced by the fact that he was a goldskin. He had grown up in Federation space on Matto, a planet in the Bedaho system where an indigenous symbiotic creature turned all the inhabitants' skins gold.

14

Jenny threw an obscene hand gesture Jonty's way. Jonty blew her a kiss in return.

'Okay, pack it in,' Orla told them. Orla was the oldest member of the crew. She had known Dane before they had both been sent to Ross 128. Ravindra was pretty sure that they had been lovers even after they had gotten out of the Warren, whatever Dane's Law had said. She was a solidly built woman of frontier-asteroid mining stock. Her long, brown hair was always tied back in a ponytail. Orla handled comms, navigation, electronic security and sensors. Ravindra was still not sure why Orla wasn't captain of the *Song*. Ravindra suspected it was because she cared too much. Orla had been the maternal figure in the Warren. She and Dane had protected and cared for the others when the predators had come. Ravindra, by contrast, was utterly ruthless. Orla was effectively first mate, as she'd been when Dane had been in charge. Since Pilot Ravindra had been voted in as captain, Orla had backed her every step of the way.

Ravindra sat in the high-backed chair and spun it to face the others, who were already sat and strapped at their stations. She touched the arm of the acceleration couch, transferring the data Newman had given her to the ship's systems. The others received the file almost instantly.

'Final details – we've run the sims, we know the score. I know we're flying by the seat of our pants more than we'd normally like but we've been out before. Any problems, I want to hear them now.'

'These people?' Orla asked.

'Newman seems to know what he's doing but yes, we're in bed with scum and we don't want to screw things up. We will not be making a habit of this, even if we did decide it was worth it for this score,' Ravindra replied.

15

'Just out of interest, could we get out of this if we wanted to?' Jonty asked.

Ravindra sighed inwardly.

'We agreed to do this, and it would be very difficult to back out now. Is that what you want to do?'

'No,' Jonty said, shaking his head. 'Just wanted to know exactly where we stand.'

'Whit's Station control has given us clearance for departure,' Orla told them all.

'Okay, let's get out of this atmosphere. I feel heavy,' Ravindra said. She raised her hands from the seat and the holographic control gloves shimmered into life around them. The information in her lenses told her that the internal doors to the docking berth had been sealed. The atmosphere was rapidly being evacuated. With a flick of her fingers she started the music as the rest of the crew went about their assigned tasks. Bach's 'Air on the G-String' started playing in the background as the doors opened in front of them. Motherlode was a curved plane filling half the view through the entirely transparent front of the bridge. The top half of their view was black and filled with stars.

Ravindra moved them to hover and brought the landing struts up so smoothly that they barely felt it. The nose of the *Song of Stone* dipped forward slightly, as though bowing, and then moved swiftly out into Motherlode's turbulent atmosphere. Ravindra triggered the manoeuvring engines, a three-quarter burn upwards. She swung the *Song* around one-hundred-and-eighty degrees. They raced up past Whit's Station and were almost immediately shrouded in a nimbus of flame. The gees forced them back into their acceleration couches, which did their best to compensate for the pressure. Ravindra didn't want to risk turning her neck too sharply at that moment so she moved her fingers in the

16

holographic control glove and a small window appeared in her vision. She could see the sleek, wedge-shaped lines of the Mk. III Cobra keeping pace with her. It was the most familiar shape in space, the most common craft, workhorse of the trade routes and the first ship that most pilots ever owned. She had flown many herself, though Newman's had been heavily modified. It was optimised for combat and boarding actions.

Stars stopped being fractal lines and became dots of light again as they dropped out of hyperspace in a burst of light.

'Running active scans harsh enough to give them cancer,' Orla muttered. Ravindra double-checked the coordinates and then found herself searching the blackness ahead of them while she waited for the result of the active scans. The Cobra appeared next to them. If the other ship had a name – and all ships should have a name in Ravindra's opinion – then she hadn't been made aware of it. But she was impressed with the piloting. Newman's pilot was holding it perfectly in formation despite the jump.

'Found it,' Orla said.

Her lenses projected the coordinates directly into Ravindra's vision. Her fingers moved slightly and the *Song of Stone* banked and went after the target ship at full burn. All of them were pushed back into their acceleration couches. The Cobra was barely a millisecond behind.

'She's running,' Orla told them.

'Juicing the manoeuvring drive,' Jenny told them.

'Missiles on standby,' Jonty said. He would wait until they had closed before triggering them.

'Fly the black flag,' Ravindra told them.

Orla moved her fingers slightly and a small data-packet was sent to the other ship. If they opened it they would see a red screen with an animated hourglass on it. The animation would show that they were rapidly running out of time.

'They're broadcasting a distress …' Orla said. 'Jamming.'

Harsh light drew a red line in space between the *Song* and the other craft as Harnack fired the military grade laser again and again, whittling down their target's shield. Ravindra could only just make out the glow of the other vessel's engines.

They closed with the other craft rapidly. Two missiles shot past the bridge, their engines burning brightly, moving at gees that would have pulped a living being.

'I hope you didn't go overboard,' Harnack managed through teeth gritted due to the acceleration.

'Me too,' Jonty said. Ravindra didn't like how unsure he sounded. They did not want to destroy the ship.

The missile payloads blossomed in light and force and were almost immediately snuffed out by vacuum, but not before they'd done their damage. There was more harsh red light as Harnack fired the military laser again.

'Their shields are down,' Orla told them.

'It's an Orca,' Jenny said. 'I've highlighted the manoeuvring engines, the jump drive, comms and weapons on the specs.'

'Targeting,' Harnack said. This time he fired the beam laser. Using the military laser against an unshielded craft would probably destroy it. Ravindra was aware of Newman's Cobra firing its beam laser as well. They were close enough to make out the beleaguered ship now. It was a once luxurious, sleek, elegant, finned, mostly transparent, multi-level yacht, a plaything of the super rich. Now it was a burnt, partially destroyed, near-wreck. There was at least one hull breach in one of the transparent areas of the upper hull. Ravindra guessed one of the missiles had done it. She was less than pleased.

The *Stone*'s shield lit up as it took multiple hits from the Orca's defensive pulse laser. Ravindra banked sharply. You couldn't dodge something moving at the speed of light but you could move erratically enough to avoid civilian-grade targeting systems. The Cobra fired its beam laser again and destroyed the Orca's pulse. Harnack had targeted the Orca's jump drive first, to stop it running, then the comms, which Orla and the Cobra had been jamming since the moment they had arrived in system. Now he was removing the yacht's ability to manoeuvre, though it would continue on its current trajectory at its current velocity.

'Prepare to be boarded,' Orla transmitted to the other ship. Her voice would be received disguised. It would have the whining accent of someone from Capital in the Achenar system, the Empire's home world. 'Make this easy on us and nobody will get hurt. Any resistance will result in your deaths and we get what we want anyway.' Orla finished the transmission and ignored the counter-threats, not even bothering to play them to the rest of the crew.

'Anyone get killed in the breach?' Jenny asked.

Orla drew patterns in light with her hologramatic control gloves, giving commands to the ship's scanners.

Ravindra was still annoyed with the excessive violence as she brought the *Song* into overwatch position above the Orca. She had no problem with killing but it upped the stakes and tended to complicate things.

'Locking missiles on,' Jonty said. It was a warning, letting the Orca know that they meant business. Harnack would keep the rest of the weapons free to deal with any other external threats.

'If they lost anyone in the breach then I can't find them amongst the debris,' Orla told Jenny. 'I'm scanning enough

19

people on board to suggest a full crew, passengers and a security detail.'

'Let's hope that they're not stupid enough to fight,' Jenny muttered. Ravindra silently agreed with the engineer.

The Cobra banked down past the *Song* and came alongside the Orca. They watched as the Cobra matched speed and then extended its docking arm,

'They're in,' Orla said moments later.

'What were they doing out here?' Jenny wondered out loud.

'Payload exchange,' Jonty guessed.

'Yeah, but what?'

'Yacht like that, the owner's got to be a collector,' Jonty suggested. 'I'm thinking alien artefact.'

'Okay, that's enough speculation,' Ravindra said. She glanced across at Orla. Normally her first mate would have cracked down on such chatter while Ravindra concentrated on flying. She did not like the look on Orla's face.

'What's wrong?' Ravindra asked. Then a flash below her caught her eye. They were about hundred metres over the stern of the Orca. The flash had come from inside the yacht.

'Gunfire,' Harnack said. There were more flashes from inside the yacht.

Orla moved her hands and the live feed from Newman's comms came over the bridge's speakers. Gunfire drowned out all other sounds for a moment, then they heard the screaming and the sobbing.

'We've given you what you want … please—' a man begged, then there was a long scream that tapered into choking sobs.

Ravindra swallowed hard.

'That's not for me. You, all of you, you're for me.' It

was Newman's voice. Everyone except Orla turned to look at Ravindra.

'Nothing's changed,' she told them. 'Orla, tell that sick bastard to get back on his ship right now.'

'Newman, if you've got the payload then we are leaving, you understand me?' Orla said over the comms link. She was answered by more gunfire.

A blinking icon appeared in Ravindra's vision. Jonty was asking permission to arm a very particular weapon.

'Arm it,' she told him. 'You drop it on my command only.'

Jonty's fingers moved within his holographic control glove.

'Patch me through,' Ravindra told Orla, who did so. 'Newman, make sure everyone's dead and get back on your fucking ship right now.'

'You'll do what you're paid for, do you understand me?' Newman said calmly over the comms link. There was more gunfire and screaming in the background.

'Listen to me, we're not leaving any evidence or witnesses behind, do you understand?' It was a direct threat. Piracy was one thing. Multiple murder was another. Right now it didn't matter if some of the passengers and the crew on the Orca were dead, or all of them – legally speaking. It did matter in terms of evidence collection and witness statements, however.

'Understood,' Newman said. Even across the comms link she could hear his begrudging tone.

They waited tensely for what seemed like a very long time, but in actuality it was only a few minutes. Then they saw the Cobra detach from the yacht. Orla was shaking her head.

'What?' Ravindra asked. The first mate pointed. Three lifepods shot away from the yacht. 'The fools. Jonty, drop it.'

Ravindra moved her fingers, preparing for a hard burn. It was Newman and his crew's hard luck if they couldn't keep up.

'E-bomb gone,' Jonty said.

Acceleration slammed all of them back into their chairs. Behind them energy connected all matter in what looked like an electrical display. Behind them space whited out, and the force of the exploding energy bomb buffeted the *Song* as it destroyed everything.

They had just blown more than half the profit they were likely to get from this job by dropping the E-bomb. Ravindra was mostly disappointed to see the Cobra make it out of the blast radius. She was a little relieved as well. It had the payload on board, after all.

Chapter Two

Ziva rammed the throttle wide open and threw the Fer-de-Lance into a tight spin, spitting out countermeasures in a classic tesseract pattern. Her wingman, a second Fer-de-Lance, shot between the incoming missiles and her countermeasure bloom, adding to the confusion, but it didn't make a difference. The Cobra Mk. III was still coming at her. Somehow it had shot all four of her missiles before they'd burst and scattered their warheads and now the Cobra was firing steadily at her with frightening accuracy. Whatever software it was running was unreal and she wanted it.

The second Fer-de-Lance twisted away. He always did that. 'Turn and take him head on you weasel,' she muttered.

A lucky shot from the Cobra punched a hole through the crystal titanium skin over the Fer-de-Lance's port engine. Several cubic centimetres of ablative armour vaporised and took most of the laser's sting, but not quite enough. Even at this range, the beam of the Cobra's military laser was still needle thin. The last vestiges stabbed into the engine's heart and wrecked a power relay no bigger than a thumbnail. A magnetic containment field, already strained to breaking point by Ziva's frantic manoeuvring, collapsed and raw plasma at eight million Kelvin erupted through the port engine, scouring everything. Damage control cut in at once, raising a magnetic shield and deflecting the plasma outward. The starboard engine started adjusting to compensate but it wasn't fast enough. The rogue plasma burst out of the ship, kicking it sideways, rupturing the port engine cowling as it went. The kick was hard, hard enough that it almost knocked Ziva out. The ship started to tumble, frantically dumping heat from the engines and ruining Ziva's perfect countermeasure tesseract.

Before she could do a thing about it, the two chasing missiles arrived milliseconds apart. Their proximity fuses triggered and both warheads burst around her into a scatter of pinhead-sized anti-hydrogen mines. Invisible and lethal. Two seconds later, the first mine hit and the Fer-de-Lance bloomed in a blaze of energy. Overwhelmed shields collapsed and the ship, missiles and mines exploded together with the gamma-flash of a dying star. That was the thing about the Fer-de-Lance: it was a true thoroughbred of a ship, but with so much performance crammed into such a tight envelope that it didn't have the backups and built-in redundancy of the more robust Cobra. Too many single points of failure.

The other Fer-de-Lance frantically ejected countermeasures of its own and darted behind the radiation burst that had once been Ziva's ship. Its fusion plume flared as the pilot floored the throttle to get away. He turned and ran. The follow-up salvo of missiles from the pursuing Cobra fused on the decoys.

Ziva crashed out of the simulation and slammed the flight panel of the *Dragon Queen* in disgust. 'Fuck! Again!'

'Would you like to try one more time?' The *Dragon Queen* was offering her a restart. Ziva took two deep breaths, considered it and then shook her head; the simulation obediently shut down and the stars of deep space filled her vision once more. The *Dragon Queen* was a Fer-de-Lance too. She wasn't the same model as the one from the

24

simulation, not even much like it under the skin, not with a hundred years of technical evolution between them, but that wasn't the point. The Fer-de-Lance was then, was now, and always would be *the* best long-range interceptor ever built. There was no way that any generation of Cobra should out-fight one, certainly not two of them and *certainly* not when *she* was one of the pilots. In the right hands there simply wasn't a better ship, never had been and never would be. Yet every time she ran the simulation of Jameson's last recorded engagement, he beat her. Yes, by then he was a legend, one of the Elite, the great name of the Pilots' Federation back when they'd been so absurdly picky about who they let in. There were probably only about six people across known space in those days who'd *really* made it to the elite council ...

She stopped herself. Took a deep breath. It rankled, that was all, being consistently beaten by a dead man. This had been Jameson's last jump. It was a mystery what had happened to him after he'd been ambushed by the two glory-hunters in their shiny new Fer-de-Lances. They hadn't taken him, that much was sure, but no one knew where he'd gone after that. His flight profile had shown him heading back to Lave but he'd never arrived. Bounced out of hyperspace by Thargoids, some said. Caught in a worm-hole, said others. Just had enough and vanished, perhaps. Ziva thought the last was the most likely. He'd had nothing left to prove, credits coming out of his ears, and it must have grated after a while, idiots picking fights everywhere he went just because of who he was.

Speaking of which ...

She took another deep breath. She was putting it off, that's what it was. That was why she'd had so much sim-time over the last two days. Putting off the choice she had to make. Somewhere within a few dozen light-years was the pirate she only knew as Newman. Newman had a nice fat bounty on his head, nice enough to get the *Dragon Queen* through the service she was due. Then Ziva could see a man in Darkes Hollow about getting the storage capacitors on the ship's twin X-ray lasers tweaked up; and *then* she'd finally be able to make full use of the black market mil-spec power circuits the two weird women had traded her in Eta Cassiopeiae a few months back. It had been one of those don't ask, don't tell back door transactions, although given the presence of the Federation Navy training facilities, it was more a case of which ship they'd been stolen from rather than whether they'd been stolen at all. She'd known that and she'd still bought them.

Even after all that, Newman's bounty would still leave enough over for a few months down-time to sort her shit out with Enaya.

The thought made her check her k-cast messages again. Micro-jumping played havoc with every piece of communications equipment she'd ever met but she hadn't missed much this time. Another very polite message from Radall Martic Holdings raising their offer of corporate sponsorship to two hundred credits per solar day plus all fuel, service and repair bills, inviting her to come and discuss freelancing for their *Federation's Most Dangerous* show. *Federation's Most Dangerous* was syndicated across pushing a hundred worlds now and Radall Martic had half a dozen bounty hunters commissioned to it, some of the best. From what Ziva had picked up, the show paid a lot better than the bounties they pulled in for it. She even watched it sometimes – checking out the competition.

The other message was from Enaya. Another one. Ziva had been tracking Newman for weeks now and his trail had gone cold. She'd been gone too long and Enaya's messages were getting irritable. *I miss you, Ziv. When are you coming back? I need to talk to you about Aisha. You still haven't caught Newman? How much longer?* En kept trying to call her when she was jumping from system to system or micro-jumping across them and Ziva hadn't replied for more than a day. Which made her a shit and a coward and she knew it, but what was there to say? *I miss you too, but I lost him and I don't know how much longer I'm going to be.* Somehow that didn't seem enough. En would smile as she always did. She'd talk a lot about her daughter Aisha and try to hide the disappointment and the anger, but she wouldn't manage to keep it at bay, not quite. The latest message was more of the same, along with a tirade about how Aisha's on-off junkie boyfriend was back, the galaxy's biggest shithead. It had started a year ago and ended with En threatening to call the police on him if he ever came near Aisha again. Six months later he turned up on the doorstep when Enaya was out. He'd told Aisha that he'd made a mistake, that he was clean, that she was all he wanted, now and forever. He had a knack for it, for turning Aisha's world on its head, and for about three weeks he'd been all that mattered again. But sure enough the drugs crept back. It had been Blast the first time but the second time he'd been pushing Antimatter too. Enaya had found out, she and Aisha had had a cataclysmic row and the shithead boyfriend got himself banned. Ziva had taken Aisha up to orbit in the *Dragon Queen* afterwards, trying to take her mind somewhere else, but she still remembered Aisha's face. Aisha had pretended it was all okay but it very obviously wasn't. She was like her mother that way.

Odar. That was his name. Odar Something. Odar Shit-for-brains, and she knew from one extremely unfortunate experience that when you stripped him down to bare skin there really wasn't very much there. *I'll track him down if you want me to*, she'd said to En afterwards. *I'll hunt him and I'll find him and see where he goes and make sure he never bothers Aisha again*. En hadn't said a word.

'I'm picking up breaking news from the Adamantine Palace,' murmured the *Dragon Queen*. The voice simulation Ziva had it running was a deep syrupy baritone, mellifluous and soothing in a fatherly sort of way. Enaya would have been all over her about the psychology of that voice, but Enaya had never heard it. Enaya didn't want anything to do with the *Dragon Queen* and the life Ziva lived inside her. *I don't want to know*, she always said. *I just wish you'd stop*.

Ziva cut the engines and let herself drift weightless. 'They got any bounties up?'

The *Dragon Queen* brought up the list. A dozen Point of Principles, the fifty- and hundred-credit bounties put up by the Federation for parole-breakers, bail-jumpers and busted non-transit orders – the petty criminals scumming at the very bottom of the food chain, the sort of bounties that didn't cover their own costs and didn't get hunted without some additional reason. At the other end you had ships like the Imperial privateer the *Red Hourglass*; and right at the top, the Veils of the Judas Syndicate, the kingpins of the most secretive and insidious organised crime syndicates in human space. A quarter of a million if you brought one in but no one ever had. The Syndicate made it abundantly clear that any bounty hunters who came after them would gain their full and fatal attention. The Syndicate would do it, too, no matter how it hurt them. The Veils' pride in fulfilling their promises matched even their murderous greed for credits.

'Go on, then. What's this news from the Palace?'

28

'It's breaking from the Pilots' Federation. They've got a ship missing and a k-cast distress beacon. Looks like an Imperial ship down in the Stopover system.'

Ziva's thoughts of Enaya vanished. Newman? 'How close? One jump?'

'One jump.'

And she was just sitting there, fuelled and ready to go right out on the edge of La Rochelle's gravity well. 'Anyone closer?'

The *Dragon Queen* purred. 'No one registered.'

That was that then.

'Take us there.'

The *Dragon Queen* turned gently, twisting on yaw and pitch thrusters before starting the stuttering series of micro-jumps out to La Rochelle's Kuiper belt and the jump to the Stopover system. The journey wasn't all that long but it was long enough to run the simulation one more time. As usual, Jameson beat her.

Stopover was one of those systems where lots of ships came to visit but no one ever stayed. There wasn't much there, just a tight binary of stars whose tidal gravity had been enough to chew up any rocky inner planets long before the first amino-acids of life had evolved on Earth. There were two distant gas giants orbiting so far out that the stars were little more than bright points of light, which made them an excellent stop for skimmers fuelling up between jumps to Delta Pavonis, Epsilon Indi, Barnard's Star, 61 Cygni, Ross 154 or Formalhaut. With so many populous systems nearby, Stopover had grown the way such systems often did; whispers among the free traders of a good place to skim that spread slowly into the corporate shipping world just a little less quickly than they had reached the pirates and freebooters and bounty hunters who took to lying in wait. After losing a dozen or so Anacondas and Pythons, the corporations got pissy enough to pay Darkwater – always and forever the Federation's favourite private military contractor – to station a corvette in the system. And then Darkwater had done what they always did: built a station and started charging everyone who wanted to use it. To Ziva's mind, it pretty much amounted to demanding protection money. It worked out well enough for the corporations who paid a monthly tariff, but the free traders hated it. The Pilots' Federation had always had a thing about Darkwater. The other corporate security groups too, but Darkwater in particular had a name for being dicks.

The *Dragon Queen* got the usual ping as soon as she arrived: a twenty credit 'voluntary charge' for using the facilities covered under Darkwater's protection. Ziva, who'd been flying solo for fifteen years and flew a ship armed with lasers, shields and engines all tuned to better specs than Darkwater knew how to spell, tended to tell them to fuck off; or rather, she told the *Dragon Queen* to tell them to fuck off and the *Dragon Queen* offered something more polite and waved her bounty hunter licence at them. Sometimes it worked, sometimes it didn't. Sometimes she skimmed free fuel in peace and quiet, sometimes she played hide-and-seek in the gas giant's upper atmosphere with a wing of irritable Vipers. They had a kind of unofficial game and they'd done it enough times that they all knew the rules: if they ever got a lock on her while she skimmed, she paid. If they didn't then they let her be the next time she came through.

'Pay it,' she told the *Dragon Queen*. This time was different. 'And remind them who we are.' Someone had stiffed a freighter under Darkwater's nose. Took some balls to do that and Darkwater were going to be pissy as a swarm of angry wasps about it. The sort of pissy that usually came with a nice fat bounty and she wasn't about to queer her pitch for that over a meagre twenty credits.

It didn't take long for someone from the Darkwater station to avatar onto her bridge either, a full hologram rendering. A commander, by the flash on his shoulder. Not some flunky but one of the station's senior officers. Could even be the watch officer. The hologram wasn't *him*, of course – that wasn't how Darkwater worked. No faces. Instead it was a complex algorithm that generated the illusion of a generic person. In this way, everyone from Darkwater looked roughly the same.

'Didn't take you long,' said the illusion sourly.

'I'm good at what I do,' shrugged Ziva. 'You got my credentials?'

'We've had them for a long time, Eschel.'

Ziva watched as the illusion looked her over – not, since it was an illusion, that that meant anything.

'You know the deal – first come, first served. The opening bounty has been set at ten thousand credits, but that's likely to rise. First respondent gets twenty-four hours before we open it up. You're flagged, though. You were a bit too damn quick for my liking.'

Which meant they'd lodged a query with the Pilots' Federation indicating her possible involvement in the attack, and it would stick to her like a dark cloud until they took it away again. 'Flagged? Fuck off!'

'Get the scum who did this, Eschel, and we'll clear it. Unless you'd like to come and work for us. Corporate are setting up their own show against *Federation's Most Wanted*.'

Ziva's eyes narrowed. The avatar was an illusion and its expression conveyed nothing, but there was something in the voice … 'Do I know you?'

'You've been through here enough times, Eschel. We all know you're trouble.' The illusion had hesitated, though, which as good as told her that she did. She racked her memory for anyone from Darkwater she might have pissed off. It was a long list. Then a grin spread over her face.

'I *do* know you! You're that Viper pilot! The one who took a pot-shot!' That had been five years ago and she remembered what fun she'd had playing with him after-wards, sitting right on his arse for twenty solid minutes through rings and around moons and in and out of the gas giant atmosphere, keeping a lock on him no matter what he did. 'Still sore because they made you apologise, or is it just because you know I'm the better pilot? I made it up to you.'

'Yeah, if by that you mean you let me pay for you to get steaming drunk. You're still flagged, Eschel.'

'I was quick because I'm already after someone. He's near.' She sent Newman's history across. 'So how about you double your bounty and drop your flag before I shove it up your arse?'

'How about I send a dozen Vipers to bring you in?'

'If you think you can, Darkwater. I flew Vipers for five years before I turned private so I might feel sentimental and let you keep a few. And of course, I do have enough fuel to jump straight back to La Rochelle if I feel like it; then maybe I might flag you right back for being a clusterfuck of shit-eating butt-plugs and we can see who else turns up to take your bounty. Corporate are setting up against *Federation's Most Wanted*? How long do you reckon it'll be between me putting the news absolutely everywhere and a hunter sponsored by Radall Martic coming this way and making you look as stupid as they can? Hey – maybe they might send two or three and make a Christmas Special out of it.'

The illusion hesitated again. 'You're bluffing, Eschel.'

Which she had been, right until he said that. She shrugged and told the *Dragon Queen* to turn about.

'Eschel! Wait! There were two ships. What they did was beyond the pale. Fifteen thousand for each captain. Not the ships, Eschel, the people. We're not the Pilots' Federation here. Another thousand for each crewman you bring in.'

Ziva stopped the *Dragon Queen*. 'Two ships? How big?'

'One corvette or cutter size, one smaller. We don't know.'

'You don't *know*? Where did they go?'

'We don't know that either.'

Ziva burst out laughing. 'You didn't get a trace on their trail after they jumped out? I hope whoever got bounced out there didn't pay their twenty credits or you're going to be looking at a very embarrassing compensation suit.'

The algorithm behind the illusion managed to look annoyed and abashed at the same time. It sighed. 'The victim was an Orca, the *Pandora*. She stayed right at the edge of the system. Barely on our sensors at all. I'd say she was there for a rendezvous and got bounced before anyone else showed. They weren't waiting for her, but they jumped in seconds later and right at the same place. They threw up jamming everywhere and all we have is what the Orca got off before they shut her down. After that we don't know. So: two ships, one corvette or cutter size, one smaller, no identity, no distinguishing marks except they knew what they were doing. They did whatever they did and then blew everything to pieces. We saw the explosion from here. By the time we got Vipers that far out, the hyperspace trails were cold. I'd say they knew perfectly well we couldn't get out there fast enough. Eschel, there weren't any survivors. They executed the crew who stayed on board and E-bombed the escape pods. All of them. Whoever did it was one cold bastard.'

'They E-bombed the escape pods? Christ!'

'Quite.'

'Could be my guy. He's clinical but he's a got a big streak of psycho going with it.'

'I don't care whether he's your guy or not, they're both your guys now. Fifteen thousand for each of them, Eschel, if you can bring them in and keep it quiet. They pissed in our yard.'

Over the next few hours, Ziva angled the *Dragon Queen* in to the nearer of the two gas giants. The Fer-de-Lance skimmed hydrogen until the ship's tanks were full. The auto-pilot could manage that perfectly well all on its own, so she reviewed what Darkwater had on the *Pandora* and her demise. It wasn't much more than the avatar had said. Private yacht, not a trader, so they had no idea what she might have been carrying. By the time the Vipers started recovering what fragments were left of the Orca, the *Dragon Queen* was already micro-jumping to the edge of the system. As expected, the Orca's black box told her precisely nothing: two ships had come in out of hyperspace running the sort of generic tran-sponders that could have been picked up anywhere, retro-engineered with black code that anyone with even the most basic connections could have fixed up. What was much more interesting was the precision of the attack. They'd hit the Orca hard and fast but only with enough to take down its shields. Then precision hits to the drives and the engines and the defensive lasers. They'd been *careful*, as though trying not to do more damage than they absolutely had to. There weren't that many crews who'd take down a freighter in a Darkwater system and whoever had done it here had known exactly what they were doing and how to do it.

She listened to the flight recording. 'Make this easy on us and nobody will get hurt. Any resistance will result in your deaths and we get what we want anyway.' The voice had the whining accent of someone from Imperial Achenar, not that that meant anything. And then they'd boarded and rounded everyone up and done whatever they'd come to do and then, before they left, they'd started beating the crew and the passengers, wilfully shooting them. It was hard to say from the audio and there was almost no surviving video, but the cries and pleading for mercy were more than enough, gunshots, more screams, swearing and shouting as though the boarders had cut down their prisoners, torturing and killing for the fun of it.

And then it stopped suddenly and they shot everyone; only they didn't quite, because after they left, three escape pods had launched. And then the E-bomb.

Ziva listened to the recordings again and shuddered. The killings had a brutality and a touch of madness to them that could have been Newman but the precision of the attack … that had a touch of someone else. Newman had a partner now? Or maybe she was chasing up a blind alley and it wasn't him at all. *Who are you?*

The *Dragon Queen* jumped and jumped again, hopping through the relative civilisation of Barnard's Star to Pethes. Pethes was one of those places where the general values of the Federation had kicked off and spiralled in the sort of unfortunate way that made the Empire point and laugh – a fractured almost-anarchy of vaguely hostile corporate enclaves and faux-democracies where nothing much had any value and credits were everything. The sort of place where no one asked too many questions about the laser scorches on your ship's hull and why you needed your ablative shields replaced or where that cargo of exotic exploding pigs had come from. But whoever had taken out the *Pandora* wouldn't come openly to Pethes. Darkwater would have their spies here; in fact, in a world like this, they probably had their own enclave where they quietly did all the sorts of things that more civilised systems wouldn't tolerate. But Newman had come here on and off in the last few months. It had been Ziva's next port of call anyway, looking to pick up his trail.

For some reason there was a Federation Farragut battle-cruiser in system today. Ziva micro-jumped in and took manual control of the *Dragon Queen*, skimming the cruiser's length carefully just outside its exclusion range. It was a thing of function rather than beauty, she thought, but you didn't get to see one up close all that often. They were very roughly the shape of an arrowhead, if you could say that about something that was two klicks from nose to tail. She took it from the bows, rolling and weaving and jinking along the length of it but veering away from the cowled engines hidden away behind their massive flat slabs of metal. You didn't get too close to something that could light up a fusion torch a hundred kilometres long whenever it felt like it. As she flew loops around the cruiser, she scanned the news feeds but couldn't gauge much of a reason for it being there. Maybe it had come to put the shits up the various local corporate dictators and presidents-for-life. The Federation did that sort of thing now and then to remind systems like Pethes that there was a wider galaxy out there and that they did, sometimes, pay attention.

Newman wouldn't be here. Not with that cruiser. No matter.

Buzzing a Farragut wasn't as much fun as buzzing an Imperial Majestic Interdictor. With the Majestics you could dive right through that rotating ring they had in the middle, although they did tend to get *really* pissy about that sort of thing. Just as well that a Fer-de-Lance was about the only ship that could outrun a squadron of Imperial fighters; still, eventually even the Farragut got annoyed and sent an irritable avatar and a squadron of F63 Condors to shoo her away. She fought the urge to play with the Condors for a bit and set the *Dragon Queen* heading for Toad Hall, the only decent orbital station in the system, launching a series of avatars ahead of her to start searching for Newman's contacts and poke around her own network of information junkies, sleaze-merchants and dirt-mongers. Not that she expected any of them to know anything about the *Pandora*. Whoever had set that up was far too smart.

'You have a k-cast,' drawled the *Dragon Queen*.

'Go.' Darkwater, she supposed, with more information from Stopover; except it wasn't, it was Enaya.

'Ziva! Love! Where are you?'

For a second, Ziva froze. 'Enaya. Um … I'm in Pethes just now. I'm … I'm still after Newman.' She waited a few seconds but Enaya didn't reply. The k-cast signal strengthened enough that she started to get pieces of low-grade grainy video, jerky and broken up. 'God! You look terrible.'

'It's been …' Enaya looked away and it was a moment before she looked back. 'It's Aisha, not me. I told you Odar the shithead was back, didn't I? … It's … Ziv, I've been trying to get hold of you for days. You never answer. Why don't you ever answer?'

'En, you know how it is. I've micro-jumped from one end of a dozen systems to the other. You know how that screws everything up.' Which was true enough but didn't explain why she hadn't replied. 'It's just … ah, En, I don't know what to say. This guy, I should have had him two weeks ago and I missed him and now he's all over the place and I know it's—'

'You could say you're coming home, Ziv.' Enaya cut her off. 'You could say you're sorry you didn't come home when

37

you promised, just like you didn't the last three times. I need you here. I don't know what to do. Aisha needs you.'

Ziva scoffed. 'Aisha doesn't need *me*. She hates me.'

'No, Ziv. She just knows that you won't put up with her shit the way I do. She's so … Oh, Ziv, you don't know how it is with her. And that … that *man*. She's talking about going away with him and I don't know how to stop her. She's sixteen, Ziv, that's all. Sixteen! And he's six years older and … You know what he's like. I found this out only yesterday: he's already been in prison!'

'I know, En. I checked him, remember?'

'And you didn't tell me?'

'He was gone, En. I didn't think …'

'I don't know what to do, Ziv. I need you to help me with this. I can't do it on my own.'

'I …' Ziva closed her eyes and took a deep breath. 'I can't, En. Not yet. Not now. Look, as soon as I've got Newman, I'll come. I promise. But I've got to get this guy. He's a—'

'I don't care what he is.'

'I got flagged, En.'

'And what's that supposed to mean?'

'It means I've got to clear this one or I might not work again.'

For a moment the video cleaned up and Enaya was looking right back at her in crystal clarity. Ziva stared, struck by how beautiful En could be. That was why they'd fallen for each other five years ago. Ziv was a skinny, scrawny fireball with a manic energy that was exactly the same now as it had been thirty years ago when she'd hit her teens, with all the strength and fortitude Enaya wished she had but didn't. And the only thing that had ever made Ziva pause was staring at En, because no one could be that statuesque. Even now, En still had that magic. She was a genetic throwback, almost pure Persian. Most people assumed she'd had chromosome therapy or been cosmetically tailored pre-birth on some back-water black-market genetic chop-shop, the sort of places that hived out in the asteroid belts in systems like Pethes and powered down and prayed every time a Federation battlecruiser came past. But Enaya was natural. There might have been some in-breeding somewhere in her past but Ziva didn't ask and didn't care. She was what she was – however she got that way – gorgeous and beautiful and a wonderful lover.

'Is that it? Is that all you've got to say?' asked Enaya.

Ziva jerked back from her memories. 'Don't you get it, En? I might not work again. I might have to sell the *Dragon Queen*.' She wouldn't, though. She wouldn't ever do that.

'Good,' snapped Enaya. 'That would be good. I'd like that. You don't need to do this, Ziv. Not anymore. We could go to Alioth and Andbephi. I always wanted to see places like that. Places where the universe shows us its colossal beauty. We could surf the chromosphere of a Canum Venaticorum variable binary and skim hydrogen all the way from one star to the next. We could find our own Delta Scuti and bathe in its wax and wane. We could see the attack ships on fire off the shoulder of Orion or whatever it is. Together. I remember, Ziv, all these things you said you wanted. We could take Aisha with us. We could go to Earth …

'He's going to ruin her, Ziv. He's going to get her into all sorts of terrible things.'

Ziva bit her lip. Thank fuck for crappy k-cast bandwidths and shitty video. 'I got to go,' she whispered. She broke the link before En had a chance to see how her eyes glistened.

39

She'd been thinking, after buzzing the battlecruiser, that she might leave the *Dragon Queen* in dock and spend an evening carousing some of Toad Hall's bars, checking for names in person. It never hurt to put in an appearance in the flesh – it was a large part of what she did and what she was, and how she'd picked up the reputation and the bounties that she had. Bar full of macho space-pirates showing off their tattoos and new bicep enhancements and in walks a skinny bounty hunter woman hardly an inch over five foot tall. They used to laugh at her and, truth was, half the men in a place like that could have snapped her in half if they ever got their hands on her. That was the trick, though. There were smarter things a canny bounty hunter could do to sharpen themselves and Ziva had a quickness and coordination that had given her the nickname Blink Dog. Here and there some people swore she could literally teleport.

She sighed. Enaya had crushed any sense of excitement she'd had. Now she just wanted to get it over with, wipe away the shit-stains who E-bombed escape pods just to cover their tracks and then go back to En and Ay, kick that wanker Odar Something into the chromosphere of the nearest star and tell En that everything would be better now. Make a whole load of promises that she'd mean to keep right up until the next itch got her and a big bounty twitched across the *Dragon Queen*'s antennae.

She left the avatars to their work after she docked and quietly got drunk, alone in the *Dragon Queen*'s cockpit, bouncing lazily around in the false microgravity of the station's core. She had a stash of Glen Halyconia smuggled from New Caledonia by a bounty she'd taken six months ago. She barely remembered his name now. Lanky white-skinned male. A pussy-cat and certainly not worth the price

40

someone had put on him, not that she cared. They wanted him for smuggling. He'd dumped his cargo of Scotch and she'd picked it up and handed it back.

Most of it, but not all. It had taken her a month to go through the first bottle. Three months ago it had become a bottle every week. At this rate, give her another three months and it would be one every day. Just as well she only had a dozen left.

Shit. Her head was starting to spin. She wrapped her hands across her face. Closed her eyes. She might even have fallen asleep. Just floating.

'Captain Eschel!' The *Dragon Queen* was speaking to her. As soon as Ziva moved and opened her eyes, it went smoothly on. 'An avatar has reported back with a lead on the information you were seeking.'

Ziva tried to focus. 'Newman? And?'

'A station maintenance supervisor claims to know who Newman is working for but he won't pass it on except to you in person.'

Who Newman was working for? The second ship? Ziva rolled her head on her shoulders. She was drunk and felt sick and slightly hungover but that wasn't a problem. She pulled a needle of Purge out of her pocket and stabbed it into her arm. It took a few seconds and then the hangover and the haze of the Scotch started to drain away. You could actually feel it happen, watch your own thoughts sharpen up again.

Oh damn and she'd done it again, jabbed herself with Purge in the cockpit. 'Shit! Water!' She pushed herself sharply out of the pilot's couch and shot down the corridor. Nice thing about micro-gravity: with a bit of practice you could get about real quick. Useful for those times when you suddenly *really* needed a piss and then to drink two litres of water because, for example, you'd shot yourself with Purge without thinking.

By the time she left the *Dragon Queen,* she was as sharp as a knife. Tight leather, tight jeans, tight boots, pockets everywhere, belt, bandoleer, two holstered guns – worn openly. In part it was a matter of being practical and not wanting anything to float off or catch on anything in the low-gravity parts of the station. In a larger part it was what people expected when the Blink Dog came by. Whoever this maintenance supervisor was, he surely had a certain anticipation of what he was going to see.

Chapter Three

'So?' Ravindra had unlocked her high-backed pilot's chair and turned to face the rest of the crew. Debussy played softly in the background. Outside the stars were smears of light as the ship traversed hyperspace. They had made a series of jumps, laying a false trail.

There was a lot of shifting and nobody was looking at her. She wondered how much of that was down to her order to kill a number of innocent people. Only Harnack looked her straight in the eyes.

'Newman's going to screw us,' the ex-Gurkha told her. She thought about this, a grimace on her face.

'Yes, he really is, isn't he?' she finally said.

'Shit!' Jonty spat. 'Why did we get in bed with these people?' he demanded angrily.

Jenny looked scared, but Orla seemed as impassive as ever.

'We talked this out and voted,' Orla reminded him. 'There's not much point in whining about it now.'

'Catharsis?' Jonty suggested.

'That doesn't matter,' Ravindra said quietly. 'The question is, what do we do now?'

'Realistically, what are our options?' Harnack asked, though it was more thinking out loud.

'We run,' Jenny suggested.

'Can you run from the Judas Syndicate?' Jonty asked. 'They're everywhere. Anyone could be a Veil.'

'For all we know you're one,' Jenny said, smiling weakly.

'Surely Ravindra's the criminal mastermind?' Jonty replied, also smiling, easing the tension just a little bit.

'We run,' Ravindra said. 'We don't go back to Whit's Station, we sell the ship, new identities, reconstructive surgery and we go our separate ways. Who we are now dies.'

'What about Ji?' Harnack asked.

Ravindra swallowed but tried very hard to show no outward reaction to the question, despite how her stomach was churning.

'There are contingencies,' she told them evenly. Contingencies that meant she never saw her son again. She had left enough money with Harlan Whit, along with instructions. She trusted the station boss to do the right thing. It wasn't a coincidence that they had settled down on Whit's Station.

'Ravindra—' Orla started.

'I said it's sorted,' Ravindra said, cutting Orla off.

'So we spend the rest of our days looking over our shoulders?' Jonty asked. Ravindra nodded. The rest of the crew went quiet as they thought about this.

'Is it just us he's going to screw over?' Jenny asked.

'You mean is he going to screw the Syndicate as well, sweetheart?' Jonty asked. Jenny nodded. Her hands moved in the holographic control gloves as she did busy work to distract herself. 'We're a lot easier to rip off than they are.'

'Are we?' Ravindra asked. Jonty looked a little taken aback.

'Well, yes.'

'We're easier,' Harnack said. 'But we are not a push-over crew. There are a lot easier crews to rip off than us.'

'We're assuming that he is going to rip us off,' Jonty said. Everyone turned to look at him sceptically. 'Just trying to stay positive,' he muttered.

'Look at what he did on the Orca,' Ravindra said. She reached for a bulb of water adhered to the control board, knocking it free. It spun up in the zero G, drops of condensation whirling away from it. She caught the bulb and took a drink from it.

'He's a sick bastard,' Jenny said.

'He's a crazy bastard,' Harnack added. Ravindra nodded. 'So if he's messed up in the head enough to do that …?'

'Then he might be crazy enough to rip off the Syndicate,' Jonty finished.

'That doesn't help,' Jenny said. 'The Syndicate still doesn't get what they want and we'll be in the frame for it.'

'He could be following the Syndicate's orders. If he screws us, I mean,' Harnack said. 'They get what they want and save some money.'

'Do that often enough and people won't work with them,' Orla commented.

'That depends on whether or not anybody finds out, and the spin you put on it, darling,' Jonty muttered.

'The Syndicate always do what they say they will, no matter what,' Ravindra pointed out.

'So we run?' Jenny said, looking less than happy about the idea. They were all looking at Ravindra. She alone had somebody she cared about she would be leaving behind.

'This is what we agreed,' Orla said. 'We don't do the stupid stuff that gets the others caught. We've made enough money. We had a good long run and we got away with a lot.'

'Except that Newman's a threat,' Harnack said. Jonty intimated his agreement.

'No witnesses,' Jenny said coldly. 'Leaving witnesses behind is part of the stupid shit that would get us caught.

Also, we deal with him, get the payload – we can still square this with the Judas Syndicate.'

'That's a lot of ifs,' Ravindra said. 'And you know the rumours – he's some kind of ex-military, special forces, with a crew of similar.'

'We have our own skills' Harnack said.

'And if we're running I don't want to leave that sick bastard in my six,' Jonty said. Jenny obviously agreed.

'Orla?' Ravindra asked. Orla seemed lost in thought.

'I don't like the options. We go to the rendezvous. It's a risk, but everything we do is a risk.'

'Okay,' Ravindra said. 'Harnack, you're up.'

'What do you think you're doing?' Newman demanded. He sounded like he was trying hard to keep a rein on his anger.

Ravindra was bringing them in low over the ice asteroid they had agreed on as their primary rendezvous point. Frozen, ugly, it was shaped like an elongated potato. They had come in low, using fissures and contours in the ancient, crystal-clear surface as cover. They had popped up over the nearby horizon, a range of jagged ice hills, and Jonty had put a missile lock on the waiting Cobra. That was when she had received the angry message from Newman.

'We don't like how it went down—' Orla said across the comms.

'*You* don't like?' Newman demanded, interrupting. Now that he wasn't getting things his way, now that she knew what to look for, Ravindra could hear it in his voice. Newman clearly wasn't as mentally well as their initial meetings had led her to believe. 'The E-bomb almost took us out! What were you thinking, you amateur bitch? Take the lock off now!'

46

'This goes down smoothly and you don't need to worry about the lock,' Orla told him. 'Any messing around and we just take you out.'

'Look, nothing—' Newman started. Orla cut the link. Ravindra brought the *Song of Stone* to a stop hovering over the small plateau of ice that Newman's Cobra had anchored itself to. She knew that, as well as the missile lock, Harnack would have the lasers targeting the Cobra.

'What have we got?' Ravindra asked. Sensor information from Orla's scans started appearing in her lenses. It showed a three-dimensional, topographical image of the surrounding landscape. There were two roughly person-shaped heat ghosts lying in overwatch positions overlooking the wedge-shaped Cobra's position.

'They're good. Their thermal signatures are well shielded and they're camouflaged; I almost missed them.'

'Snipers?' Ravindra asked.

'At least one of them will be,' Harnack said. 'The second one could have a support weapon.'

'And there's no guarantee I found everyone,' Orla said.

'Give them a chance,' Ravindra instructed as her hands moved slightly, working the manoeuvring engines, keeping them in place. Newman was still shouting when Orla reopened the comms.

'Newman … Newman … Shut up. We've got two heat signatures, both a little more than a klick from your position. Want to pull them back in?'

'I don't know what you're talking about!' Newman declared.

'Sure?' Orla asked.

'Of course I'm sure' Newman said. Orla cut the comms link.

'This guy's a moron,' she muttered and looked over at Ravindra.

47

'Do it,' Ravindra said.

Port and starboard pulse lasers fired. The least accurate and powerful of their laser weapons, they were more than enough to turn two ten-metre radiuses of ice into steam. The steam almost instantly re-froze, creating multi-trunk tree-like structures of ice rising up from the surface of the asteroid. Some of the ice was red.

'He seems angry,' Orla said. She hadn't bothered putting Newman's ranting over the loudspeakers. She would handle comms now. She didn't want to distract the rest of the crew.

'We should take him from here,' Jonty said. 'Cut our losses.'

'Jonty,' Harnack said softly to his lover, 'we agreed that we were going in to get the payload and confirm a kill on Newman.'

'Quiet,' Orla told a furious Newman over the comms. 'You said they weren't yours, we took you at your word. No more pissing about. We're going to come down, get our pay and then we don't ever have to have anything to do with each other again. Mess around and everyone dies, understood?' Orla listened to Newman's reply. 'Okay, we're on,' she told the rest of the crew.

'You think he realises we're playing a zero sum game?' Jenny wondered.

'I don't think empathy's his thing,' Jonty muttered.

'Tell him he delivers our money,' Ravindra said. Orla nodded and repeated the instruction.

'He wants to see you as well,' Orla said.

Of course he does, Ravindra thought as she brought the ship into land.

The loading ramp airlock's inner doors slid shut behind them. The air cycling out of the airlock made them sway in their armoured spacesuits. The monomolecular hooks on the griphook soles of their suits kept them solidly anchored to the loading bay ramp in the asteroid's microgravity.

'Ready?' Harnack asked. Ravindra and Jenny nodded. Affirmatives came across the secure comms link from Jonty and Orla.

'Lower the docking ramp,' Ravindra told the ship. Harnack knelt down, the griphook kneepad on his space suit adhering to the ramp. Ravindra and Jenny stood to either side of him. All three of them were holding their EM carbines ready. Crosshairs appeared in their vision, either on the heads-up display on the helmets themselves, or, in Ravindra's case, on her lenses.

There were five of them positioned in a rough semi-circle around the Cobra's ramp. Ravindra was reasonably sure that it was Newman in the centre of the five. Four of them had carbines levelled at the *Song*'s crew. Ravindra was gratified to see that they were only lasers. There was a reason her crew carried EM carbines. Jenny, Harnack and Ravindra brought their own guns up. The targeting systems showed them the best places to point them. The ice all around them glowed deep blue, reflecting the landing lights of both ships.

'I thought you were professionals. Where's the trust gone?' Newman asked. He *was* the man stood in the middle, his hands behind his back.

Harnack stayed kneeling on the loading ramp. Ravindra and Jenny edged down, carbines snug against their shoulders, and then moved to either side of the ramp.

'Professionalism includes torturing the passengers on the yacht?' Jenny demanded. Ravindra cursed the engineer. There would be no closure here. No point in discussing it.

'What about the ones you killed in the escape pods? I'm not sure you're in a position to morally judge me.'

49

'Just give us our credit packs and we'll be on our way,' Ravindra said through gritted teeth. Even in Alliance space all electronic financial transactions could be traced. The best way to move around large amounts of credits unnoticed was using credit packs. They were little more than specialised, secure, electronic storage devices.

'You killed two of my people—' Newman said angrily.

'We gave you a chance …' Jenny pointed out fiercely.

'The E-bomb nearly killed all of us.'

'We had to clean up your—' Jenny started.

'Are we doing this?' Ravindra demanded, cutting the engineer off.

'I think you need to—' Newman began to shout.

'Now,' Ravindra said.

It was difficult to say what happened first, though Ravindra knew the order of events. The night turned an angry hot red as the *Song*'s military laser punched a hole through the Cobra's armoured hull and the Cutter's pulse lasers fired. Two of the five mercenaries in front of them just became so much red steam, which then instantly refroze into root-like, red ice sculptures. Black score marks appeared on the front of the Cobra.

Then everything in front of them turned into glittering silver as Orla fired all the front-facing reflective chaff launchers. The return fire from the Cobra's pulse laser batteries was refracted into so much red light and heat. Ravindra's suit's expert systems transmitted warning icons to her lenses as it partially melted. She ignored them and moved forwards firing, the griphook soles of her suit keeping her adhered to the ice.

Harnack fired the underslung grenade launcher on his EM carbine. The recoil rocked him back but the griphook pads kept him on the loading ramp, the suit's servos compensating and returning him to a firing position.

The grenade shot through the glittering silver rain of anti-laser chaff and exploded in the hail of ice fragments. Newman's remaining mercs were thrown into the air and bounced off the underside of the Cobra. The targeting systems on Ravindra's EM carbine tried to compensate as she followed one of the bouncing figures, firing short burst after short burst of needle-like, electromagnetically powered, low calibre rounds at the merc. The needles hit home, penetrating the suit's armour, destroying its integrity, letting vacuum in and ripping into the man's flesh.

Ravindra glanced around through the chaff, which was rapidly floating away at its initial launch velocity. Newman was nowhere to be seen. He'd been Harnack's job, but Harnack's bio readout on her lenses had flat-lined. She risked a glance behind her. Harnack was still adhered to the loading ramp, but it looked as if he was swaying in an invisible wind. The visor on his suit had been smashed. There was something that looked not unlike a red bonsai tree growing from the hole in his visor, where leaking blood had flash-frozen.

Refracted red light filled her vision and she felt heat on the side of her helmet. They'd missed a sniper. Somewhere out on the ice one of Newman's people had a powerful longlaser and was targeting them through the thinning chaff. Worse, Newman had made it back into the Cobra.

'Sniper on the ice, starboard,' Ravindra said over the secure comms link. 'Jenny, Newman made it back to the Cobra.' She knelt down, aiming the carbine out into the ice. Jenny ran across in front of her, and Ravindra raised the carbine as she passed. Any moment now the Cobra's pulse lasers would have a clear targeting solution through the chaff, and she and Jenny would be nothing more than a cloud of red steam.

There was another flash of red and part of Jenny's armour glowed. It looked as if smoke was pouring off it, but the smoke was actually particles of superheated carbon being blown off the suit's armour. It was enough. Ravindra had seen the beam. The carbine's targeting systems interpreted the visual data from Ravindra's lenses. Ravindra triggered long burst after long burst, suppressing the area where the shot had come from. At the same time, she sent the targeting information to the *Song*.

'Rav, get out of there,' Jonty called urgently over the comms link. Ravindra started running towards Newman's Cobra. The *Song*'s pulse laser started firing. The ice to the starboard of the cutter exploded upwards in geysers of steam, which subsequently refroze into a beautiful, glittering, and structurally fragile wall of ice.

Behind her, too, something similar was happening, as the Cobra's pulse laser tried to target her through what was left of the chaff. Her world was red. She could feel the heat through her suit. Armour plate was starting to run like melted toffee. She was aware of, rather than saw, the *Song*'s military laser stabbing out into the Cobra until the other ship's pulse lasers stopped firing.

Ravindra made it to the Cobra's loading ramp. She could feel the ship shift underneath her. Jenny was holding a thermal cord frame charge in her left hand, her EM carbine at port in her right. She adhered the frame charge to the inner airlock door the moment its assembly program had finished. Behind and beneath them the loading ramp was rising and closing to form the external airlock seal.

'They're rabbiting,' Ravindra said over the comms link. A moment later she felt the Cobra judder as the ice shook. The *Song* had just vertically launched a missile. Ravindra and Jenny stood either side of the frame charge and Jenny sent the detonation sequence. The thermal cord glowed white hot and part of the inner airlock door turned to molten metal as the cutting charge burned a large rectangular hole in it. They felt the unmistakable sensation of a ship taking off as the Cobra left the ice asteroid.

'Through!' Jenny shouted over the comms link.

Ravindra delivered a suit-servo assisted kick to the rectangular piece of blast door. It slid out with a clang onto the cargo bay floor and then fell forwards. The edges of the hole were still glowing bright white. Jenny was already diving through, firing a fragmentation grenade from the underslung grenade launcher to clear the Cobra's cargo bay. The recoil kick on the grenade launcher was almost enough to halt her forwards momentum in the microgravity. Ravindra fired the underslung grenade launcher on her carbine. The recoil bounced her back, the suit servos compensated for a degree and the griphook soles kept her anchored. Then she dived forwards following Jenny. Someone fired a grenade at them from inside the cargo bay. One of the incoming grenades clipped her, sending her spinning, as it flew into the airlock compartment. Even through her armoured suit she felt the burning heat as the spin made her leg contact the white molten metal edge of the newly cut hole. Then all four grenades went off.

Because they had been in freefall, the first of the concussion waves from the two fragmentation grenades they'd fired kicked them about, bouncing them off walls and the ceiling. Shrapnel embedded itself in their suits' armour. Then the two grenades in the airlock went off. The airlock contained most of the explosion, but it didn't stop them from getting another battering.

Ravindra triggered the magnetic element of the griphook soles and shot up to the corner of the roof and the wall, one foot on each. She had a moment to take in the cargo bay. It was the usual large open space – rails running along the roof, connections for winches and containers. Empty tool shelves ran up either side. The far door, the one that led into the crew compartment and bridge of the Cobra, was sliding shut.

The two mercenaries left in the cargo bay were starting to recover. Their armoured suits were a mess; Ravindra was pretty sure that one of them was no longer functioning. They were trying to bring their laser carbines to bear on the two intruders who would have no reflective chaff to help them this time.

There was a strobing burst of red light. Ravindra screamed as her skin burnt, even through the insulating layers of the suit. One of the ceramic plates on the front of her suit turned red for a moment and then superheated and exploded. She brought the EM carbine up and fired another grenade, the recoil throwing her back into the ceiling. It hadn't been her best shot, but it was a trick that Harnack had taught her. Hundreds of razor sharp flechettes burst from the grenade launcher's muzzle and spread out. You only had to be so accurate when you fired the equivalent of a thirty-millimetre shotgun cartridge loaded with armour piercing needles. She caught the merc who had been firing at her. He staggered back. She saw his visor crack but not break. She steadied herself, moved the EM carbine until the crosshairs settled on his visor, fired a short burst, adjusted her aim, fired again, adjusted her aim, and fired again. Blood and bits of helmet went flying away from the merc in slow motion in the micro-gravity. He went windmilling backwards, but his magnetic boots kept him anchored to the deck.

Jenny had anchored herself to the floor and was firing at the other merc, who was using a small, square crate as cover.

'Brace,' Orla said over the comms. Ravindra triggered the magnetic application on the griphook pads on her knees and elbows and tried to flatten herself against the roof.

The missile had been forced to take a circuitous route above and around to hit the Cobra's main thrusters at the rear of the ship. The impact forced the rear of the craft downwards towards the asteroid. Even attached to the superstructure, Jenny and Ravindra received a thorough battering – both of them would be black and blue, Ravindra had chipped a tooth and felt like passing out. Ravindra, with a pilot's instincts, was pretty sure that the Cobra was in a spin.

The other merc was floating free. The impact had torn him off the deck, his magnetic boots notwithstanding. Something about his posture told Ravindra that his neck was broken.

'Double tap,' Ravindra told Jenny. The engineer climbed groggily to her feet and advanced, firing two bursts of electromagnetically propelled rounds into the last merc's face through his visor.

Ravindra kicked off from the ceiling and floated down to the deck. Just as her magnetics attached themselves to the hull there was another impact, this one considerably less hard. Ravindra guessed that the Cobra had spun round and bounced off the asteroid.

They moved up to the internal door.

'Is that the payload?' Jenny asked, meaning the square crate. It seemed likely. It was the only thing in the cargo bay. The door was closed and locked. Jenny sent an override signal through her suit's comms and the door slid open. Ravindra stepped into the interior of the Cobra checking all around her, the EM carbine's barrel moving where she looked. They were in a narrow stairwell. Bare narrow steps led up, though there was room for crew to pull themselves up in the zero G. She and Jenny moved up the steps and found themselves in the crew quarters. There were eight bunks attached to the floor and the walls, and everything was neatly packed away – necessary in the zero G environment. It was empty, but they could see through into the Cobra's bridge/cockpit. There was a woman silhouetted in the doorway to the bridge.

'Shit!' she exclaimed and then disappeared back into the cockpit. Through the transparent front of the cockpit they could see the surface of the asteroid coming into view as the Cobra spun round for another bounce.

Ravindra clipped the EM carbine to the front of her suit, drew one of her burst pistols and advanced with it held in both hands. The pistol was loaded with frangible rounds and was less likely than the EM Carbine to damage anything important. Jenny was right behind her. The door to the bridge started to slide shut.

'Don't be stupid!' Ravindra shouted through her suit's loudspeaker. The door halted and then slid open. There was another thud as the Cobra's nose impacted with the asteroid in a slow motion explosion of ice. The Cobra started to spin slowly the other way.

Ravindra advanced on the cockpit with Jenny following, moving backwards, covering their rear.

The woman in the cockpit was a little younger than Jenny, dark haired and was wearing a leatherish jacket over a flight suit. She had her hands up and was cringing away from the gun.

'Newman?' Ravindra demanded.

'He ejected,' the woman told her. If she was lying, then she was a good actor; she seemed too frightened to lie.

'Orla, did you guys see a pod ejecting?' Ravindra asked

over the comms. Jenny was swearing quietly under her breath, unaware her suit mic was picking it up. 'Jenny,' Ravindra said quietly. The engineer stopped swearing. Outside the cockpit the stars had come back into view.

'Nothing,' Orla said.

'Any chance you could have missed it?'

'Was it stealthed?' Orla asked. Ravindra swore. That meant yes, they could have missed it.

'Is the crate in the hold the payload? The score?' Ravindra asked the Cobra's pilot.

'Yes,' the pilot said. She was shaking now, tears leaking out of her eyes.

'What's in it?' Jenny asked.

'I don't know. I swear!' the pilot said.

'Why didn't Newman take it with him?' Ravindra demanded.

'I don't know! Too big?' the pilot suggested desperately.

'Where'd Newman go?'

'I don't know! Please!'

'Are you lying?' Ravindra asked.

'No,' the pilot said miserably.

'I believe you,' Ravindra said.

'You're going to kill me, aren't you?'

Ravindra pulled the trigger on the pistol. Twice. The frangible bullets disintegrated in the pilot's skull, but only a little bit of her head spattered against the Cobra's cockpit. The pilot slumped forwards.

'Sorry,' Ravindra said as smoke curled out of the burst pistol's barrel. She closed her eyes, allowing herself a moment, though she knew how sloppy she was being. Harnack was gone. She had known him for the better part of twenty years. He had taught all of them how to fight.

57

It had been him and Marvin that had looked out for them all in the Warren. One second he had been there and the next he was dead. She had to blink back the tears. She swallowed hard.

'We need to search the rest of the ship,' she told Jenny. 'Orla, can you get grapples on this piece of crap, get it to stop spinning?'

Ravindra and Jenny were back on the *Song of Stone*. They had searched the Cobra thoroughly but they hadn't found Newman. They had brought the cargo on-board. As far as they could tell it was the payload, but it was armoured and shielded against scans. It also looked as if any attempt to open it without the correct codes would result in the destruction of the box's contents. This suited Ravindra. It was best not to know the Judas Syndicate's business.

Jenny and Ravindra had looked after their own wounds. It was mainly blistering from first and second degree burns and lots of bruising. Ravindra would need to get her tooth capped at some point.

Orla had gone over the *Song*'s sensor logs. She had found enough tells to suggest a stealthed pod ejection, possibly during the missile impact. Ravindra had wanted to be angry with her first mate, but frankly, even if they had detected the pod, they would have been hard put to scratch it with the military laser. Little short of an energy bomb could hurt escape pods.

They had brought Harnack's body on board, put it in a body bag and strapped it to one of the shelves in the cargo bay. Jonty had watched all this not saying a word, his face an expressionless mask. It was all in his eyes. Fury. Jenny had wept. Orla had held her but there had been tears in her own eyes.

They were sitting on the bridge again. They had destroyed the Cobra to leave as little trace as possible and then put several random jumps between themselves and the ice asteroid. They were in the middle of nowhere. Space had a lot of that.

Ravindra had turned her pilot's chair around and was looking at her remaining crew. She wanted to apologise to them, but every choice they had made they had agreed upon and she couldn't risk appearing weak now. She would cry for Harnack when she was on her own. A bottle of brandy would be company enough.

'Well?' she asked.

'*We* attacked *him*,' Jenny said. There was just the slightest hint of accusation in her voice. Ravindra thought back, running through what had happened. It had seemed obvious that he was going to turn on them – the snipers, the insistence on meeting on the asteroid when the payment could have just as easily been handled on Whit's Station. As certain as she had been then, after the fact she was finding explanations for everything. The snipers were reasonable operational security to an ex-military mind. To the paranoid, the crew of the *Song*'s close relationship with the 'authorities' on Whit's Station was too much of a risk.

'It was a burn. There's no question of it,' Orla told the engineer, glancing over at Ravindra as she did so. 'We start second guessing and we'll screw up. Harnack had seventeen hard years at this game, more before he ended up in the Warren. We all know the risks.' Jonty's head had jerked up at the mention of his lover's name but the goldskin remained silent.

'Do we run or deal with the Syndicate?' Ravindra put to them.

'Can we offload the cargo anywhere else?' Orla asked.

'It's too hot,' Ravindra said.

'If we run, we may as well leave the cargo for them somewhere. Maybe they'll leave us alone,' Orla said.

'I don't think they knew what Newman was planning,' Ravindra said.

'I think we should contact the Syndicate. Give them the cargo, get paid, smooth things over. This mess isn't our creation,' Ravindra stated. *And then we don't have to run,* she added silently.

'You think they'll care whose mess it is?' Jenny asked bitterly.

'I think it's worth the risk. We still have the option to run if it all goes wrong,' Orla said.

We do, but the longer we leave it the less chance we have, Ravindra thought, though she kept it to herself.

'We agreed?' Orla asked. Jenny nodded but didn't look happy. Ravindra nodded as well. The three of them turned to Jonty.

'Newman,' was all he said.

Orla was shaking her head.

'That's exactly the shit we don't do,' she insisted.

'Never personal,' Ravindra said. 'Dane's L—'

'Fuck Dane's Law and fuck Dane. Where'd that get him? Dead, that's where, just like Harnack!' Then Jonty's face crumpled and the tears came. He slammed his fist into the edge of the control panel before slumping back in his seat. Jenny was closest to him. She reached over to squeeze his arm.

'In time, brother,' Orla soothed. 'In time, we promise.'

Chapter Four

You got all sorts in this job. Maintenance supervisor John Graham turned out to be one of the harmless ones. He lived in a decently sized multi-function cabin in a slightly low-gravity section of the station. Not prime real-estate but close enough to show he had credits to his name. He had a nice smile and bright eyes under greying black hair, and the easy happy manner of someone who'd largely had what he wanted from life because what he'd wanted had never been too much. From Ziva, all he wanted was to be able to say he'd met the infamous Blink Dog. After five minutes of fan-boy awe and asking all sorts of dumb questions about whether this, that, or the other was true, he asked Ziva if she was as fast as they said she was. Ziva drew her pistol on him and he spent the whole next minute gawping and gasping and asking her to do it again – and could he make a recording of her doing it, please? She told him that would be just fine as long as he didn't mind it ending with her shooting him and could he please tell her what he thought she might like to know.

'That guy you were looking for. I heard a couple of his crew. I didn't know they were with him until your avatar came showing their pictures. Didn't think anything of it at the time, but I heard them talking about the Black Mausoleum. Kind of pricked my ears, that. That's why I remembered them.'

'How long ago?'

'Couple of weeks.' When he'd told her the rest of what he'd heard, it wasn't the wasted trip she'd feared it would be. Putting Graham's story together with what she already knew, Newman was working with the Judas Syndicate – with the Veil of Beta Hydri – and if Newman was working with a Judas crew then there was a very good chance the Syndicate had been behind the destruction of the *Pandora*. The Syndicate's involvement brought its own problems. The smuggler she'd jumped with his Glen Halyconia six months ago had probably been working for the same Veil and she'd been to the Black Mausoleum before; but figuring out who was the Judas Veil in a thriving system like Beta Hydri would be like finding a needle in a haystack. The New Caledonia police already had an entire task force dedicated to nothing else. Which left her two courses: ask them, or find Newman and ask *him* instead.

Graham didn't want money or any sort of reward. When he was done and Ziva had finished pacing his flat, talking to the *Dragon Queen* and using his bandwidth to search the Federation systems archives for anything they might have on the Syndicate in Beta Hydri, she felt almost sorry for him. She took him to a bar as thanks – on the promise that he stopped acting as if she was some kind of celebrity. He was fun enough company for a while, drinking and quietly listening to her stories. It felt good telling someone else about what she did and how things had gone down and the scrapes and squeaks she'd been through. Nothing confidential, nothing the world didn't already know if it had cared to read the news reports, but it felt good having someone listen, *really* listen and pay attention the way Enaya never did. She might have stayed with him longer if the drink hadn't got him. He told her she had beautiful eyes and she pointed out they were top-range Fresnel Technology implants that had cost her a small fortune and so they'd damn well better be beautiful. She left not long after that. The Purge still in her system made being in a bar rather less fun than it ought to be.

There was a message waiting for her back on the *Dragon Queen*. Darkwater had finally managed to reconstruct the outward jump trails of the two attacking ships. They'd followed one out into deep space and the other to the outskirts of 61 Cygni, but after that they were a dead end. No telling where the attacker ships had gone.

61 Cygni. Another place to add to her list.

Ziva left Pethes and Toad Hall, made the jump to Beta Hydri and docked in orbit over New Caledonia. Every civilised system had a few cracks and crevices that people like the Judas Syndicate could slip into, but Beta Hydri was special in that regard: Beta Hydri was home to the infamous Black Mausoleum, an old research station in its own weird elliptical orbit sharply offset from the ecliptic of the system. The Mausoleum had been built as the hub of an array of X-ray telescopes, but that had been almost a millennium ago and the station had been abandoned for centuries. With its odd orbit, it had been all but forgotten. No one remembered its original name any more. In the sketchy history that followed, it had been home to all sorts, largely ignored until it was taken over by a smuggling ring that had brought it all the wrong attention.

And there things got interesting. The New Caledonia police had tracked the smugglers, seized the station and that had looked like being that – a nice clean bust. But when they went to trial, New Caledonia had their arses handed to them: in the back and forth of politics between the Federation and the Empire and the formal incorporation of New Caledonia into the Federation, the Black

Mausoleum had never been included in the treaty papers. An oversight, no doubt, but technically the station was still an Imperial outpost. The smugglers counter-sued the New Caledonia government. The Empire, when it eventually realised it had been invaded, gleefully backed them up and shouted about illegal acts of war. The Mausoleum had reverted to being a hideout for smugglers and pirates for a while as the Federation and the Empire argued, until the Lupus Group had moved in with the grudging backing of both sides. And now, as far as Ziva could tell, it was exactly what it had been before – a hideout for smugglers and pirates, but now with all the hull breaches patched and with breathable pressurised air through most of the station and a thin veneer of law and order painted over it for the benefit of the New Caledonia authorities. Everyone knew you didn't have to scratch very hard to make it flake.

All of which made the Mausoleum not the sort of place where a bounty hunter in a Fer-de-Lance showed up, parked her ship, went to a bar, asked a few questions and then came back and expected to find her ship still there. In fact she probably shouldn't be expecting to leave the bar at all, at least not in one piece; so for this, Ziva sent the *Dragon Queen* ahead without her and switched her identity. She gave herself a flimsy backup that wouldn't take too much scrutiny and then a more solid second one beneath. The new her – Olivia Red – bought herself a berth on the *Myla*, a dubious Python almost certainly fitted out for low-rent smuggling. The *Dragon Queen* would wait, running silent out in empty space, until called for. Which would make for an interesting exit, if it came to that.

Olivia Red kept herself to herself aboard the *Myla*. She stayed in her cabin and spoke to the crew as little as possible and generally gave the impression of wanting to be left alone. When they reached the Black Mausoleum, she paid in credit packs and found herself somewhere cheap to stay. The station was a hole, tiny, barely managing to fake half a standard gravity even around its rim. No matter. With a bit of luck, someone would have the curiosity to poke around and realise that Olivia Red was a fake. The Judas Syndicate had their fingers all over the Mausoleum. If she'd guessed right then someone would poke through the flimsy false identity to discover a dubious past calculated to stir the Syndicate's interest in a vaguely unfriendly sort of way. Enough to provoke a visit from station security, at least.

Of course, there was always a chance that they'd poke through the second false identity too and work out who she *really* was, at which point life would quickly become very interesting in a particularly shitty sort of way.

Three hours after closing the door of her room behind her, down in the low-rent, low-gravity inner ring of the station, a pair of steroid junkers burst in on her. They were big men, six foot six and easily twice her body-mass. They towered over her as they walked in, full of their own strength. Three million years of evolution still hadn't done the male brain many favours when it came to size and its apparent importance, but Ziva backed away anyway, duly putting on a façade of female fear. The junkers made themselves at home, one sitting on the corner of her bed, the other drawing up a chair in front of the door so she'd have to go past him to get out.

'What do you want?' She had an open link to the *Dragon Queen*. Eventually the *Dragon Queen* would start trawling databases for who these guys were and who they worked for and all that sort of thing; the only snag being that the *Dragon Queen* was currently fifteen light-minutes away. By the time it got the question, found an answer and sent it back, chances were it wouldn't matter anymore.

One of the junkers studied her hard. It was a look meant to be fierce and intimidating. It might have worked better if his eyes weren't just a little too squashed together. 'Olivia Red, is it?'

Ziva nodded and quivered. It was hard to resist hamming the act up just to see how far she could take it before they twigged they were being played.

'What's your business in the Black Mausoleum?'

'None of yours. What do you want?'

The two junkers exchanged a glance. One reached inside his jacket and pulled out a card. Most places people just swapped electronic tags as a matter of course, but the Black Mausoleum had started life as a science station so long ago that they'd still used physical cards. No one had ever bothered to change the system. Physicists, Ziva had discovered, liked swipe-cards. She had no idea why.

'Cameron Sweet. Station security.' The junker passed his card. Ziva took it and pretended to look at it while the sub-dermal reader in the tip of her left index finger quietly cloned its magnetics and her Fresnel eyes snatched an image. She slipped a Sly-Spy microdot tracker onto it for good measure. She'd have a clone of Cameron Sweet's pass card in about thirty seconds and she'd be able to to monitor his movements too. She passed his card back. 'What have I done? I only just got here!' She paced nervously around the far corner of the room, keeping her distance. Keeping the façade.

'We have a policy on immigration.'

Ziva laughed. 'Last I looked, your policy was not caring who came here.'

'We have a stricter policy on people like you. We have some questions. We'll start with who you really are. Then some people might like to talk to you about how you can pay off the debt you owe.'

'My name is Olivia Red!'

The junkers exchanged another glance. 'You think about that, *Olivia Red*. While you do, you'll come with us.'

Ziva tried arguing but the two junkers simply got up and grabbed hold of her. Feigning fear came easier with their fingers wrapped around her arms. They were strong, and she normally dealt with strong men by not letting them touch her. The first time she'd come to the Black Mausoleum had been ten years earlier, on the trail of a milli-credit hustler who'd called himself Hombas the Fish and had apparently thought that wasn't stupid. It was the last assignment she'd done in uniform. She'd come in the Viper she flew back then, made no pretence of who or what she was, and had been lucky to get out alive. If it hadn't been for her partner, chances were she'd still be rotting in the same cells Sweet was taking her to now. Her partner hadn't made it out. Three months and the New Caledonia police did nothing but shout and make noises and get laughed at. Politics. Demarcation. Limits of authority. That was when she'd quit, not that it hadn't been coming for a while. Made a down-payment on her first ship, a battered old Cobra on its last legs. She'd come back to break her partner out but they'd ejected him into space months ago.

Once burned, forever learned. The cloner in her shoe already had a copy of Sweet's card ready to go.

The two junkers pinned her arms and clamped her wrists in magnetic cuffs – the cuffs were linked to Cameron Sweet's card too, which was going to make him look even more stupid than he actually was – and took her out of the hotel and shoved her in an elevator. She felt herself getting lighter as they moved towards the hub; then the elevator stopped and shifted sideways. It crawled along one of the gossamer circles of the great metal spiderweb that joined the Black

67

Mausoleum's docking hub to the station's habitation rim. She could hear metal creak and groan and remembered how decrepit and old this place was. Eight hundred years? Nine? It had been falling apart for centuries.

The elevator reached the next spoke and started moving rimward again, drawing to a stop in some administrative section off-limits to the general public – if, that was, the Black Mausoleum could be said to have a general public. They checked her in at a desk and took fingerprints and retina scans, both of which were fakes. They took pictures, not that anyone looked at that sort of thing nowadays. The pictures bothered her. They just might still have records of her in a New Caledonia uniform from ten years ago, if they troubled to look. She hadn't worn much of a disguise to her face, assuming it would be found out too easily. If the drill hadn't changed, they'd put her in a holding pen, come back after a few minutes for a blood sample and then leave her for twelve hours while they checked her records. Then came the part where they'd pull her out, strip her and depilate her, force her into a chemical shower and then into a convict jumpsuit that stank of other people's sweat. The Black Mausoleum had its own law. It hadn't been much fun going through it once and Ziva had no intention of enduring it a second time.

The junkers lost all interest in her as soon as they had her in the holding pen. There were two other people inside, one an impish man who eyed her over the sort of absurdly overblown Zapata moustache that said he either came from the Moon or that he wished he did. The other was snoring on the floor, passed out and stinking of cheap rum. Ziva ignored them. She had to be quick and get the next minutes exactly right. Get them wrong, get trapped here until they figured out who she *really* was, and the best she could hope for was that they'd eject her into space without a suit.

She crouched against the wall and pulled her knees tight into her chest until she could reach her shoes and then extracted the clone of Sweet's card and flipped it across the magnetic cuffs. They popped free. Moustache watched with interest. Ziva put a finger to her lips and swiped the card across his cuffs as well, but nothing happened. They exchanged shrugs. Ziva sat down again. They really could have done a better job of searching her. She bit her thumb and popped out the spring razor hidden behind the nail, then used that to nick the seam of her shorts and eased out three little black drones the size of apple pips. She licked a finger and wiped it over them, opening their DNA-locks. As they sprang into life, she slid them under the cell door. They fluttered into the corridor outside. It took the drones about thirty seconds to find and latch onto the three cameras out there and to take over their tiny algorithms.

The two junkers came back together right on cue. Sweet swiped his card and opened the door. As soon as they were in, Ziva triggered the drones latched to the cameras and kicked Sweet between the legs hard enough to rupture both his testicles. She had the shocker rod off Sweet's belt while the second junker was still staring in disbelief – until she smashed his ankle with it. As he went down, she touched her copy of Sweet's card to the base of the shocker, unlocking it, and zapped them both. The junker with the smashed ankle collapsed as though someone had cut all his strings. For Sweet it was more of a mercy than anything else.

Her heart was racing. She was half listening out for the first alarms or for the hiss of tranq-gas. *You got no back-up here, not this time.* She had to keep telling herself that.

She pulled the bodies away from the door and propped them up on the cell's one bench, then practically tore their uniform jackets off. She tossed one to Zapata along with the second guard's keycard and stuffed the other underneath the bench. If she'd put one of them on herself, it would have been like wearing a tent.

Still no alarms and the cell door was wide open. Ziva grinned. Couldn't help herself. That was the thrill of it, the danger. They'd be out for hours. It was all so easy, like it was supposed to be. Amateurs.

Moustache man helped himself to the second junker's shocker. The card had unlocked his cuffs. He gave Ziva a nervous glance.

'Try not to be seen,' Ziva said. 'And try not to set off the alarms.' She patted Sweet on the head as she left. 'Don't worry. It's the thirty-fourth century. They can grow you a new pair.'

She headed deeper into the Black Mausoleum's restricted arc, worming her way to their data cores, flicking her little seed-drones ahead. The drones were expensive but worth it: they fed every camera they infected into her Fresnels and put them on a loop for everyone else until she'd passed out of sight and called them back. It wasn't a cloaking device but it was as good as one – unless she met someone in the flesh. How long before they found she was missing from the cell? Minutes? Hours? How long before someone started to wonder why Sweet and his friend hadn't come back? Then they'd come looking …

The cameras showed a pair of junkers coming the other way. She had a few seconds, that was all. She flashed Sweet's card against the nearest door but it didn't work. Probably kicked off a warning of an unauthorised access attempt. She looked wildly for a place to hide and darted into another corridor a moment before the junkers came round the corner. There was nowhere to hide there, either. All she could do was press herself against the wall, shocker at the ready, and hope they didn't look. She could hear them. The junkers were talking, laughing, one of them telling the other some story or other that apparently was hilarious. Ziva stayed perfectly still and quietly prayed that they'd walk on by.

'... And then he gets out this bucket, right, only it's not just a bucket ...'

Cloaking device. Bloody Jameson again. There was a story – more of a legend – that he'd got his hands on a prototype cloaking device once. She couldn't remember whether it was supposed to be Thargoid or whether it was some secret corporate military thing.

'... It's the biggest bucket ever made. You could hide a whole person inside it ...'

And it obviously wasn't true either, since a hundred years had passed and neither the Federation nor the Empire were flying around in invisible ships. Nor, as far as she knew, were the Thargoids.

'... And he slams it down on the table in front of Christoph, and the look on his face ...'

As far as she knew.

The junkers passed the end of her corridor, one of them gesticulating wildly, the other laughing with his friend. They didn't turn and they didn't look and they didn't see her. Ziva listened as they walked away. For a while she stayed where she was. Catching her breath. Letting her heartbeat slow. It had seemed like such a clever idea back on the *Myla*. Trick them into bringing her through all their front-line security and then snoop about.

She set off again. *Snoop about?* She hadn't thought this through, not properly. If the Syndicate caught her here, they'd kill her. It wouldn't trouble them much, either.

71

A minute later, the cameras spotted someone coming towards her again. A woman on her own, walking quickly – seemingly in a hurry. The choices were better this time. Ziva slipped around an unlit corner and watched the woman rush past.

Close to the data cores now. Fuck knew what security they'd have on the cores themselves. She turned a corner and a door opened right beside her and she almost collided with another uniformed steroid-junker. He stared at her and started to open his mouth ... Speed. That was always her edge. She snap-kicked him between the legs and whatever he'd been about to say died in a whimper. As he doubled over, she grabbed his hair with one hand, pulled his head down further and slammed the heel of her other hand onto the nape of the junker's neck. He dropped and didn't get up.

Cameras. Check the cameras. But the corridors around her were clear for now. She crouched and checked the junker's pulse. Still alive, which was something. Whether he'd walk again without some expensive nerve surgery was another matter. That was the trouble with junkers – you never knew quite how hard you had to hit them to take them down. If she hadn't almost walked into him, she could have used the shocker ...

The camera behind her flashed a warning. Two men approaching from behind. *Damn it!* She had about five seconds. The open door was right there; she dragged the junker inside and closed it just in time. Now the camera ahead of her was flashing a warning too. Another pair of junkers, coming the other way. She looked about for a weapon. The unconscious man on the floor had a burst pistol but the grip would be coded to his palm print and probably to his DNA. He had a trio of stun grenades that wouldn't be, though. Ziva bared her teeth. You could never go wrong with a stun grenade or two.

The junkers coming from behind passed the door where she was hiding and met the junkers coming the other way. They stopped and started to talk. Ziva made herself breathe slow and steady, forced her fingers to unclench. Sitting silent in the dark. *No reason to be anxious*, she told herself. *Patience. Patience. That's all.* They couldn't possibly know she was there but she couldn't help herself willing them to move on …

A last exchange of nods and smiles and laughter and the junkers went their separate ways. Ziva let out a long, slow sigh and then made herself wait until they were out of range of the cameras. She waited another minute more to be sure, counting out the seconds. Each one seemed to last an age. While she did, she used the card from the junker she'd taken down to access the Black Mausoleum's network and find out just how much further she had to go. Not far now. That was a mercy, at least.

Her ear buzzed. The *Dragon Queen*. The ship must have come in a lot closer and now it was riding the station's network to find her. Which pissed her off, because if the *Dragon Queen* could do that then so could anyone else who happened to know she was there. And someone would be wondering, right now, who the hell was sending a signal in from empty space and who they were talking to.

'What the fuck?' she hissed, squatting in the pitch black. 'Get off this channel …'

The delay was several seconds before the *Dragon Queen* replied. 'You asked me to give priority routing to any call from Enaya.' And yes, she had, and just hadn't remembered to take the order off. *Shit.*

'Take a message and make her go away. Don't call me—' but it was too late. The *Dragon Queen* had already patched the link.

'Ziv!'

'En.' Shit. 'En, I'm hiding out in a dark room on a station full of people who want to hurt me. There's a body on the floor right next to me. Now isn't the time. I'll call you when I can.'

'Ziv, It's Aisha ...'

'Not here, not now. I'm sorry, En.'

'Aisha's gone, Ziv.'

'Sorry, En,' Ziva whispered. She cut the link.

The drones infecting the cameras told her that the corridor was still clear. She slipped outside. Three doors further down she found what she was looking for: the Black Mausoleum's data cores. The card from the junker she'd taken down let her in: that's what you got for having such archaic piss-poor tech. She had her drones infect the cameras outside, keeping watch for her while she crouched in the dark. At least the data cores themselves were only a few decades obsolete. She took off her other shoe and took the heel apart, slipped a wafer into one of the access sockets and bit her other thumb. A tiny wire popped loose. She plugged it into the wafer. *And here we go ...*

It was mundane stuff. Maybe that was why they didn't have much protection on it. The attack-ware on the wafer ripped through the server's firewalls and quasi-sentient security algorithms like a knife through paper. *Yes. Good. Come on ...* She passed over the personnel lists and the staff files and went for the station docking records, arrivals and departures, skimming as fast as she dared, looking for anything that might be Newman's ship or that had come here shortly after the *Pandora* had died. *Come on, come on, where are you?* Any moment now, some sort of alarm would go off. Someone would come. Something ...

She got what looked like it might have been Newman's Cobra passing through a month before – there for a few days and gone again – but that was no news. Didn't look like he'd come back. She couldn't see anything with an obvious connection to the *Pandora* either.

Fucksticks.

She sat back, wondering what to do next. She'd have to leave fast – the moment anyone came looking for the junkers she'd left in the holding cell. She'd pushed her luck too far already …

There *was* one odd thing in the docking records. An Adder, the *Unkindness,* had come in from 61 Cygni carrying an escape pod it hadn't had when it went out. There was nothing in the Pilot's Federation bulletins about a ship going down in 61 Cygni but Darkwater had tracked one of the *Pandora*'s raiders there. Ziva knew the *Unkindness* of old, a Judas runner. She tried to find anything more about the pod, but whatever records there might have been were missing. It wasn't that they were too well protected for her attack-ware to penetrate, they simply weren't there at all. Odd.

She pulled what she could on the pilot of the *Unkindness* and carefully put everything back as she'd found it. The attack-ware wafer returned to her shoe, the wire under her thumbnail. She crept out of the data cores and returned the way she'd come, pulling the drones out of the cameras behind her as she went, hiding whenever anyone came the other way. Moustache Man might have done her a favour. When they found he was missing and then found the junker in the office, maybe they'd think it was him …?

Yeah, right. Until the junker woke up and told them he'd been taken out by some crazy dwarf woman. No, that wasn't going to fly. *Face it girl, you're blown here.*

She reached the holding cell and there still weren't any alarms but, dammit, she hadn't the first idea how to get out without being seen. Christ, the tension was killing her!

Well, there was always the straightforward way.

She carried on, out to the front doors of the enforcement offices. There were a dozen or so junkers between her and the exit and so she didn't exactly leave quietly, but the shocker rod was just perfect for seeing they didn't give her any trouble. It was a relief taking them down, burning off all that suppressed adrenaline. She left the last one on his feet and flipped him an identity tag. Who she *really* was this time. 'The guy you had in the cells back there? Mistook him for someone with a price on his head. My bad. I'll be leaving now. I might stop in a bar or two on the way out. We can continue this argument if you like or you can just be glad to see the back of me. And yeah, I know, whichever Veil runs this place could evacuate a whole section of the station into space if he wanted to, but you might like to consider that I let you have me and I could easily have left bombs tied to my life-monitor in all sorts of places down in the hub before I came up. So there's that.' She looked about. 'From the state of the place I should have left smaller ones.'

She walked out. Before they could put a lock on her, she tapped her ear and bounced a message to the *Dragon Queen*.

'Get here. Now.' That was all.

It was easy enough to find the pilot of the *Unkindness*. He was in a bar that some arsehole had called The Jameson, as if the real deal would ever have come to a shit-hole like this. A retro flat-screen took up a whole wall inside, running a loop of spectacular space accidents. Most of the ones here were of Cobra's fucking up their roll-rate and crashing into the entry gate of one of the old-school rotating cuboctahedral Coriolis stations. There had been a whole spate of that when the Coriolis stations were first introduced. Was always a problem with the Cobras for some reason, fitting them through the letterbox opening and the pilots back then … well, these days no one got a licence without showing they could roll-match a station whether they were drunk, stoned or stone-cold sober.

Ziva threw a handful of camera drones into the air and gave them their thirty seconds. After the way she'd left the enforcement office, there didn't seem much point in subtlety. Give them another five minutes and they'd have a whole posse of junkers hunting her; this time they'd be armed with a damn sight more than a shock-rod. She fired hers at the ceiling. That got the attention of every spacer in the bar quick enough. Once she had it she asked, 'So which one of you fuckers flies the *Unkindness*?' All it took was one glance and she knew who it was. She shocked him as she ran at him, vaulting tables, and he hadn't even finished slumping to the floor by the time she reached him, picked him up and slung him over her shoulder. *Heavy fucker.* She was thankful the fake gravity of the Black Mausoleum was only about half Earth-standard. She stuffed a pair of anti-stun plugs in his ears and then let off one of the grenades from the junker she'd neck-chopped. That gave her about fifteen seconds while no one else in the bar would know their arse from their elbow, enough to drag the pilot into the gents – no one ever put a camera up in the men's toilets, not ever – and barricade herself in. Next, she sent the camera drones off to create a moving blind spot through the station that would make it seem as though she was heading for the hub. Then she jabbed the Adder pilot with a half dose of Wakey-Wakey and enough Demon to put the shits up a horse. She slapped him; the moment his eyes opened, she pinned him down onto the tiled floor by his throat. The air stank of stale piss. A thousand years and some things just didn't change.

'I don't know your name,' she spat, 'but I know you fly a Judas runner and I know you came in with an escape pod not long back. Who was in it?'

The pilot would have screamed if Ziva hadn't stifled it with a balled-up sock in his mouth. That was the Demon. Put the living fear of Hell and Armageddon straight inside you. Instant bad trip.

Ziva hissed at him. 'Tell me who it was or I'll eat you alive.' She pulled the sock out and leaned into him, pressing her arm across his throat, their faces inches apart. 'Who?'

The pilot pissed himself. He mouthed the words more than spoke them. 'I never knew his name.'

'Was he tall? Short?' Ziva slapped him again. As far as the Adder pilot was concerned, she'd look like some hideous nightmare creature from the worst corners of his own imagination. He wouldn't have the first idea she was even human. Demon. Weird what people got off on these days. 'Nod or shake your head. Was he tall?' No. 'Short?' Not that either. Useless fucker. 'Was he pale-skinned?' Yes. 'Dark hair?' Yes. 'Short hair?' Yes. 'Real short?' Yes! Getting somewhere at last. 'Accent? Maybe a touch Imperial? Ex-military? Pale watery eyes?'

Yes and yes and yes and yes. Newman. She asked a few more to be sure, but it was definitely him.

'Why were you there?'

'I was told to go and get him.'

'He was in an escape pod?'

Yes, in an escape pod. A stealthy one, powered right down and hiding against the dark side of an ice planetoid. No traces of any ship-to-ship in the last few minutes, no jump trails and Newman hadn't talked. When she was done, Ziva jabbed the pilot with NightNight and left him there. She squatted a moment, wondering what to do – until someone started pushing on her barricade. They'd have recovered from that stun grenade by now and probably had station security on the way. She opened the door, smiled at the bemused man waiting outside and lobbed out a second grenade before slamming the door in his face. She put her hands over her ears a moment before the detonation shook the room. The Adder pilot screamed. Then he started to buzz. She thought it was his life-alarm at first, that she'd overdone the Demon and killed him; but it wasn't that sort of shrill piercing wail, it was the loud incessant alarm that every spacer knew – the alarm of a ship preparing to leave without you. Apparently the *Unkindness* was trying to leave without its pilot.

Newman. He was on the station and he knew she was after him and he was running. She raced out of the bar, hurdling the handful of men and women reeling sprawled about the floor, and dashed outside. She didn't know how much time she had but it wouldn't be long. The camera drones might have bought her the few minutes she needed at the bar but the junkers would know that trick by now. They wouldn't fall for it a second time.

'Where are you?' she shot the question to the *Dragon Queen* as she sprinted through the station.

'Half a million kilometres away.'

'When you get here I need an out. The way we did on Tau Ceti.' She reached the closest of the spindle elevators that would take her towards the hub. A squad of junkers was milling about, presumably watching out for her. They were dumb enough to be clustered together and the shocker took out three of them at once before the last pair realised she was there. One of them swivelled, bringing a shotgun to bear. The other started talking urgently into his hand. Most places Ziva went, everyone started screaming and running at the first sight of a gun. On the Mausoleum people ran, right enough, but they didn't run screaming. They ran with the grim, silent speed of people who'd seen this sort of thing too many times before.

The elevator doors were closing, the handful of passengers inside dashing out between them as the evacuation alarm sounded. Ziva raced the other way. She ducked behind a roving refreshment bot as the junker fired his shotgun, then she darted out and shocked the other one. He went down like a falling tree while she ran on, dodging and weaving. The junker with the gun got off another shot before she threw herself through the elevator doors. Ziva felt the sting of a pellet tear her shoulder, turned, fired the shocker one more time as the doors closed and then sat back. She heard the hiss of the vacuum seal close around the elevator and the bump as they started to move. She had it to herself. In some ways this was a good thing, in other ways … not so much. She released her drones to take out the cameras.

They couldn't have gone more than a dozen metres towards the hub when the elevator lurched to a stop.

'Ziva Eschel.' Ziva didn't recognise the voice but it was too smooth to be some junker. 'This is how you stay alive: put the weapon down. Get on the floor and put your hands on your head and say very clearly the words *"I surrender."*'

Ziva sought out the elevator cameras and pouted at the nearest. Hopefully, it was blind by now. Hopefully, whoever was doing the talking couldn't see her. 'But I don't want to.'

'How exactly do you think this is going to go, bounty hunter?'

'To whom am I talking?'

'I run the Black Mausoleum. That's all you need to know.'

'Ah. A Veil, then.'

80

'You could be useful to me, Eschel. Give me a reason not to kill you.'

'Actually, I was thinking something more along the lines of threatening to start executing hostages unless you let me descend to the hub, board my ship and leave.' She smiled. 'Or threatening not to blow up some bombs I left around the place. That sort of thing.'

'You're in a sealed elevator out on one of the spindles. How about you do what I say and I don't evacuate you into space?'

'Hey, maybe there's a dozen other people here!'

'Eschel, even if I cared, you don't have any hostages and there aren't any bombs. You might have blinded the cameras in there but really, how stupid do you think we are?'

'Well, actually ...' She'd barely got the words out when a soft alarm went off behind her Fresnel eyes. Every spacer carried a pressure monitor.

'And the bitch of it, Eschel, is that I'm not planning on killing you, just on dropping the oxygen level enough to make you pass out and then having a whole shitload of fun getting you to do my dirty work. I'm thinking a really exotic genetic disease to hold over you and your loved ones, but I'll settle for a tiny sub-cranial anti-matter bomb if I have to. What do you think?'

'I think that whoever you are, you're a fucking arse.' *Ship! Where are you?*

There was a sudden flicker as the elevator lights went out. Lines of ultraviolet scintillation scarred space outside, the tell-tale of military-grade X-ray beam lasers. Dim red emergency backups switched on at once. The elevator shuddered. The intercom went dead and then something deep within the metal spindle snapped as the lasers cut it apart. The fake gravity of the station's rotation vanished and the elevator, floating free in space now, shot sideways straight at the station rim and then lurched as a sleek dark shape flickered past so close that Ziva flinched. The *Dragon Queen*. The ship had cut the elevator right out of the Black Mausoleum.

Gravity came back hard. Ziva slammed in a heap into the elevator wall, which had taken over as the floor, then toppled and tumbled as the *Dragon Queen*'s fuel scoop reeled her in like just any other cargo container. 'Careful,' she howled. 'Remember I'm not in an escape pod or acceleration couch here!' Unprotected as she was, the *Dragon Queen* could easily kill her with the scoop, with the sheer force of snatching her up.

Everywhere outside was full of bright light like fireworks now, the *Dragon Queen* dispensing cloud after cloud of countermeasures, aerosols and flares, while the station opened up with a handful of ancient pulse lasers. As soon as the ship had her inside, the *Dragon Queen* flooded the hold with air and burned open the elevator doors.

'Tactical,' snapped Ziva, launching herself for the cockpit, wincing at the sting in her shoulder. She'd have more bruises than she cared to count from this.

'The Black Mausoleum is firing on us from increasing range and poses no threat. Several pursuit ships have launched but will not be able to draw sufficiently close to engage us as long as you are within an approved acceleration cocoon within the next thirty-seven seconds.'

'Where's the *Unkindness*?'

'We're following. What shall I do with our new cargo?'

'Dump it.' The weight would slow them – not much but it all counted.

She reached the Fer-de-Lance's cockpit and strapped herself into the pilot's cocoon. As soon as she did, the ship's engines ignited and five gravities of acceleration slammed into the back of her. The cocoon was already jabbing her with its needles, dosing her up for the harder accelerations to come, flooding her with repair nanites.

A bounty notice flashed up. Someone from the Black Mausoleum had put two thousand credits on her head. There was an irony in that. She considered paying it off from what she'd get for bringing in Newman – thirty-five thousand credits now, if he really was one of the pilots Darkwater were after. One the other hand, maybe the Judas Syndicate could just go fuck themselves. People like them didn't raise bounties – they put a price on your head and paid the first assassin to claim it.

The *Unkindness* was micro-jumping now, racing off to the inner edge of the Kuiper belt. The *Dragon Queen* set after it, burning hydrogen as only a Fer-de-Lance could. She didn't quite catch him before the Adder jumped.

'Follow him!' The Fer-de-Lance hit Newman's departure point sixty seconds later; his hyperspace trail was still pristine fresh. Child's play. Ziva felt the momentary tremor of the *Dragon Queen*'s jump-drive and then the stars stretched into lines.

The jump was a short one. As soon as she emerged back into real space, Ziva had alarms sounding all over the cockpit. Mines. The fucker had left mines for her and the *Dragon Queen*'s two point defence pulse lasers were already in overdrive, firing constantly. The nearest mines had spotted her and fragmented into a storm of tiny darts. She took a moment – just that and nothing more – to see where she was. They'd emerged in the outer fringes of an unclaimed system with no name, just a designation, and the *Unkindness* was less than a hundred thousand kilometres ahead of her, streaking for a Neptunian gas giant with a vast and complex string of rings and moons. Ziva snapped a pair of missiles off after the Adder; then she flipped the *Dragon Queen* so she hit the minefield tail first and lit up the main engines for a few seconds as she did. A plume of fusion-heated plasma kilometres long scoured a path for her through the wave of dronelets. When she was done, she flipped the Fer-de-Lance back around and let the point defence lasers deal with the rest.

The *Unkindness* raced for the system of rings. Clear of the minefield, Ziva fired her own engines hard. The *Dragon Queen* had the best customised drives that money could buy but the Adder was up at maximum burn. Inside her cocoon, the *Dragon Queen* flooded Ziva's system with adrenaline and a swarm of nanites to keep all the capillaries open in her brain while they shut off most of the blood to her arms and legs and forced her heart into overdrive. The only time Ziva had ever wished she wasn't built the way she was had been the day she'd discovered that big men like Newman could push the limit just that little bit more. The *Dragon Queen* would grudgingly let her sustain an acceleration of about sixteen gravities if she was in the cockpit gel-couch and let it take over her blood-chemistry and circulatory system. Grudgingly.

Even with stretched engines, the *Unkindness* was maxing at ten gravities. At that sort of acceleration, Ziva couldn't move and couldn't speak and the *Dragon Queen* pretty much had to fly itself. It watched her eyes and took a few basic commands from the way she moved them. Sometimes from a sequence of blinks.

The *Unkindness* abruptly flipped, decelerating at full burn as it neared the ring system and suddenly Ziva was closing fast. The Adder fired a salvo of missiles. Ziva switched the laser targeting to her Fresnels and started taking them out before they could get close enough to fragment into submunitions. She held her fire on the Adder itself until she knew she could hit it exactly where she wanted to. Newman was wasting his time. He was hopelessly outgunned. He had to see that, didn't he?

The *Dragon Queen* autonomously launched a salvo of interceptor dronelets. The defensive pulse lasers opened up again. A lone rogue broke through and a pinhead-sized anti-hydrogen warhead detonated a few metres from the *Dragon Queen*'s skin. The ship shuddered as its shields absorbed the sudden storm of high-energy exotic particles.

Another few seconds and she'd be on top of him. Ziva flipped the Fer-de-Lance, matching the Adder's deceleration. The *Unkindness* fired another salvo. By now, the two missiles she'd fired from the minefield were keeping station with him but he still wasn't getting that he was beaten. She had one of the two missiles target the Adder's own salvo and blew them to pieces close enough to junk his shields and scorch his hull. *Give it up, Newman.* But she couldn't talk to him with the engines on full burn and he wouldn't be able to answer even if he wanted to.

The Adder's beam laser began firing. The *Dragon Queen* twisted into corkscrewed flight, making herself harder to hit and spreading the damage as widely as she could; but a single beam laser wasn't going to hurt a Fer-de-Lance in a hurry. Half the time the Adder was firing through the plume of her engines anyway, wasting itself.

They were down to less than a thousand clicks between them but the Adder had almost reached the rings. Newman launched another salvo of missiles — as though he somehow hadn't noticed what had happened to the one before.

What the hell are you doing? Ziva took out his salvo and this time she fired back, beaded up on the Adder's engines, keeping the power low on her dual military X-ray lasers, not wanting to do any more damage than she absolutely had to …

The *Unkindness* exploded as though every containment field inside its fusion core had failed at once. The *Dragon Queen*'s reactive cockpit went opaque and space turned utterly black. Displays lit up smoothly around Ziva, following her eyes. The Fer-de-Lance cut its acceleration to a more tolerable three gravities.

'I didn't hit him *that* hard!

'The detonation of the *Unkindness* was a self-destruct device.'

'And the pilot?'

'There is no escape pod beacon. The pilot is gone.'

Along with her thirty-five thousand credits, unless she could prove he'd been on the ship. Which would mean cutting a deal with that jackass Veil back on the Black Mausoleum and that didn't seem too likely. 'No. Newman's not the blaze of glory type. He didn't blow himself up out of spite. He's out there. Start scanning those rings and moons.' *Shit! Unless he wasn't on it in the first place. Unless she'd got it wrong …*

'That will take a very long time.'

'Do it anyway. Do all the trajectory maths stuff, whatever you need to do. He came out of that explosion somehow.'

'That is highly improbable.'

Which made it all the sweeter when the *Dragon Queen* finally worked out how the pilot had done it – how he'd collapsed all the magnetics in just the right way to create a funnel in the middle of his miniature nova and catapulted his escape pod out through the vortex and straight into the mess of rings and miniature moons, and how he'd used the explosion to mask his manoeuvring. He was sitting in the middle of a ring system now, powered down and silent. The *Dragon Queen* was right – searching the debris would have taken a year or more. But if you started with the premise that Newman *hadn't* blown himself up, if you reconstructed what else had to have happened, no matter how unlikely, in order for him to survive, then there weren't so many places he could have ended up. It only took the *Dragon Queen* half an hour to pick him out.

There was always the chance he was carrying an antimatter warhead in there with him.

Ziva took him the quiet way, letting him think she'd missed him and then dropping a salvage and recovery drone as she passed by. A dozen tiny bots detached themselves from the *Dragon Queen*'s hull and swarmed over to Newman's pod. Three of them bored into it, slow and steady, while the others sealed the breaches the first left behind so the pod wouldn't register even a microscopic loss of pressure. Once they were in, the bots found the pod's single passenger and sedated him. The rest was easy. The recovery drone brought him back to the *Dragon Queen* and Ziva reeled him in with the fuel scoops. She took a good long time sweeping both him and the pod for any kind of radiation, for viruses, bio-contaminants and anything that might possibly explode. When she was done, she took a good look at him. Thirty-five thousand credits, sleeping like a baby in front of her.

'Hello, Newman,' she said.

Chapter Five

'The station's just hard scanned us,' Orla said. Jenny looked up from her control panel. Jonty remained slumped in his chair. He had been drinking steadily since the ice asteroid. Ravindra should have said something but she didn't want the fight right now. She felt her heart sink.

What now? she wondered. A nimbus of flame surrounded them as they made re-entry, dropping towards the bands of colour that were Motherlode's surface. Whit's Station looked tiny against the backdrop of the gas giant.

Harlan Whit's face appeared on the comms screen monitor. The image was covered in static. Orla used her hologramatic control gloves to throw the image up onto the cockpit. Part of the transparent hull became the screen. The static cleared as they completed re-entry.

'What happened to you?' Harlan asked.

'What's up, Harlan?' Ravindra responded.

'Looks like you took a bit of a beating.'

Ravindra moved her hands and brought the *Song of Stone* in on a longer approach than normal. They had switched their transponder back on, which was normally more than enough for Whit's Station. This time, however, the station had hit them with a scan so active it had probably lowered Jonty's sperm count.

'Is there a problem?' Ravindra asked, then she cut the comms link and turned to Orla. 'Any weapon locks?'

Orla glanced back at her. 'That's probably something I would have mentioned,'

They were all tired. The adrenaline had worn off and left them edgy and narky with each other. Well, that and the death of one of their own.

'That's not how I play, you know that, girl,' Harlan told them when Ravindra came back online. He must have guessed what she had asked Orla. He was one of the few people that Ravindra would let get away with calling her 'girl'. 'We've got some things to discuss, though. You need to come and see me when you land.'

'Sure,' Ravindra said, not liking where this was going. The *Song* hit some turbulence and Jonty made a complaining noise from behind her as her hands traced patterns in light to minimise the effects of the chop. 'I'll speak to you soon,' Ravindra told Harlan and then nodded to Orla, who cut the link. Ravindra thought for a moment. The *Song* was flying smooth now. Below her she could see thunderheads gathering. Lightning crackled, electrical displays thousands of miles long. Ahead of the *Song* the huge mushroom shape of Whit's Station was getting closer and closer.

'This is a long way from over,' she said. She glanced behind her. Jenny looked absorbed in going over the damage control reports from the fight on the ice asteroid, but Ravindra knew the engineer well enough to know that she was worried. Then she glanced at Jonty. He was a drunken, red-eyed, tear-stained mess, which wasn't what she needed right now. She glanced at Orla, who was looking back at her.

'I'll get some Purge down him,' Orla told her. 'He'll be fine.'

Ravindra nodded, unconvinced. Still, she turned back to the station, which now filled their view through the transparent part of the hull.

The elevator doors opened and she stepped in. The elevator sent a signal to her ring computer letting her know that it would be taking her up into the restricted section.

Security, in the shape of a couple of Harlan's dependable old hands, was waiting for her in the carpeted hallway as she stepped out of the elevator. Ravindra knew them both and they exchanged friendly greetings. To her surprise they didn't take her direct to Harlan's office. Instead they took her to the station's control centre. Inside there was a raised platform that ran between rows of sunken control panels where all the workings of the station, from financial and life support to the automated hydrogen mining operation, were handled. A significant part of the personnel present ran air traffic control and looked after the port facilities. They used hologramatic control gloves and a mixture of glasses and monocular heads-up-displays, though much of the wall was covered in flat screens and holo-projections of various control systems for ease of use by the section supervisors. The rest of the wall was a huge transparent window looking out over Motherlode's planetary horizon.

From the station's position Ravindra could see an Anaconda, wreathed in flame, making a classic flat-bottomed entry into the atmosphere. The spearhead-shaped craft was an old design, but this one looked new. Sleek, for such a large ship, it displaced more than nine hundred tonnes, and it was heavily armoured. Although nominally a freighter, Ravindra knew that some navies still used the Anaconda in a frigate or light cruiser role. They were fast for their size and could be modified to pack quite a punch. Although Ravindra would never consider trading in her Cutter, she had always thought that the Anaconda were magnificent craft. That hadn't stopped her attacking a few in her time.

Harlan was standing in front of the large window. He

was wearing his trademark white linen suit, holding his cane behind his back. An argument with a knife-wielding smuggler just over ten years earlier had left him with nerve damage in his left leg. The medical facilities on the station just weren't quite up to repairing the damage, and Harlan never left the station long enough to get it fixed elsewhere.

'Hey, Harlan,' Ravindra said, walking up to him. Harlan just nodded. Then she noticed the comms link icon blinking in her lenses. She opened the connection and found a link to sensor information coming in from the station and the results of a lidar scan from one of the orbital defence satellites. It showed a corvette in high orbit. Made by the Federation, the corvettes were multi-role warships comparable to the Imperial cutters. They were a little slower but more heavily armed.

The station's sensors showed that the Anaconda docking with the station was heavily armoured, had a shield projector and carried enough firepower to give a frigate a run for its money. It wasn't as fast or as manoeuvrable as the *Song of Stone* but it certainly packed a far heavier punch. Ravindra was beginning to get a sinking feeling as she looked at the converted freighter. There was something wrong with the ship's configuration. The cargo hold looked like it had been extensively modified.

'See the hangar doors?' Harlan asked. Ravindra had noticed them. She was looking down now. The Anaconda was too big to come into the station proper and a docking umbilical was extending from the station to mate with the ship.

'Fighters?' Ravindra asked. Harlan nodded. The Anaconda was a large ship. Ravindra was trying to do the math. If the cargo hold had been completely converted to a flight deck how many fighters could it hold? She didn't like the numbers she was coming up with. Ravindra opened her mouth to ask if the corvette and the Anaconda were here for her, but Harlan held up his arm.

'Let's talk in my office,' he said

'Brandy?' Harlan asked. Ravindra shook her head. She had a feeling that it was going to be a very long day, to the point where she suspected an offer of stims would be more useful.

Harlan took some time fixing himself a drink and then sat down behind his hardwood desk, ownership of which would probably have gotten him executed for crimes against the environment in the Sol system.

'They're here for us, right? The Corvette's back up for the Anaconda?' Ravindra asked, sitting down in one of the comfortable green leather chairs on the opposite side of the desk.

'You've chipped a tooth,' Harlan said. 'You're walking a little stiff and the *Song*'s E-bomb is missing. I take it things didn't go well?'

'I'm not going to talk about it,' Ravindra said wearily. 'And the hard scan was out of order.'

'I didn't know what was coming back. There are some very concerned people who want to speak to you.'

'Is this where you tell me you told me so?' Ravindra asked. The leather chair felt so comfortable. She wanted to go to sleep in it and then wake up, have a drink with Harlan and see Harnack off properly. She knew it wasn't going to happen.

'Who'd you lose?' Harlan asked.

'Harnack,' Ravindra finally told him. He just nodded, not saying anything else, his expression hard to read.

'Are they Syndicate?' Ravindra finally asked.

'The ship that just docked is the *Omerta*, there's a Veil on board.' Ravindra was suddenly very much awake. Just for a moment fear was written all over her face, before she managed to regain control. 'Sure you don't want that drink now?' Harlan asked. She accepted the drink.

'They here to talk?' Ravindra asked.

'They are. Will you listen, girl?'

This time being called 'girl' rankled her.

'What does our protection get us?' Ravindra asked.

'A polite request to them not to kill you and mess up my station.'

'You hanging us out to dry?'

Harlan's expression softened. There was sympathy there, but not guilt. He took a sip of his bourbon.

'No,' he finally said. 'I'll sit in your corner, but let's be clear about one thing, I … we … can't stand up to the Syndicate.'

'Like we couldn't stand up to the Empire?' Ravindra asked. It was a low blow and she knew it, but she had to do what she could for her crew. *Now* she could see the guilt in his face. *Now* he suddenly looked old and tired.

'The Empire gave us a stand-up fight. The Judas Syndicate will already have people on the station. They don't like what they hear, they'll just murder me, put one of theirs in my place and nothing is very much fun anymore. You know that.'

Ravindra nodded.

'I'll do what I can. I'll fight your corner, run interference.'

'Make sure Ji's okay?'

Harlan stopped for a moment. He just looked at her. Then said. 'I'll look after the boy.'

Ravindra opened her mouth to ask about refitting the

Song, but Harlan had the distant look of someone who was receiving information via his lenses.

'There's a number of very serious-looking people making their way towards the *Song* right now,' Harlan told her. Harlan forwarded the security feed he was receiving to Ravindra.

They didn't waste any time, Ravindra thought as she turned and ran for the door.

She made it to the elevator and called it. It seemed to take forever.

'Orla,' she said over her comms link. She could hear Harlan limping after her, talking into his own comms link. 'You've got the Syndicate incoming. Looks like about eight or so, fully armed. Lock up the berth, lock up the ship, do not engage.'

The elevator arrived as Harlan caught up with her.

'Security override on berth 44D. Lock it down tight,' he said into his comms link. 'I want Taylor and two squads of security there, armed for bear.'

Both of them stepped into the elevator. Orla hadn't replied.

'Orla! Orla, respond!' Ravindra shouted, as though raising her voice would make a difference. 'Run a diagnostics on comms,' she told her computer ring as she drew and checked both burst pistols. 'Have you screwed me?' she asked Harlan evenly. Harlan didn't even glance down at the two burst pistols.

'No,' he said, looking her straight in the eyes.

'Then why are the comms down?'

'I don't know, but the security override on your berth isn't working either.'

'They walk up on the *Song* like that, Jonty's going to turn them to red steam with the pulse lasers.'

'I can't have your crew killing Syndicate on my station, darlin', I just can't.'

'Then you need to get between them and my people, and do it quickly.' If Harlan was telling the truth then someone had screwed them both. The elevator door opened and Ravindra started running. Those that knew her well enough, and saw that she was armed, got out of the way. Harlan came limping after her.

Ravindra could see the station's security running towards the corridor that led to the fourth level of docking berths. The security was mainly made up of wandering gunmen and women, most of them with a price on their heads, who had settled in Whit's Station and who Harlan had decided to put to good use. They were competent or Harlan wouldn't have hired them, but they weren't going to get there in time, either.

This doesn't make sense. Ravindra sprinted into the docking berth. The *Song of Stone*, high on its landing struts, filled the berth. Even scarred up with blackened score lines from the Cobra's laser, she still looked majestic. A technological bird of prey, sleek, proud and deadly. There was no sign of violence. The ramp to the ship was down and the airlock door was open, as it normally was when they were berthed and working on the ship.

Ravindra advanced into the berth, both pistols up, scanning left, right, up and down. She heard them before she saw them. The sounds of boots falling on the ramp. Ravindra moved quickly behind a packing crate that some of the *Song*'s missile components had come in. Both her pistols were levelled at the ramp.

They came down cautiously. They had projectile carbines at the ready and were scanning all around them. These weren't low-level criminal enforcers. These were clearly military contractors. If Ravindra had to guess, then she thought they were probably slave auxiliaries from one of the contract military Ludi.

They were onto her immediately. Three of them emerged from the ship. Two of them had their carbines levelled at her, the third was checking all around the berth.

How did they get onto the ship? Why hadn't they been taken out in the berth? Why hadn't the ship been buttoned up?

They were shouting at her to drop the pistols and put her hands on her head.

'Not going to happen! Put the guns down, lie face down on the deck, lace your fingers behind your heads!' she shouted back. It was a waste of time. She had been here before. This was the moment before a gunfight. She resolved to start it. It was the closest thing to an edge she would get. She started to squeeze both triggers.

'Enough!' The slave-soldiers went quiet but kept their carbines levelled at her as they moved to better cover. The voice hadn't sounded like a shout, but it had carried, and it was a voice that was used to being obeyed. 'Captain Khanguire, I would like to speak to you. Reason with you. I want to see if I can impress upon you the seriousness of this situation. I, with the rest of my men, am going to come down the ramp. You are going to see some things that will upset you. I implore you not to overreact.'

'Just you!' Ravindra shouted back.

'That's not how this is going to happen, I'm afraid. If you shoot then nobody gets what they want. We're coming down now.'

The contractors wore civilian versions of dark-coloured military clothing. All of them had their weapons up, several had them pointed at her and she found herself looking down the barrels of underslung grenade launchers. Ravindra saw one of them pushing a battered-looking Jenny in front

98

of them. Her hands were locked in front of her neck, attached to an explosive slave collar. Ravindra felt her gorge rise when she saw the collar.

The man whom she assumed had done the talking wore an immaculately tailored suit that she guessed came from one of the Imperial houses on Capitol. He had a bowler hat on, and from under the hat flowed a white veil that obscured his features. Even with Harlan's warning, her heart still sank. Somehow she had struggled to believe that the Judas Syndicate would actually send a Veil.

The last two slave contractors out of the *Song* were carrying a collapsible stretcher with a body bag on it. Ravindra desperately wanted to shoot someone. With a whisper she switched the burst pistol in her right hand, always her more accurate, from fully automatic to semi-automatic. She shifted it by increments until the crosshairs settled over the slave-soldier that was holding Jenny. She knew she could kill him, but then a shot from a grenade launcher would turn her into so much flying meat.

'Can I assume that you now understand the gravity of the situation?' the Veil asked. Somehow his voice seemed quiet, though it carried and she had no problem understanding every syllable.

'I'm sorry, Rav,' Jenny said miserably.

'It's all right,' Ravindra lied to the engineer. 'Who's in the bag?'

Jenny looked confused for a moment.

'Harnack,' Jenny told her. That didn't make sense to Ravindra. She couldn't understand what the Syndicate would want with Harnack's body.

'Orla and Jonty?'

'They are both fine,' the Veil informed her.

'I'm not talking to you,' Ravindra told him.

99

'They got shocked pretty bad but they'll live,' Jenny said. 'There was nothing, no warning, just suddenly they were in the ship …'

'Decanus, please gag Miss Storrow,' the Veil said. The slave-soldier holding the diminutive engineer grabbed her by the head and forced a self-expanding ball gag into her mouth. Jenny's nostrils flared and Ravindra could read the anger in her eyes.

'Okay,' Ravindra said. 'So I kill you, and the rest of your guys get me – assuming they're still interested in the contract and being a slave after I've sprayed your head all over my pretty ship.'

The Veil was shaking his head as she spoke.

'Do you really think this is just another frontier gunfight? Do you honestly think that I would waste my time, these resources, for that?'

She had to concede that he had a point.

At that moment, Harlan and the station security turned up. Ravindra remained behind the crate and the Veil stayed standing where he was. There was some more shouting and gun pointing.

'Enough!' Harlan finally yelled before limping into the berth to stand, leaning on his cane, between the station gunmen and women, and the slave-soldiers. He did not block Ravindra's view of the Veil. Her arms were starting to hurt from holding the pistols up.

'Let's see if we can't settle this with a conversation,' Harlan suggested.

'Ah yes, good old-fashioned common sense masquerading as folksy frontier wisdom. The peacemaker. The compromiser. I am afraid not,' the Veil said, walking forward beyond the protective cordon of his unhappy-looking slave-soldiers. Ravindra felt some of the station security personnel shift

100

slightly, nervously changing the grip on their weapons. She suspected that nobody wanted to be the one that killed a Judas Syndicate Veil.

'We are an organisation that prides ourselves on anonymity. Our whole point is that we could be anyone. This encourages people not to mess with us, because they never know who we could be. Their dentist, a man sitting next to them on a park bench, a woman in a bar, their oldest friend, a lover. You get that, right?'

Ravindra wasn't sure who he was talking to, but she kept her left pistol on him, her right pistol on the slave-soldier closest to the gagged and furious Jenny.

'So can you imagine how unhappy we are when one of us actually has to appear in public? I mean, this is a media event. By now someone will have told someone else, who will have told someone else and then everyone will be trying to trace me, find out who I am, because – for cop or journo – discovering the identity of a Veil would be a major coup. We will almost certainly have to kill a few journalists over this. And do you appreciate how much I value my anonymity?'

Harlan cast a glance at Ravindra. It was the first time she could remember Harlan being short of words. Actually, it was the first time she could remember him not being in control of the situation.

'No?' Ravindra suggested.

'Well, I'll tell you. I probably have a lower standard of living than you. Oh, don't get me wrong, it's not bad – but I do not live the swashbuckling high-life of a frontier space pirate. Do you know what I do?'

'Obviously not,' Ravindra said through gritted teeth, tiring of this game.

'I go to PTA meetings. Now, you've got a child, haven't you, Captain Khanguire?' the Veil asked. Ravindra almost

pulled the trigger. 'Seventeen years old, called Ji, right?'
Ravindra swallowed hard. 'Have you ever been to a PTA
meeting' All Ravindra could see was the silhouette of his
facial features through the white silk-like material of the
veil, the movement of his mouth. 'No, of course you haven't.
It's the social equivalent of root canal surgery, if the surgeon
went in through the anus. That is how boring my life is.
Unless, of course, I have to take two heavily armed ships
full of military-contractors, hired through a bewildering set
of blinds, and jump out to the absolute middle of less-than-
nowhere to retrieve something that I've already paid for.'

'Good speech,' Ravindra said.

'You like it?'

'I think you just made all that up.'

'That would seem likely, wouldn't it? I want my cargo.'

'I'm sure we can work something out here, we're all
civilised people,' Harlan said. Ravindra could make out the
shadow of the Veil's face contort under the silken veil.

'No,' the Veil said, his tone suggesting it took a real effort
to control his anger. 'If we were civilised people then we'd
be in a civilised place, doing civilised things. Clearly, that is
not what we are doing. We are going to get what we want
and then we are going to remind people why they do not
mess us around like this.' He was shaking his head. Then he
turned to Ravindra. 'About two thousand years ago they used
to use these clips to hold eyes open for surgery.' He reached
into his pocket and pulled out what looked like two twists of
wire. 'So the patient didn't blink. Now, you're going to want
to shoot me, and I have two children so, believe me, I can
empathise with that want, but it is in your best interest not
to do so. You see, you'll be wearing these when I have your
son raped to death in front of your eyes, and your head will
be in a vice so you won't be able to look away.' Ravindra

102

swallowed. She felt her hand go numb. She tried not to squeeze the trigger. 'It's hard to imagine a more complete failure as a parent than one who would allow that to happen.'

'Newman tried to burn us,' Ravindra said.

'I don't care,' the Veil told her.

'You might not,' Ravindra said, trying to control her anger. 'But you can see how we'd maybe respond in a certain way to that, right? As far as we're concerned the deal hasn't changed. We get paid, you get the cargo and everyone walks away…well, less than happy. There is no need for any of this.'

'If you weren't pulling a burn then why'd you dump the cargo? Good job, by the way, we couldn't find a thing in the nav's memory. The only thing on the table is the life of your crew and your son.'

Ravindra realised that the Veil couldn't have known that the cargo was still on the *Song* in a very well-hidden smugglers' compartment. In fact, somebody had misled him, made him think that they had dropped the cargo somewhere else. She just couldn't work out why.

'Okay, this is how it's going to go down—' Ravindra started.

'Do you really think you're in charge of anything?' The Veil was shaking his head. 'You care about everyone involved. I'm here on a matter of principle.'

'Expensive principle,' Harlan said. The Veil's head shot around. He must have been staring at Harlan. The station boss didn't flinch.

'I'll shoot her in the head,' Ravindra said nodding at Jenny. 'To spare her your tender mercies, and then take my chances.'

The Veil turned to look at Jenny. The engineer just glared at him defiantly.

'Ask around, she'll do it in a heartbeat,' Harlan told him.

'Then what do you have to bargain with?' Ravindra asked.

'You know you can't run far and fast enough, right?' the Veil asked her.

'You know you've always got to leave people with something to lose, right?' Ravindra asked. 'You're going to take Jenny, there's nothing I can do about that, but you had better treat her good because I'll want proof of life. I set the rendezvous point, just one ship.' Her comms link icon started blinking in the corner of her lens. Ji was trying to speak to her. She severed the link. 'I go get the cargo, we meet, you put Jenny in a pod and eject her and I'll need proof that's happened. I eject your cargo. We pick up Jenny, you pick up the cargo, and if you're quick enough then you get to try to kill us when we make a break for it.'

'You're not in a position—'

'You don't like it then let's roll the dice, right here, right now.'

The Veil looked at her for a moment and then glanced at Harlan.

'You don't gamble, Captain Khanguire,' he said.

'You've left me with a zero sum game.'

The Veil gave this some thought.

'Agreed,' he said finally.

'This only works with you off my station,' Harlan told the Veil.

The Veil walked past them followed by his security team, dragging Jenny with them and carrying Harnack's body on the stretcher. Ravindra stared at the body bag as it was carried past.

'We'll be in touch,' the Veil told her.

Ravindra lowered her pistols. Her arms were aching, the

104

muscles felt as if they were on fire. She had no idea how she had managed to stop her arms from shaking.

'They shouldn't have gotten in as easily as they did. Someone sold us out.' Ravindra changed the subject, shouting over her shoulder as she started running towards the ship. 'If it's one of your people—'

'You can talk to them before I kill them!' Harlan shouted after her as she ran up the ramp into the *Song*.

Ravindra was in her home now. She all but fell over Jonty. He was lying in the corridor that led from the cargo bay to the cockpit. He had his burst pistol in his hand. Ravindra reckoned he had heard something and been heading towards the ramp when they jolted him. He was going to be out for a while. They had jolted him pretty extensively.

She found Orla coming to on the bridge.

'You okay?' she asked. Orla nodded, her expression grim.

The comms icon in Ravindra's lenses started blinking. It was Ji again.

'I just turned around and they were there. I don't understand how …' Orla started.

No, none of us do, Ravindra thought suspiciously. 'They've got Jenny,' Ravindra told her, then opened the comms link to Ji. His image appeared in a window on her lenses. He was looking into the camera on his comp ring. He wanted her to see how angry he was. Ravindra kept her side of the conversation voice only.

'What the fuck, mum? You just shunt the call? What do—'

'Are you in the apartment?' she demanded, interrupting him.

'No, I'm at Alice's,' he said. Ravindra mentally ran through her list of Ji's friends. *Shit!* She was pretty sure that

Alice was one of Merkel's crew, a pirate groupie that Merkel kept around to make himself feel good.

'Okay, stay there until I come and get you. Where is it?'

'What? You're not coming here—'

'This is important, Ji.'

'It always is when you're talking, mum, never when I am. Well, fuck you!'

'Don't talk to m—' Ravindra snapped, the tension finally getting to her as she felt her temper start to slip.

'Want to know what it feels like?' Ji cut the comms link.

'Shit!' Ravindra screamed.

Orla was staring at her. Ravindra shook her head.

'I'll be back,' Ravindra said.

'We need to talk,' Orla told her. Ravindra acknowledged this while striding out of the bridge. As she walked through the ship and out onto the berth past the remaining station security personnel, those that weren't escorting the Veil and his people off the station, there was still something nagging at her mind. Someone had sold them out to the Syndicate that was clear. She hadn't wanted to say anything that would reveal her ignorance, show her hand, but what she didn't understand was why they wanted Harnack's body.

Chapter Six

Usually Ziva kept most of the *Dragon Queen*'s cargo hold fitted out with a collapsible internal fuel tank and a holding cell for the bounties she took. The *Dragon Queen* had collapsed the tank and jettisoned the cell when it had swooped in to snatch the elevator and so Ziva was left with no option but to keep Newman in the *Dragon Queen* herself; not that there was very much room in a Fer-de-Lance once you replaced the factory fitted luxury cabins with more fuel space and warheads. She let the ship drift while she pulled Newman, unconscious, out of his escape pod and floated him down the forward passageway that ran between the two tiny cabins, the head, and the cockpit. She put a tag on him, and a bracelet and a collar so that the moment he did anything she didn't like she could shock him into unconsciousness, dosed him with so much Antimatter that he wouldn't know who he was when he woke up, and locked him into the half of the spare cabin that she'd rigged as an emergency containment cell.

And then there was the Truth. Truth was illegal throughout the Federation, the Empire and the Alliance but every bounty hunter worth their salt carried some. Truth did what it said. No need for long tortuous physical interrogations, no need for psychology, no need for anything except a nice chat over a cup of something hot and sweet and a camera sitting in the background recording it all. The Federation really didn't like Truth; nor did they like people getting juiced on Antimatter but there wasn't much they could do about either in an empty system outside their borders. Once she had Newman locked up, Ziva took him out to Witches' Reach. It was a nothing system and as far as she knew no one had ever claimed it or given it a proper name. There were some basic survey records but nothing more. Simple binary star system with two Sol-like main-sequence stars and a single gas giant for fuel. Every bounty hunter had their backwater systems where they could go and hide for a while, where they could get on and do things in peace and quiet. Every pirate had them too. She'd start with that, she thought: with Newman's safe systems, with his ship and his crew.

When she was ready for him, she went back to his cell and drone-jabbed him with Wakey-Wakey, then tossed a bottle of water through the bars. This bit was the worst, the first confrontation, the part that always made her nervous. She was careful – extremely careful – when searching the bounties she took before she let them wake up, but she could never be *quite* sure they hadn't smuggled some trick past her.

She waited for his eyes to focus on her. 'Hello, Newman.'

He blinked a few times. 'Who are you?'

'Bounty hunter.' That was all he needed to know. 'You got any threats you want to make, deals you think you can cut, you make them now.'

Newman leered at her. 'You crossed the Syndicate, bounty hunter. Open this cage and when I'm done with you I'll put in a good word.'

'*That's* your best offer?' Ziva snorted. 'No sub-cranial anti-matter bomb? No tailored viruses? Although I do scan for those, of course.' Newman, as best she could tell, was a proper shit. Some pirates saw themselves as anarchists, as freedom fighters. Most were simply jerks who wanted to have something on the quick and easy. And then, right at the far end, there were the Newmans, the thrill-seeker sadists who took pleasure in what they did and just didn't know how to stop. The Pilots' Federation had put a bounty on him for a couple of stop-and-board raids but it was the tip of an iceberg and Ziva had known it as soon as she'd seen what he'd done. There were murders in at least three systems that had his name all over them – bloody, senseless, brutal things. She reckoned she was about to discover a good half dozen more.

Newman shook his head. 'Threats, bounty hunter? What for? You want my cards on the table? You know who I work for. You know what they're like. I don't have a ship anymore, so that Pilots' Federation bounty on me has gone. I'm worthless to you. I'm just one motherfucker of a liability now, because my people don't leave loose ends.'

'What happened to your ship, Newman?'

He stretched out in the zero gravity and pushed himself to the bars, as close to her as he could get. His eyes were wide, dilated from the drugs. He was shaking. *Too much Antimatter.* 'That bitch Khanguire,' he spat. 'That's what happened to it. Ravindra Khanguire.'

Ravindra Khanguire. She didn't know the name. She asked the *Dragon Queen* to cross-reference but it wasn't in any of her databases. Maybe that was the way to do it with Newman, then. Disassemble his life backwards instead of forwards. Darkwater would pay if he'd been one of the captains in Stopover, but he was right about the Pilots' Federation: Whoever this Khanguire was, she'd taken that bounty when she'd taken out his ship. Twenty thousand credits. All that work pissed away. No point in grilling him about what had happened before Stopover.

Backwards, then. 'The *Unkindness* brought you back to the Black Mausoleum in an escape pod. Where did it find you?'

'61 Cygni. What's a nice little girl like you doing hunting bounties? Where's your boss? I want *him* here, not you.'

'No, you don't,' said Ziva. 'Partly because I don't have one, and partly because even if I did, you'd still want me. You want to think about how much you could hurt me if you got out of there, don't you, Newman? How big and strong and tough you are, and how small and fragile I look. You like to imagine how it would be if those bars somehow vanished and you got those beefy hands on me. That's about right, isn't it? Luckily for me that clouds your judgement – well, that and the drugs I put in you. But you don't want someone else. You want to keep thinking about all those things.' Ziva smiled at him. 'You do that.'

Newman laughed a low throaty laugh and grinned, baring all his teeth. 'Is that what *you're* thinking about?' He sucked in a sharp breath. 'Does it make you afraid?' Truth didn't let you lie, but it wasn't perfect.

'Not really. What were you doing in an escape pod in 61 Cygni?'

'It was our rendezvous ...'

'Whose rendezvous?'

'With Khanguire. Like I told you. She was supposed to meet me after we took the *Pandora*. Ravindra Khanguire. Bitch. I went there to pay her off like I was supposed to, and she took my ship and I want her dead. I'll kill her if I find her.' He cocked his head. 'Tell you what, bounty hunter – I'll help *you*. Plenty of bounty on *that* ship. We'll take her down together.'

'The job that got you in this mess: who set it up?'

She listened impassively as Newman ran through the attack as though it was nothing. The Orca was carrying a cargo and the Judas Syndicate wanted it. The Veil of the Black Mausoleum had hired him and given him what he needed to get it. He didn't know what the cargo itself was except that it was in a sealed secure crate. Didn't know and didn't much care. And of course he had no idea who the Veil really was.

'Tell me about the *Pandora* and how you hit it.'

Newman grinned again. 'It was sweet. We jumped into the Kuiper boundary and she was right in front of us. Khanguire might be a bitch who's going to die slowly and in a world of hurt, but she was all over that Orca. Cut it open for me with the precision of a surgeon and so quick and far out there was no way the Darkwater Vipers were going to get to us before we were in, out, and gone – with our trails all evaporated.'

'So Khanguire stood overwatch while you and your crew went in? Who blew the ship?'

'I had a bit of fun with some of the crew and then I had to take them down. Couple of pods got away. Khanguire went mental and dropped an E-bomb. She nearly took me out. That's what you get when you deal with amateurs.'

'But you're not an amateur, are you?'

Newman laughed. 'I trained with the best, bounty hunter. Fifteen years. I'll show you a trick or two if you like. Or are you still scared?'

'With these bars between us?' asked Ziva drily. 'Terrified.'

It took a bit of poking to get at the whole of everything that had led up to the *Song of Stone* letting off her E-bomb, but by the end she thought she understood. Newman had started on the Orca's crew. His reason for it had been that he could; and that was the Newman she'd been hunting, right enough, the Newman who thought laws and morality were for the weak and stupid, who was probably responsible for a string of savage murders across Federation space. Executing the crew changed the game, made the bounties a whole lot higher, and so Khanguire had been minimising her risk. Newman had made it the logical choice. A cold one, though – Newman might be a sociopath but this Khanguire, if anything, sounded worse. And then, as Newman told it, Khanguire had tried to take him down too.

'Why'd she do that, Newman?'

'Because she's a stupid amateur bitch who doesn't know who she's dealing with, that's why.'

'She knew she was dealing with *you*, didn't she?'

'61 Cygni was our rendezvous. I was supposed to pay her off. If it had been down to me then I'd have wasted her there, her and her whole junk crew for what they pulled. But this was a Syndicate deal. They like quiet and people sticking to their scripts. So I was ready to do my bit and do what I was told and everything looked sweet. And then the next thing I know she's wasting the men I've got on overwatch and turning her ship's lasers on us.' He spat. 'We barely even got off the ground before she hit our engines. Bitch had a missile loitering right from the start.' He glared at Ziva as he told her how Khanguire had dismantled him. 'My Cobra against an Imperial cutter? Hardly an even fight.' He looked about. 'Now this ship, though – a Fer-de-Lance. Didn't get to have much of a look at you when you were chasing me but you'd have a much better chance with this.'

'I'm quite sure you're right. You went straight to 61 Cygni from Stopover?'

'Yes. You want to cut a deal? I'll help you get Khanguire. The Syndicate will want her head on a stick for what she pulled. *I'm* not worth anything to you, but *she* is. I'll tell you where to look, you take her down. You keep the bounty, give me the cargo and let me go, and I'll split the credit packs that were meant to be hers.' He grinned. 'Yeah, I still got them safe. The Syndicate gets what it wants and we both get to keep our heads.'

'We do, do we?' Ziva chuckled. The Syndicate wasn't known for being forgiving.

'Maybe. I don't know. But it's the best chance either of us has, bounty hunter.'

'Khanguire didn't go straight to 61 Cygni. She went somewhere else first. Another rendezvous?' But Newman only shrugged. 'Tell me about this cargo.'

'I've got no idea. Khanguire has it now.'

'You want to deal? You go first. Where will I find her?'

'At Whit's Station, probably. If she doesn't vanish.'

Ziva had a micro-drone bite Newman with a sedative, then returned to the cockpit and told the *Dragon Queen* to jump back to Beta Hydri. Newman had said he wasn't aiming to burn Khanguire at their rendezvous. He'd been dosed up with Truth so he probably meant it but Ziva could see how it might have looked the other way. First impression? This Khanguire was cautious, clinical and cold. Newman looked like a risk and so she'd taken him out. Good girl. If she'd done the job properly then no one outside the Syndicate would know the first thing about her and she'd be clean. As it was, Khanguire had the Syndicate's cargo and the Syndicate were going to be hopping mad. They'd go after her like wolverines. Khanguire would either deal or vanish.

Or maybe she'd roll over.

Ziva paused to consider this. She had Newman cold for the *Pandora*, which made him good for the Darkwater bounty and worth too much money to simply eject into space, tempting as it was. Most of the rest of what she'd been chasing him for had gone when he'd lost his ship. Irritating, but that was the way the Pilots' Federation worked. Maybe if she dug and probed she might find stuff he'd done that no one had linked to him yet but it would be pocket change compared to Darkwater.

Fifteen thousand credits for each made this Khanguire very interesting too.

The *Dragon Queen* arrived back in Beta Hydri and micro-jumped to the gas giant Endl. While the Fer-de-Lance skimmed fuel, Ziva sent avatars across to a handful of people who'd known her back when she flew a Viper. There was some explaining to do about what had gone down on the Black Mausoleum, although technically she ought to be doing that explaining to the nearest Imperial ambassador. She told them anyway, gave her side of the story and made sure everyone knew she wasn't about to run anywhere. When she was done, she traded in a few old favours and looked into the law enforcement databases, trawling for anything she could find on Ravindra Khanguire. Whit's Station made for an interesting dilemma. The Black Mausoleum operated under a façade of order and compliance to Federation ordinances because the rest of the system would have swept it away otherwise. Whit's Station didn't give a fuck about any of that shit. Reddot was an anarchy system and proud of it. Pirates operated openly, some of them quietly sponsored by the Federation to be a nuisance to the Empire, some of them the other way round. Both sides talked loudly about shutting the place down, wading in with a battlecruiser or an interdictor and rousting everyone out; but neither did any more than rattle their sabres because they both had the place riddled with their own spies. A pirate who made Whit's Station their home normally didn't last long, but there were plenty of others who would flit in and out and use the place for supply and repair.

Ravindra Khanguire. The name didn't mean anything. If she was as good as the *Pandora* take-down made her look, what was she doing in a place like Whit's Station?

Ziva checked the bounties open on Newman again. She didn't need to take this Khanguire down as well. She could haul Newman back to Stopover, claim the reward and go home. Put her feet up for a few months. Get the *Dragon Queen* serviced. Pass on the capacitors for the *Dragon Queen's* lasers. Give Enaya what she wanted.

Yeah. Until the itch bit her again.

Shit! Aisha! Right in the middle of the Black Mausoleum En had been trying to tell her something about Aisha. She deserved some time, a call … but …

Fifteen thousand credits for taking Khanguire to Darkwater. And maybe that was only the start of it. It wasn't the money. She didn't need the money. It was the itch. The not being able to let a thing rest when she had it in her sights.

The *Dragon Queen* drifted on through Endl's upper atmosphere. Dozens of avatars crawled through archives and open-access databases. A few more showed off her credentials to the authorities and begged and wheedled their way into more classified records, the sort the Federation didn't mind sharing with the handful of bounty hunters they'd come to trust. Ten years and she'd kept her nose clean. Maybe she pushed to the edge of the line sometimes, pulling stunts like the one on the Black Mausoleum and stuffing the bounties she caught full of Truth; but none of that was any secret, and however much she walked the line, she never actually crossed it. Most bounty hunters did, sooner or later. Most of them had a streak of pirate but not Ziva. She'd never taken down a ship that didn't have a bounty on it, never killed anyone she didn't absolutely have to and, even then, never anyone who didn't deserve it. There was no collateral damage in her past, no fire-fights in crowded space-station lounges, no scattering of anti-matter minelets in busy shipping lanes. She was meticulously clean and careful, always tidied up after herself and never got into a fight she couldn't win. In fact she rarely got into a fight at all until she'd manoeuvred her target into a corner with no one else around and the odds stacked heavily to her advantage.

She thought about running the Jameson simulation again but hesitated. Enaya deserved better. She closed her eyes.

'Start a k-cast,' she sighed. 'See if you can raise Enaya.'

It took a while. Setting up a k-cast always did. Ziva almost cancelled it twice. The words were right on her tongue when the link crackled open and a grainy video feed fizzed across the *Dragon Queen*'s screens.

'Ziv?' Enaya looked like shit. She looked like she'd crawled out of bed and was nursing the god-emperor of all hangovers. Which didn't make sense because En didn't drink on her own and it was the middle of the day back on Delta Pavonis.

'En. Christ, what happened to you?'

'Ziv, it's Aisha. She's …'

'What? What's happened?'

'She's gone, Ziv.' Shit, were those tear-streaks on En's face? Damn video bandwidth was too crappy to tell.

'*Gone*? En … What happened? Some sort of accident?'

'No. She …' Enaya's head sank into her hands and she started to shake with sobs. It took her a few moments to

116

find her voice again. 'She ran away with that Odar. She didn't even say anything. She left a note, Ziv. A *note*. Is that what I'm worth? She can't talk to her own mother? And then she got herself arrested.'

'Arrested? Aisha? What the fuck for?'

'Pills, Ziv.'

'Pills? What fucking pills?'

'I don't know.'

'Well, how did she get them?'

'I don't know!'

'What sort of pills?'

Enaya almost screamed at her. 'I said I don't fucking *know*! They let her go but they … She didn't want to come. She started screaming at me. She's sixteen. They wouldn't let me take her with me. She didn't want to … I don't know where she is, Ziv. I try to call but she doesn't answer.'

Ziv made herself count to ten. 'En, I've got Newman in my hold. I need to take him in. Give me a couple of days and I'll be home.'

The uncertain hope that washed over Enaya's face left Ziva feeling as though she'd been stabbed. 'For how long, Ziv? Because if it's just a day or two and then you're gone again then I don't …'

'A while, En. A while. I don't know. Long enough. However long Aisha needs. We'll talk about it when I'm there. The *Dragon Queen*'s due a service anyway. So there's that.' She winced. It was the wrong thing to say. 'And and we need to talk, En. I know that. About … things. And how they are.'

Enaya nodded slowly. 'Yes. We do. But okay. A couple of days, then.'

'You'll let me know if you hear from Aisha?' Ziva tried to bite back the anger but she just couldn't. 'She's really with that shit Odar again? After everything he's done to her?'

'I'm pretty sure. I don't know. I sent him a message. I haven't heard anything. He despises me.'

'I'm going to find him and I'm going to break his knees.'

'Ziv!'

'No, En. I told you he was bad news. Look, he's not going anywhere. He's got a non-transit order which means he can't leave Delta Pavonis without picking up a Point of Principle that would let me fuck with him to my heart's content. No, Odar Shit-for-brains can't go anywhere.' Ziva shook her head. 'I almost wish he would. I'll put as many credits as you like down on him being the one who gave her whatever it was that got her arrested. He needs to hurt for it.'

'Ziv, no, that's …'

Ziva snarled. 'If you *do* talk to him, tell him I'll gouge his eyes out when I catch him.'

'Ziv!'

'You know he's a piece of crap!'

'And how would *you* know? You've hardly seen him! You've hardly seen her! For months!'

'I know because I spent ten years dealing with shit-bags like him before I traded my Viper for my first Cobra! I *know*, En. He's a shit and he's bad for her, and you should never have let her see him.'

'So it's *my* fault now?' Enaya's face twisted in rage and pain. 'It's *my* fault that Aisha's run off with a junkie?'

'I didn't say …'

'Fuck you, Ziv. Just … just fuck you.' The link broke.

It took another hour for the avatars to come back and compile a file. It wasn't much. Ravindra Khanguire. Captain of the *Song of Stone*. Born and bred an Imperial slave pilot

118

and probably involved in a genetic manipulation program from conception. Convicted in her absence for a murder in the Empire but by then she'd escaped – for a slave, almost as serious a crime, and both would carry a bounty. No records in the Federation until she was taken in for piracy at the age of eighteen. Did some time in Warren Prison, came out almost two decades ago – and had come out pregnant too, though Ziva couldn't find any record of any offspring. Nothing more until she showed up as a registered trader in the Pilots' Federation, not that she ever did all that much trading. The *Song of Stone* itself was an Imperial cutter. There weren't any official records of modification but you didn't need to be an expert to look over the bulges in the hull and know it had undergone some extensive rework. There were hardpoints on the outside for a fistful of drones and a turret where most cutters had never had a turret. It was impossible to tell what the *Song of Stone* was packing beneath its weapon nacelles. The whole shape of the back of the ship had been changed at some point and that had to mean a serious engine modification.

Getting much on the crew was like getting blood out of a stone. The avatars dug out the former captain, Marvin Dane, and that was about it. The *Song* had done a couple of things it shouldn't. Dane had attracted a bounty. Not a big one, but someone had gone after him for it, caught him in Tiolce and taken him when he was away from the *Song*. He'd gone down fighting. The only other name she could get was Jonty Davis. He had a partner, a Gurkha by the looks of him. Jonty and Dane and Khanguire had all been in Warren Prison together, so there was the connection. Dane had made a crew in there and they'd stayed together after he'd died. At a guess, from the prison records, that made the Gurkha Harnack Sahota.

'*OK, Khanguire, but how do you make your money?*' A fast, armed cutter was perfect for a pirate. There were records of the *Song of Stone* moving about Federation and Alliance space and even flitting into the fringes of the Empire, but there was no way to tell what the *Song* had carried and traded. The Federation and the Empire would both have records; but the Federation wouldn't have shared them even back when Ziva had worn a uniform; and as for the Empire, well, that would all depend on getting the right Senator interested in being helpful. The Alliance was even worse, a case of going to each world one by one and trying to get access. There was something off about the *Song of Stone*'s movement, though. It wasn't the pattern of a working ship. There was no back-and-forth of a steady trading circuit and she frequently loitered in the same system for days or even weeks, or else vanished into empty space for a while. Not the sort of thing a regular trader could afford to do. The *Song* moved as though she were a ship of leisure, a ship not tied to any needs.

The *Song* moved, Ziva suddenly realised, like a bounty hunter. There was nowhere it kept going back to, no apparent home, but it did keep vanishing from the records within a jump or two of Reddot.

Whit's Station.

'*And you don't hunt bounties, do you?*' Ziva checked with the Pilots' Federation on the off-chance but Ravindra Khanguire had never claimed a single bounty. Didn't mean she hadn't done it under another name, of course.

Not one record of the *Song of Stone* being involved in any sort of attack after she changed hands. Not even a hint of it. Every official record came back as unremarkable. A clean bill of health. Nothing of note. Nothing except the time Khanguire had done on Ross 128 and what Newman had told her with his brain hazed by Truth.

120

Something caught her eye. Three years back Khanguire had been in Barnard's Star and vanished for a month. Ziva cross-checked against the public record to be sure, but yes – a few days after the *Song of Stone* vanished, the infamous *White Star* incident had kicked off. The battlecruiser *White Star* had been en route from Earth, heading out towards the Alliance with a collection of old-Earth artefacts and pieces of art. A goodwill voyage to the Alliance worlds after which the *White Star* had continued on into the Empire, which was how everyone remembered it now. But Ziva remembered it for the débâcle at the start of the journey, the fuck-up around the convoy of freighters that tailed around with it.

A Federation battlecruiser on a well-publicised route from the centre of Federation space to the rim and beyond had inevitably attracted dozens of free traders hoping to travel under its protection. And of course they had, and it was only when the *White Star* was almost at the edge of Federation space that it discovered three Pythons had gone missing during the course of the journey. The convoy travelled fifty light years before the first of the missing ships eventually turned up without the first idea what had happened. The others, eventually, had had the same story: they'd jumped, following the *White Star*'s route, and arrived straight into a storm of jamming and under attack from what appeared to be an Imperial privateer. The *White Star* confirmed the events, reporting that on three occasions a Python travelling as part of the convoy had been attacked, that it had sent Condors to assist and that the attackers had immediately withdrawn and jumped away – leaving the Python apparently unharmed to continue on its way. The Pythons had responded appropriately to hails and the Condors had turned back each time.

121

Except what had *actually* happened was that some enterprising privateer had built collapsible Python shells around the chassis of some long range reconnaissance drones and filled them with enough response circuitry to give all the right sort of answers to basic hails. The *real* Pythons had been boarded and jumped before the Condors could see through the jamming and the pirates had left one of their decoys behind. Every time the *White Star* was due to jump, the decoys would attach themselves to one of the innocent Pythons and then detach at the other end and that way the numbers had looked right and no one had twigged that anything was wrong. Doing it once was audacious enough but getting away with the same trick three times was a scandal. Whoever was behind it had had the sense to stop and quit while they were ahead, too, which was more than most pirates managed.

The Federation had quietly brushed the whole affair under the carpet. No one ever knew who had jumped those Pythons except that it had been an Imperial cutter; but they called her the *Red Hourglass* for the red pirate timer the cutter had broadcast in the seconds before each attack.

The *Red Hourglass. That* rang a bell. Ziva checked the logs from the *Pandora*'s data recorder and there it was: the same thing.

She looked further. And yes, now and then, whenever the *Song of Stone* dropped off the radar for a while, somewhere in the surrounding systems a ship vanished, taken out by the *Red Hourglass*, the Imperial privateer. Now that Ziva knew what she was looking for, the pattern was obvious. It was clinical and clean. Ships ambushed right on the edge of a system straight after jumping in. By the time any Vipers got there, the jump trail was cold. The cargoes vanished, the crews were left drifting in escape pods and the *Red Hourglass* was a ghost. No one had a clue who she really was.

Khanguire had been doing this for years. And no one had caught on.

'Captain, refuelling is complete. I have a course prepared to take us to Stopover.'

Darkwater. Hand over Newman and then to Delta Pavonis and Enaya and home. Ziva shook her head. 'Take us to Reddot, to Whit's Station.'

When she checked, the bounty on the *Red Hourglass* was up at a hundred thousand credits.

Chapter Seven

'How did you meet Khanguire?' Ziva asked. 'I don't mean who set up the hit and brought her in on it, I mean how did you first actually meet? Did you go to her ship? Did she come to yours?' She had Newman awake for the jump and now the *Dragon Queen* was making its way warily in from the Kuiper belt. There wasn't much point in pretending she was something she wasn't, not in a place like this. Commercial ships didn't come to Reddot. Pirates did. Pirates and bounty hunters with more balls than brains. She was coming in quiet, hoping to get close enough to Whit's Station without being seen to set her attack-ware against their data cores, and maybe see whether Newman was right and Khanguire was here. She doubted either part of that plan was actually going to work which left plan B – pay Harlan Whit's protection money, dock with the station and brazen it out. Doubtless there would be a few people less than pleased to see her.

Newman sneered at her. 'What do you care?' She hadn't bothered with more Truth this time, just had him locked up in his makeshift cell and piped him into the cockpit via a screen.

'I don't. I'm curious. She seems too meticulous.'

'What the fuck's that supposed to mean?'

'It means I'm curious to know how you met.'

But if he answered, Ziva didn't hear. The *Dragon Queen* cut him off and all her displays snapped to tactical. Two

Sidewinders and what looked like a heavily modified Asp II had micro-jumped to less than a thousand clicks away. They hadn't actually opened fire but it was about as clear as a fuck-off could be without dressing it in a nice anti-matter wrapping. Whit's Station wasn't the Black Mausoleum. A bounty hunter coming to Reddot in the open was as good as asking to be used for target practice.

Ziva sighed. So much for silent running.

'Alice, Merkel's groupie, where does she live?' Ravindra demanded. Harlan narrowed his eyes but let her speaking to him like that pass.

'Why?' Harlan asked.

'Ji's there, I need to get him,' she told the station boss evenly.

Harlan regarded her for a minute, trying to make up his mind about something. 'Merkel and his crew's paid up,' he said. 'And the station's had enough excitement for one day.'

Ravindra took a step towards him. Harlan didn't move. He was standing there, in the shadow of the *Song of Stone*, both hands on his cane, looking at her impassively. A few of his more observant security people had noticed the exchange.

'He's my son, Harlan. I need to go and get him, make sure that he's okay. You know me; I don't want trouble unless it's absolutely necessary. Now you can tell me, or I'll go and find out myself.'

'Jonas, Harrelson, go with her. Make sure everyone plays nicely with everyone else,' he said, turning to two of his security detail. Harrelson was a massively built female who looked as if she had only just managed to squeeze into her suit, and Jonas was a thin, sly-looking man who moved with nervous energy and had mean eyes. Harrelson nodded.

Jonas turned and headed for the door. Ravindra watched them leaving and then turned and looked at Harlan.

'They'll take you there,' he told her. Ravindra looked as if she was about to argue but thought the better of it.

The two Sidewinders and the Asp were ignoring Ziva's hails, but they couldn't hide their transponders. She had nothing on the Sidewinders – the *Lemming's Wrath* and the *Jon Wood* – but the Asp was the *Nephilim* and she had that as part of the Harris Gang, wanted in the Alliance for three hit and run attacks. Which probably meant the *Nephilim* was working with a corporate Federation backer, but she wasn't about to say no to an extra two thousand credits for taking it down.

She sent an avatar across. 'Whoever you are in there, I'm not strictly working. So wave and say hi and keep your distance and we'll all get on fine.' While she was talking she brought the power plant up to maximum and engaged the tracking systems on the four missiles currently latched to her external hardpoints. She put them all on the Asp and had them go active in case that helped make her point.

The Asp kept coming straight at her. The two Sidewinders split away. Slugging it out at short range made it all about who had the best shields and armour and not much else, and on that basis the Asp, as modified as it was, was probably going to shave a win. Which meant breaking off and letting them chase her away or calling his bluff and shooting.

Ravindra hammered on the apartment door. It was one of the inner apartments, no porthole looking out over Motherlode. The corridor outside stank of urine, the floor was covered in refuse and the walls were covered in graffiti. The graffiti often contained the artist's opinion of the people who lived in the corridor. The words on Alice's door, for example, said: 'Try-too-hard whore'. Ravindra almost smiled. She reached up to hammer on the door again. Jonas grabbed her wrist.

'Take it easy,' he told her quietly. His voice was a low rasp. It sounded affected.

'Take your hands off me right now,' Ravindra told him. He held on just long enough to make a point but not long enough to get beaten.

The door slid open.

'Do you know who I …' The blonde woman who answered the door tailed off when she saw them. She was wearing only a T-shirt and her underwear. Blonde hair, blue eyes and well-endowed, she had a shop-bought prettiness to her, was an unimaginative wet dream. She also had a large auto-pistol held loosely in her right hand. It looked too heavy for her to use properly.

'I half expected a cutlass,' Ravindra muttered and pushed past her.

'Hey!' Alice shouted and started to bring the pistol up. One of Harrelson's massive hands enveloped the heavy pistol and took it.

The Asp had a bounty on him. So there was that. But it was more that she'd be fucked forever in Reddot if she let the Harris Gang chase her off.

Ziva let the *Dragon Queen* jab her with a nerve booster then fired all four missiles. After that everything got interesting very quickly.

Ravindra was in the apartment, looking around. The place was a shithole, beanbags and thread-worn sofas covered in fast food cartoons, empty booze bottles and various bits of drug paraphernalia. The main room was lit in red, the smaller rooms in other colours. Blue was the kitchen, a worse mess than the lounge; green was the bathroom and Ravindra didn't investigate that too thoroughly. She found Ji in the purple room. Alice's bedroom. In her bed, smoking a bowl of some herbal narcotic.

'Mum! What the fuck?'

Ravindra slapped the bowl out of his hand in an explosion of sparks and hot ashes. She tried not to look too closely at the filthy room. Outside she could hear Jonas and Harrelson speaking in low tones to Alice.

'That's the last time you speak to me like that!' Ravindra snapped. 'Get up, get dressed, you're coming with me.'

'Like hell,' Ji said and glared at her defiantly. 'Or what? Going to choke slam me again?'

Ravindra had to force herself to control her breathing. She also had to resist the urge to slap Ji, very, very hard. 'I'm going to yank you out of that bed and march you through the station in whatever you're wearing.'

'Go ahead,' Ji said and crossed his arms. 'We could have talked about this yesterday. We could have talked about this on the phone earlier. If you wanted me to be reasonable, you had your chances then.'

Ravindra glared at him, took several deep breaths and forced herself to calm down.

'Look, you want to hang out with scum, that's up to you—' Ravindra was trying not to raise her voice.

'They're my friends!' Ji protested.

'No, they're—'

'How're you not the same kind of scum? How is you being friends with Orla and Jonty any different to me being friends with Merkel and Alice?'

'I know it seems the same—'

128

'Oh yes, everything's okay when you're doing it, but not when I'm—'

'Shut up!' Ravindra screamed at him.

'Everything okay in there?' Harrelson asked.

'Mind your own business!' Ravindra shouted, a little too shrilly for her own liking. She slammed Alice's bedroom door and turned back to Ji. 'Fine, I'm scum, my friends are scum, but I know they have my back ...'

'Merkel's just the same ...'

'No, he's not. I know this. I signed on with a captain like Merkel when I was just a little bit younger than you. They're friends until it comes to the crunch. That's how I ended up in prison. That's when I learned how to read people a bit better.'

'Oh right, so I'm too immature to work these things out for myself?' Ji spat.

Yes, of course you are. We all are when we're seventeen. Ravindra decided not to voice her thoughts.

'I don't care who you hang out with,' Ravindra lied. 'I just don't want you to do something that will get you arrested, hunted or killed,' she said. *I want a better life for you. Why can't you see that?*

'Mum, I know you want what's best for me,' he said rather coldly. 'I really do. I know you want me to avoid making the same mistakes that you did but I have to make decisions for myself. There's no age of majority on the station. I'm old enough to make those decisions. You have to loosen your grip.'

Then make better decisions! 'Look, we can talk about this ...' Ravindra knew right away that it was the wrong thing to say. She watched his face harden, saw the anger back in his eyes.

'When, mum, when? Even when you're here, all you're thinking about is the ship, the crew and the next score and you keep shutting me out.'

Is that why you want to be a pirate? Thinking that made Ravindra reflect. She'd provided for Ji, but was that all she'd done? Was that enough? It seemed so ridiculous to her that her soft, sensitive boy wanted to take down scores in the spaceways. He hadn't the slightest concept of what the life was like. What it took to do it successfully. What it took to not end up in the Warren, somewhere worse, or dead.

'Okay, I'm sorry. I'm having a bad time at the moment and I need you to cut me some slack,' she said, trying to appeal to him rather than hector. 'I think you should leave it a few years. Maybe university and then decide …'

'I don't want to go to university – I know what I want to do! I have done since I was seven years old. I've grown up around it!'

No, Ji, you haven't. You've no idea how much I've fought to keep this life from you.

'All right, you want this life. Fine! I'll tell you what this life means: I've pissed off some bad people. They may come looking for you. We are probably going to have to run. In the meantime, I need you safe so I can concentrate on fixing the mess that I've made, because if I have to worry about you, I'm likely to get myself and the others killed. *That's* what this life means.'

'I can look after myself.'

'No, you can't. *I* can't look after myself against these people, and I've got seventeen years of experience on you, plus a hardcore crew and a warship behind me.'

'I've got friends and I'm not leaving.'

Friends likely to sell you to the Judas Syndicate without a second thought.

Ravindra noticed the blinking comms icon in the corner of her lens. Harlan was trying to contact her. She cut the link without answering it.

130

'This is what you wanted, did you? This is what it means. Only dealing with bad people, and law enforcement and bounty hunters after you. Always having to run. Or did you think it was going to be the glamorous fantasies that Merkel spins, or like it is in the holos? Because I have some bad news: that's all bullshit. Now put your clothes on and let's get going.'

'No.'

'Ji, I don't have—'

'I'll take my chances.'

'It's not a fucking chance!' Ravindra screamed. There was a knock on the door.

'Everything okay in there?' Harrelson demanded again, with a bit more menace in her voice this time.

'I mean it,' Ravindra told Ji.

'Or what? More violence?'

'I'm going to do whatever I need to, to make—'

'Go on then,' Ji said, crossing his arms. Ravindra considered going to get a shock rod and shocking her own son until he was a drooling mess on the filthy carpet. There was another knock on the door.

'Fuck off!' Ravindra screamed, almost losing it.

'I'm sorry, Captain Khanguire,' Harrelson said. 'But Boss Whit wants to speak to you and I think you should take the link.'

'It'll be more important than me, anyway,' Ji taunted.

'It'll be a bloody sight more important than arguing with you,' Ravindra snapped and opened the link. Harlan's avatar appeared in her vision.

'I think you've got more trouble,' the avatar told her.

What could be more trouble than the Judas Syndicate? she wondered.

* * *

131

Ziva was almost impressed. The Asp didn't pull the novice manoeuvre and turn away, and he didn't start firing either; instead the pilot cut his main engine and started course adjusting with attitude thrusters, dumping heat from the ship's skin into a scatter of inflatable canisters strewn behind him. The *Dragon Queen*'s infrared trackers lost his hull signature, but picked up his thrusters, and the Fer-de-Lance continued trajectory predictions from estimates and basic Newtonian physics. It was an old trick and a simple one – if you could make yourself as cold as the vacuum of space then you made yourself invisible. Ziva had fitted a set of attitude thrusters to the *Dragon Queen* that vented liquid helium specifically to do what the Asp was trying to do, only better.

The Sidewinders did the opposite. They curved away from the Asp at full throttle. The *Dragon Queen* rotated a new salvo of missiles into position and set up estimated target tracks on all three ships. Ziva fired a drone, this time loaded with a cloud warhead, but held back on the rest of a second salvo. A pair at each Sidewinder would have set things going nicely but the Sidewinders didn't have a bounty on them, not yet. Things like this had to be done right. That was the discipline. The line between pirate and hunter.

The Sidewinders changed course again, steering hard back across her bows. They'd dropped the range to five hundred clicks now. They passed right between the *Dragon Queen* and her estimate of where the Asp was hiding and Ziva was quite certain the Asp would have put out a short burst from its own thrusters while the Sidewinders' fusion plumes were blinding her. The *Dragon Queen*'s track-error estimates grew steadily wider.

Fuck you, Ziva thought, and allowed herself a smile.

* * *

132

Ravindra stood in Whit's Station's control centre. The footage from the high orbit surveillance satellite showed the Fer-de-Lance pilot kick the ship into a corkscrew and spray low-intensity laser fire all over where the Asp might be. The Fer-de-Lance didn't have much chance of hitting; her pilot was trying to spook the Asp into giving himself away, that was all. So far it wasn't working.

'That Harris?' she asked Harlan. He was stood next to her on the raised platform over the Command and Control workstations. The station boss nodded. 'Harris is a good pilot,' Ravindra conceded.

Ziva checked the missiles had all lost their locks on the Asp and then had them decelerate and position themselves along her best estimate of the Asp's trajectory, lurking to pounce as soon as she had a solid lock on him again. The last missile she'd fired raced on.

Warnings flashed across the cockpit. Someone was lasing her. She cut the Fer-de-Lance's fusion plume, dumped heat and twisted the *Dragon Queen* sideways, tumbling momentarily. In part the tumbling spread the laser damage over more of her shields, in part it helped her get a better fix on where it was coming from. Not that she much needed one. A Neo-Technik pulse laser, the standard factory armament of a Sidewinder.

When she was sideways on to her own trajectory she let out a hard burst from the main engines. It was the same trick as the *Nephilim* was trying only without bothering to hide it, and the trajectory shift from a main engine burn made for bigger prediction errors. While she was at it, she dropped the second salvo of missiles, one after the other. They kept their engines cold, drifting inert along a narrow spread towards the oncoming Asp. The drone with the

133

cloud warhead was in the lead now, heading for the *Dragon Queen*'s estimate of the Asp's position.

The Sidewinders both launched missiles at last. Ziva smiled, nodded her thanks to them for making themselves legitimate targets and threw out a snow cloud around the Fer-de-Lance, a fine spray of hydrogen and methane crystals close to absolute zero. It had the side effect of acting a little like a cloak but what it was really for was—

… The missile with the cloud warhead reached the *Dragon Queen*'s prediction spheroid for the *Nephilim* and ejected anti-hydrogen. The spent drone powered on. With a bit of luck whoever was in the Asp didn't have the first idea what was about to happen. At the same time, the *Lemming's Wrath* opened up with a pulse laser again …

—that. Lines of scintillation ripped through the ice around the *Dragon Queen*, giving Ziva a track-back on where the Sidewinder was coming from and confirming she wasn't being lased by some other ship she hadn't yet seen. The *Dragon Queen* projected lines of light directly into her heads-up displays, marking the laser strikes across Ziva's view of space. It added the scintillations to its targeting solution and flipped over. In her acceleration cocoon, Ziva fired back with a sustained burst hard enough to make her cranked-up power circuits smoke. The *Dragon Queen*'s two coherent military-spec X-ray beams raked over the Sidewinder's skin. The Sidewinder's shields stopped them for a moment, and then they punched through and the port side of the *Lemming's Wrath* broke apart. A flash of fusion product lit up space and momentarily blinded the *Dragon Queen*'s trackers. A beacon started flashing, the pilot's escape pod, damaged but functional. That was Sidewinders for you. Small and fast and agile and armed to the teeth, but they broke if you as much as looked at them in a funny way.

The Asp drifted into Ziva's cloud of anti-hydrogen. The particles of the cloud were too small and scattered to actually hurt it, but the nano-flashes of hard radiation that flared from its skin pinned it for the *Dragon Queen*'s fire control array. The Fer-de-Lance flipped again, end over end and let off another volley of laser fire while at the same time the four lurking missiles Ziva had launched in her first salvo, now only a few dozen clicks away, burst into life, bracketing the Asp's position. Ziva's shot scorched away some of the Asp's ablative shield. Its engine lit up, full torch now, but it was already too late and it knew it. The missiles silently went off around it, a perfect bracket, flinging anti-matter minelets everywhere. The pilot ejected a moment before the first one hit. A second later, the Asp vanished in a flash of hard radiation.

The *Jon Wood* turned tail and screamed away as fast as it could go. Ziva could have caught it if she'd wanted, but she let it be. Instead, she swept up the Asp's escape pod and had the *Dragon Queen*'s drones put the pilot in restraints in the cabin with Newman. Then she picked up the pilot of the *Lemming's Wrath*. 'I'll let you go when we get to Whit's Station,' she told him. No bounty. That made him lucky. The Asp pilot was another matter. Harris himself, was it?

When she was safely away, she sent out remote detonation orders to any minelets that had survived the Asp's destruction and retrieved her second salvo of missiles. Finally she turned the *Dragon Queen* back to Whit's Station and lit up the Fer-de-Lance's fusion flare. Stealth had gone out of the window. Plan B, then. She sent out an avatar and paid Harlan Whit his protection money.

'Well, Khanguire, were you there to watch the show?'

'Well, they can fly, whoever they are,' Ravindra conceded as she watched the death of the *Nephilim*. 'What's this got to do with me – or did you just want me to see the pretty lights?'

'Her name is Ziva Eschel and she's a bounty hunter.' Harlan said and sent her a data packet across their open comms link. Ravindra opened it and information started cascading down her vision. Ten years in the federation police in Beta Hydri, five years as a Viper pilot. Ten years as a bounty hunter. 'She's taken down some heavy ships as well: the *Broken Heart*, the *Widow Maker*, the *Red Goat*.'

'She was the one that took Vanos down?' Ravindra asked, impressed despite herself. She was scan-reading the information. It was telling the story of a pilot who was a bit more than competent but also someone who was careful, clever and thorough and, unusually for a bounty hunter, had always kept on the right side of the law. She didn't want this woman on her six, not at the moment. 'What makes you think that she's after me?'

'I've got some data rats in a number of different systems working for me. They're paid to look for certain keywords, including the *Red Hourglass*.'

The *Red Hourglass*, the name their victims had given the *Song of Stone*. Most people who were even aware of the ship's existence assumed that it was an Imperial privateer. It wasn't enough in itself but Ravindra didn't like the coincidence that this Eschel had done a search on the *Red Hourglass* and then come to Whit's Station.

'There's more,' Harlan said grimly. 'She pulled your records. Imperial and Federal.'

Shit, Ravindra thought. 'I'm going to have to kill her,' she said.

'Not here.'

'For someone I've given a lot of money to over the years, you're saying no to me a lot.'

'Because you keep wanting to break the rules, the ones that make this place work.'

'What, no preferential service for loyalty?' she asked, knowing the answer. She could see the fusion torch of the *Dragon Queen*'s engine now as the ship fell towards Motherlode's atmosphere. Harlan turned to look at her.

'If I make one exception, everyone knows they can't trust me.'

Ravindra turned to face Harlan. 'She's a bounty hunter.'

'She's paid up. You want to take her, you do it off my station. It'll be made clear to her, in no uncertain terms, that the same applies. She can't hunt here. If she does, she gets spaced. Same goes for you but it would piss me off a lot more.'

Ravindra nodded, rubbing her face.

'Look,' Harlan said. 'Everyone's going to know what she is. Maybe you'll be lucky and someone else will take care of her for you, and then I'll have to come down on them for breaking the rules.'

Ravindra was of the opinion that she'd been lucky many times in her life, but she didn't think that today was going to be one of those times. She walked away and stood on the observation deck over the docking berth levels, looking down as the Fer-de-Lance, the *Dragon Queen*, came in. The piloting was done with the grace of economy. No unnecessary movements, no flourishes, just like the ship itself, a utilitarian, armoured spearhead whose modifications promised speed, manoeuvrability and a prodigious capacity for violence. She didn't like the sound of the pilot. Or rather, she did – Eschel sounded careful, confident and capable. To Ravindra's mind she was what a bounty hunter should be, she just didn't want Eschel hunting *her*. This was not what she needed right now; although it was difficult to imagine when she *would* need to be pursued by such a capable bounty hunter. Ravindra turned and headed up towards the main concourse. As she walked she checked both her burst pistols. A moment later she received a comms request from Harlan. Ravindra glanced up at the security cameras and then opened the link.

'Keeping kind of a close eye on me, aren't you?'

'Remember what I said – she paid for protection,' Harlan told her.

'Before or after she took down Harris and those idiots in the Sidewinders?' Ravindra asked. As if she didn't know. That had been a message. Ravindra decided she would re-watch the footage of the dogfight. She would analyse the other woman, look for weaknesses. 'If she tries to take me or kill me, then she's going down, otherwise I'll play nice.' Ravindra cut the comms link.

She looked up to see McCauley sat at a table outside one of the 'coffee' stands, sipping from a small cup, looking straight at her.

What is his problem? she wondered. She was angry enough to go and get in his face but she just didn't have the time. She sent out a comms request.

Whit's Station kindly gave the *Dragon Queen* the sort of welcome scan that scorched paint. Ziva returned the favour, careful to keep her own active arrays in their commercial-zone mode so that anybody who happened to be paying attention wouldn't know how hard the *Dragon Queen* could burn back if she wanted to.

'You've paid up, so you can come in,' shrugged the avatar of Harlan Whit. 'If you hunt on my station or even lie in wait, I take your ship and then I space you. You might not be very popular or very welcome, but that's your problem, not mine. You pay me and behave, no one touches you or your ship. That's as far as it goes. Cross my lines and God help you.'

Ziva raised an eyebrow. 'Anyone touches my ship, my ship will get very cross with them, and none of us would like that. I have a Sidewinder pilot with no bounty on him and I'd like to release him back into the wild. See if he can find some new friends who can take better care of him this time. I'm keeping the other one. You have a problem with that?'

'*I* don't. Can't promise he hasn't got friends here who might think otherwise, rules notwithstanding.'

'I suggest you keep an eye on them, then. I won't be here long.' Ziva shut the channel. She'd paid and Whit had a solid reputation, and that was that. It wasn't going to be much of a stay anyway. Let the Sidewinder pilot out, a quick check around the docking bays for the *Song of Stone*, send a few avatars out into the station to see if anyone had anything they wanted to say about Khanguire. Then out and gone and back to Stopover to ditch Newman. She nosed the *Dragon Queen* in closer to the station, lightly scanning all the other ships in the area. In high orbit overhead, five thousand miles above the aerostat of Whit's Station, a refitted Federation corvette scanned her back. She pinged it for a transponder signal and got nothing. She had the *Dragon Queen* memorise its configuration to compare against Federation data cores when she was back somewhere more amenable. *Another pirate?*

She pulled back the fuel scoops and took over manual control of the Fer-de-Lance, feeling the tiny nudges back and forth from the whirls and eddies of the gas giant's upper atmosphere. She slipped the *Dragon Queen* gently under the aerostat's mushroom canopy and the balloon that held it aloft as the station opened a bay for her. The *Dragon Queen* kept her lasers primed and engines hot ready for a quick and nasty getaway if needed, but no one had locks on her. Ziva glided into the station, keyed the ship's energy bomb to her own life-monitor and adjusted the *Dragon Queen*'s safety protocols so it would look like the E-bomb would go off if she were killed – it wouldn't, but maybe the appearance would give any trigger-happy pirates who came her way at least a momentary pause for thought. The ship settled into its docking cradle. It had been a while since she'd landed in an aerostat. All the fun of docking with an orbital station and gravity as well. At least it wasn't spinning.

She hadn't even unstrapped when a blank avatar winked into life beside her and a disembodied voice spoke.

'I hear you're looking for me,' the voice said. It was probably a woman, deep and perfectly controlled, although that didn't mean anything. Avatars had algorithms to create voices just as much as they did to create faces.

'Really? Who are you and how much are you worth?'

'There's a bar on level four. It's called Hope. Meet me there – I'll buy you a drink.'

Ziva snorted. 'Shall I wear a shirt with a big cross-hair on it too?' *Who the fuck was this?*

'If you like.' The avatar winked out as the link broke. Ziva made a face.

'I don't suppose you have any idea who that was?' she asked the ship. 'Any way to trace it back to whichever one of the several bounties I'm sure are here?'

'We have voice transcripts of Ravindra Khanguire's exit hearing when she was released from Warren Prison. There is a good match. Would you like to hear them?'

Khanguire? For a moment that stopped her dead. But it was hardly likely, surely? 'Go on then. While you're at

140

it, start crawling around all the station subsystems and see if the *Song of Stone* is here.' While the *Dragon Queen* piped Khanguire into her ear, she set up a dozen avatars and cast them out into the station, hunting for anyone who might have information they'd like to sell. 'Really? You think that was really Khanguire?'

'The match is a good one. Not excellent.'

'Show me the pictures we have of her and get me surveillance on that place she mentioned.' *She*. Damn. Ziva *wanted* it to be Khanguire.

Pictures flashed up across the cockpit monitors. Ravindra Khanguire as she was almost twenty years ago. Slender – wasted from her prison term – dark skin, tall, statuesque. Unsettlingly like En.

'There is no surveillance available,' said the ship.

'Marvellous.' Ziva let off an irritable sigh. 'Send a spy drone ahead of me, then. Patch it to my Fresnels.' She got up and collected her pistols. Chances were it wasn't Khanguire waiting for her. Whoever it was, what she was about to do was really stupid. *We'll see how much that protection money was worth then, shall we?*

Hope was one of the oldest bars on the station. It had the most history. It was a small cramped place made of various nooks and crannies amongst the support struts of the station. Enough to provide a degree of privacy, as did the countermeasures that Harry – barman, owner and oddly taciturn stim junkie – had installed. Hope wasn't a party establishment, it wasn't where crew and captains gathered to drink and tell stories. Hope was where you did business. On one of the few occasions that anyone had coaxed more than a few syllables out of the jittery Harry, he'd told them that was why he'd named it Hope.

Ravindra had a reasonably central table looking at the door. One hand was on the glass of brandy that she felt she both needed and deserved, the other was under the table close to one of her burst pistols. She watched as the door opened and a small robot floated into the bar and had a good look around. Harry reached under the counter and drew his EMP pulse projector.

'It's all right, Harry,' Ravindra told him. 'That's with me.'

'I don't care,' Harry groused. 'It'll make the other customers nervous.'

Ravindra glanced around at the completely empty bar.

'It's the principle,' Harry explained.

Ravindra looked up at the robot. 'Lose the bot. *You* don't try anything, neither will I.'

The robot finished looking around and then left. Ravindra imagined that with all the jamming and countermeasures in the bar it hadn't found much anyway. She tapped her comp ring on the table transfer pad, spending some credits as she did so.

'Disappear please, Harry,' she said. Harry nodded and made himself discreet.

She hadn't been sure what to expect. Most bounty hunters she only saw from the outside of their heavily armed ships. There weren't that many who had the ovaries to set foot on Whit's Station, regardless of whether they'd rendered unto Caesar or not. What she saw was a small wiry woman dressed in a T-shirt and a pair of jeans. Ravindra assumed that she was concealing significant armour under the clothes, although if she was, it wasn't at all obvious how. A burst pistol hung from her hip and her belt had a number of little loops and pouches that could hide all sorts of nasty little tricks. She had short spiky black hair and there was something vaguely feral about her. She looked like a fighter.

'Eschel?'

The bounty hunter nodded. 'Khanguire. You didn't change your face when you came out of prison, then?'

No, Ravindra thought. She was older, a little fuller in the body because she wasn't having to hunt for mine-rats to supplement meagre prison rations. Otherwise she looked much as she had when she came out; except now she had her hair again. It was held in a braid all the way to her waist. Gods, how she'd missed her hair. It was her one concession to vanity. She gestured at the seat in front of her. Eschel looked at the chair and then glanced at the door; clearly she didn't like having her back to it.

'Drink?' offered Ravindra.

'What have you got?' Eschel kept a wary distance.

'You look like a whiskey girl to me, bourbon – not Scotch. Harry keeps some good stuff here for Harlan. That do you?'

'Half right.' Eschel came slowly closer and eased into the chair directly across the table. 'Scotch though, not bourbon. I took a bounty a few months back who was smuggling it out of New Caledonia. Gave me a taste for it.'

Ravindra tapped the transfer pad on the table again and then got up and walked behind the bar. 'I need my life to get significantly less complicated.' She poured a generous Scotch and brought it back to the table. Eschel stared into the glass as she swirled it. She seemed oddly hesitant.

'Don't we all?' she said at last. 'But I can help you there. Turn yourself in. It's all about as simple as it gets after that.'

'Trust me, that's just not the case.'

'Then what's to talk about? I chose not to wear the shirt with the cross-hairs, by the way.'

'Sure?'

The bounty hunter blinked and cocked her head. 'I spend half my life around shit-stains and scum and junkers. But to be honest, I thought you were better than that. I'd admire the professionalism if it wasn't for the people you killed.' She gave a little shrug. 'Also, you can never be *quite* sure I haven't got a little bit of anti-matter somewhere tagged to my vital signs. We can start shooting at each other if you'd like to find out.'

'Harlan really would kill me.' Ravindra ignored the counter threat. 'I need you to go away. I need you to do it quickly and I'm prepared to take the most expeditious route to achieve what I want. How much do you cost?'

'That's not how I work.'

'No? Pity. Worth a try, though.' She took a good long look across the table. Eschel held her gaze. 'The Imperials will pay a lot for me,' she pointed out. For some reason Ravindra wanted to know where this Eschel stood on hunting escaped slaves. She hoped she already knew the answer.

'Yes. Runaway slave and a murderess, too. Did you do it?' Eschel asked. Ravindra said nothing. 'I don't think you did. Even at fifteen, I don't think a crime of passion was quite your thing. Not that it particularly matters.'

'At fifteen I was capable of murder.'

'I don't doubt it.' Maybe Eschel was impressed that she didn't balk at the word; but Ravindra had never been one to hide from what she was.

'If you want to hear excuses then I'm afraid I don't have any.'

'I haven't heard you deny anything.'

'That's true.'

'But I think even then you were too careful.'

Ravindra almost laughed at that. *Careful?* 'You know I was in the Warren, right?'

'I don't hunt slaves, if that's what you're asking.'

'Principled?'

Eschel shrugged. 'Just doesn't feel right.'

Both women took a sip of their drinks.

'What's the bounty like on me?'

'You don't check?' Eschel asked. She was smiling now.

Ravindra shook her head. A lot of pirate captains used the bounty on themselves as a measure of their notoriety but she'd always thought that was dumb. It was a measure of how well known they were, how many mistakes they'd made.

Eschel put her glass back on the table. It was a slow, careful gesture. 'A hundred thousand for the *Red Hourglass*, though I don't know if anyone else has figured out that was you. Darkwater put another fifteen each on you and Newman for what you did to the *Pandora*. You'll be a name-maker for whoever takes you down, Khanguire.'

Ravindra gave this some thought. 'That's certainly a lot of motivation.'

'There are better ones.'

'Such as?'

'I imagine the families of the crew you killed with that E-bomb would have some suggestions for you.'

'I hadn't realised your work was so altruistic. Will you be giving my bounty to charity?' Ravindra rubbed the base of her nose with her thumb and forefinger. She was tired and cranky and she knew it.

Eschel pursed her lips. 'Actually, I had my eye on a new Zyfon reactor core.'

For a moment Ravindra stared, then her mask cracked and an unfamiliar smile spread across her face. 'The Zyfon's pretty good. If you're using a military grade laser – and you'd better be if you plan on coming after me – then be careful. The cyclic rate can create feedback in the reactor.

145

Fools the diagnostics into thinking you've got radiation leaking into the coolant system.'

'Ha! You try feeding in a trickle of anti-matter to boost the output and see what happens *then*.' The bounty hunter laughed. 'I'm afraid I have a bit of a thing for anti-matter.'

'Last time I tried a stunt like that I had to vent plasma during a dogfight. Caught it with one of our own lasers as it came out and kicked off a fusion reaction. My … one of my crew said I'd set fire to space …' It had been Harnack. Ravindra went quiet, tried not to show any of the emotion that she felt. 'So it'll be you coming after me, then?' Her voice had hardened.

Eschel stared across the room, lost for a moment. 'Radiation's a bitch too.' She closed her eyes and shook her head. 'Yes. I suppose it will.' There was no suggestion of threat. It was a simple statement of fact. She sounded almost … reluctant?

'You know that's not going to be as easy as the other bounties you've taken down, right?'

'I've taken down all sorts. You'll take more effort than some dipshit novice in his first Cobra, eh?'

'Remember what I said about expedience. I've got other things I need to worry about.'

'Then how do you expect to deal with me?'

'Are you that committed to making my life difficult? You must have nothing in your own.'

Again Eschel looked distant. She didn't smile this time. 'Right now, not that much.' The words came with a bitterness not quite hidden. Eschel drained her glass and looked Ravindra in the eye. 'Right now, how can *you* have anything to worry about that isn't *me*? Or someone like me? How do you do that?' She pushed the glass to Ravindra. 'Refill?'

Khanguire nodded, took the bounty hunter's glass to the bar and poured another generous measure.

'What I *should* be doing is being somewhere else. What I *should* be doing is spending time with my lover helping her to sort out her damn teenage daughter before she falls off the tracks completely. But I'm not. I'm here.' Eschel took the glass as Ravindra handed it to her. 'You want to make my life easy, hand yourself over and let me get on with that.' She laughed. 'But we both know that's not how this plays. You'll be as hard as you can be and I won't let go until one of us loses.' She raised the glass. 'Here's to being a single-minded daughter of a bitch.'

'Go and look after your woman and her kid,' Ravindra suggested.

'That what you'd do?'

Ravindra had to stop and think. 'You've seen my files from the Warren?'

'I know you left prison pregnant.'

'I've got a kid too.' She caught Eschel looking at her expectantly. 'And this game's messing him up. So if I've got to go through you so I can be the one who's looking after him, that's the way it'll be.'

'Good luck with that. You've made your choices. Leave him money. Turn yourself over. Spare him any more of this shit.'

'Or *you* could walk away.'

Eschel shook her head. 'I could, but even if I did, then what? Someone else steps up, that's what. Once your name's tagged to the *Red Hourglass*, you'll never be clear. You know that. They'll come for you in droves. Maybe one of those wankers from *Federation's Most Wanted*. They'll make a game out of killing you. A bit of mass entertainment. That how you want to go?' Eschel shook her head again and took another drink. 'What about your boy – you want him to see that? You want someone like me coming after *him* one day?'

'Don't talk about my ...' *No*, Ravindra thought, *you let her in.* 'He's not making good decisions ... He needs ...' Suddenly it all came rushing over her. Harnack, the betrayal, Jenny taken, Ji, this bounty hunter. She was just so tired.

'Then show him what one looks like. Turn yourself over. You know how it ends, how it *always* ends if you don't. Maybe it's me this time, maybe it's not, but there's always going to be someone coming for you. One day ...' The bounty hunter shrugged. 'You have to know that.' Ravindra's face hardened. 'Sorry. That was cheap. True, but cheap. Of course you know.'

'Spend some time in the Warren and then we can talk about good and bad decisions. See, here's the thing you need to remember if you want to come after me. I'm *not* going back.'

'I hear you.' Eschel stood up. 'Good Scotch. And here's the thing I need *you* to remember: if I see you out there, I won't hesitate. If I have to burn your ship and your crew to take you down, then I won't like it. But I'll still do it. Whoever you've got with you.'

Ravindra just nodded. She watched as the bounty hunter left, downed the rest of her brandy and sat in the empty bar for a bit longer.

Chapter Eight

Ziva let the Sidewinder pilot go and got out of Whit's Station as fast as she could. She left a Sly-Spy behind on the off-chance that Khanguire was stupid enough – distracted enough, perhaps – not to notice and she was already micro-jumping back to the Kuiper belt when Enaya tried to reach her. She didn't take it. She didn't know what to do about Khanguire either. Bloody woman had rattled her cage. *Go and look after your woman and her kid.* She had a point.

While the *Dragon Queen* flickered in and out of normal space, alternating between lower and higher dimensions according to a physics Ziva couldn't begin to understand, she went back to the spare cabin to see Newman again. He was sitting up and alert against the back wall of the makeshift cell. Ziva wrinkled her nose. He was starting to smell a little ripe. 'You didn't tell me Khanguire had a son.' Harris, the Asp II pilot, was still there too, tripped out on the *Dragon Queen*'s sedatives.

Newman spat. 'You didn't ask.'

'Close, are they?' Maybe the son was a way to get at Khanguire? She had a weakness there.

'Didn't look like it. Seemed to me they were at each others' throats.'

Which only went to show how little Newman understood. He wasn't going to be much more use. 'He have a name, this son?'

'Of course he has a name, bounty hunter.' Newman held out his hands. 'You going to let me out? I'll help you find the bitch and take her down.'

'Yes, yes, you said. Dear God but you can be dull and besides, I found her already. We had a nice little chat.' *And now I have to keep reminding myself that she murders people in deep space and E-bombs escape pods.* 'What's his name, Newman? Or do I have to get the Truth out again?'

'Ji.' Newman turned and spat on the unconscious Harris. 'Upstart toe-rag. Thinks he wants to be a space-pirate. Clueless as they come. He wouldn't last a day.' A smile broke across his face. 'You're going to use him to get to her are you? I wouldn't count on it. Bitch is too cold. No heart there. Nothing.'

Ziva turned away and left him there. She had other questions about Khanguire; and maybe Newman knew some of the answers or maybe not, but right now he made her sick. No, she wouldn't use Khanguire's son against her. '*Dragon Queen*, if I have a momentary impulsive lack of judgement and ask you to open the passenger cabin into deep space, don't let me. Talk me down. It would be unfair on Harris.'

'And also in violation of the Mars treaty.'

She looked over the files she'd made on Khanguire again. Hunting her down and catching her out was going to be a bitch. Going toe to toe with the *Dragon Queen* against the *Song of Stone* didn't look promising either, especially not in a hostile system, and so lurking outside Whit's Station to jump her when she left wasn't going to fly. She'd have to catch Khanguire off guard, and Khanguire didn't look like someone who was easily caught that way. She'd need a lure and an ambush. Months of work. A bucket-load of patience and a fistful of frustration; and Khanguire had the smarts to slip out from under her nose if she made even a single mistake, the patience to simply sit and do nothing at all for months, waiting her out, possibly the discipline to vanish entirely and forever. Ziva couldn't really want that, could she? Newman had been bad enough. Hunting Khanguire would devour her.

Perhaps she could release what she knew about the *Red Hourglass*? Let someone else do it … Except most hunters in the top league had corporate sponsorship deals and their own news feeds and weekly shows k-cast across the Federation. They hunted the bounties their sponsors thought would make the best entertainment. Never mind what she'd said back on the station, the cold truth was that stalking Khanguire would be a slog. She wouldn't make for compelling viewing. No one capable would actually do it.

She murders people in deep space.

The *Dragon Queen* was flashing a light at her, telling her she had a k-cast waiting. Ziva closed her eyes. She'd always turned the offers away. She didn't need them. She didn't need an audience, didn't *want* an audience, didn't want to be another smiling empty celebrity. She should take Newman back to Stopover and take the bounty off Darkwater, that's what she should do. Then sell them the file she'd amassed on Khanguire providing they took the flag off her with the Pilots' Federation. They could set their own hunters after the *Song of Stone*. Presumably they had them. They wouldn't be the best otherwise they wouldn't be working for Darkwater, but there would be a lot of them. Maybe that was what it took. A great big dumb corporation with endless resource and persistence.

Yeah, and maybe she should send Khanguire a message while she was at it: *Good luck. Keep to what you're doing and no one's going to come after you.* But then presumably she knew that already, which was why she did what she did.

'Play me the message.'

It was short and hard from En. 'She left me another note, Ziv. A *note*. Why doesn't she talk to me anymore? He's taken her off Delta Pavonis. I don't know where. I thought you said he couldn't do that. Anyway, he has. I'm scared, Ziv. I'm in Alioth. I tried to go after them but I can't find out where they went. I don't know where you are, but I want to see you again. If we can't make this work then we can't. But … He took her away from me, Ziv. I just want to see you.'

The anguish in Enaya's voice settled any doubts. Khanguire could wait. The *Red Hourglass* wouldn't be going anywhere. The *Song of Stone* might vanish without a trace but Khanguire would be back before long, dressed up as something else.

'Tell her we're coming.' Ziva had the *Dragon Queen* set a course for Alioth, then went back to her cabin for some sleep. The *Dragon Queen* could find her own way, jumping from system to system as she needed, micro-jumping in to skim fuel from gas giants as and when she wanted and with standing orders to avoid any trouble. She could cross the whole of human space that way without Ziva ever having to lift a finger, plotting her own cautious course from one civilised world to the next, keeping away from any trouble; and if the ship ever got that part wrong, she was a Fer-de-Lance. When she ran, almost nothing could catch her. When she powered down to hide, almost nothing could see her. When she turned to fight, few ships could match her.

Ziva lay back in her cocoon and closed her eyes. She'd lost track of how long she'd been up. Kept doing that. Odar wasn't supposed to leave Delta Pavonis. And *that* gave her an excuse, and something unquestionably better to do.

* * *

She woke up again to find they were closing in on Alioth. She'd half-expected En to go for Wicca's World and the Lost Gardens of Antipi-Hymbos but no, she'd gone to New California, the symbolic capital of Something New. Alioth had quite a history, but what most people knew about it was that this was where Mic Turner and Meredith Argent had turned a thousand years of history on their head by leading a revolt against both the Federation and the Empire at once and founding the Alliance. For the first time in a millennium, every world suddenly had a new choice. It had started here.

The *Dragon Queen* stopped its micro-jumps and locked in to one of the orbiting stations. Ziva didn't know which one. She hadn't been specific. *Take me to En.* That was about as much direction as she'd given the ship. Ziva floated, weightless, as the *Dragon Queen* drifted in. She tried going through her files on Khanguire once more; but she couldn't focus and her thoughts kept slipping through each other like a knot of eels. She reminded herself that Khanguire didn't matter, that she'd come here because she'd made that decision. She'd come here with Newman still sedated in her spare cabin because she'd chosen En and Aisha.

She looked at the files for a last time and then told the *Dragon Queen* to delete them, wipe them out, erase them utterly. Seconds after they were gone she was checking there was an archive after all, a backup, something the *Dragon Queen* could recover. There was. She wanted to kick herself. Maybe En would do that for her.

'Prep Harris for transfer,' she snapped. Alliance territory. She could off-load *him*, at least, and so she sent an avatar to start the claim for his bounty. The *Dragon Queen* had been complaining about the state of its jump drive after so many trips on skimmed fuel and so she booked a posse of Zorgon

Peterson maintenance drones to come aboard as she docked. She'd need a temporary holding arrangement for Newman, too, while she had a proper self-contained prisoner-transport module fitted into the cargo bay again. The law said she had to hand Newman over to the station authorities and pay for him to be held in 'proper and fitting conditions' until she left. Hardly any bounty hunters ever actually did that when a jab of sedative served just as well, but it would be a relief to have him out of her ship for a while. That done, she took over the docking with the Golden Gate. It would be nice to spend a little time in a system like Alioth. The *Dragon Queen* could slumber in her station berth, safe and sound without any worries. Ziva could walk the corridors of the station's rim in a full comfortable standard gravity and not be constantly on edge, wondering who was waiting for her around the next corner …

'We appear to have been followed,' said the *Dragon Queen*, and showed her the corvette that had scanned her from above Whit's Station.

'Send an avatar. Find out what they want.' No one would bother her in a system like Alioth. It didn't surprise her when the corvette didn't reply, turned and powered away. One of Khanguire's friends, Ziva supposed. So be it – let them watch her. It wasn't like she was going to be hard to find.

She matched the rotation of the Golden Gate's hub and drifted leisurely into its cavernous heart. The *Dragon Queen* had already negotiated a docking bay; Ziva guided the Fer-de-Lance in and settled on the landing pad. She felt the jolt as magnetic clamps engaged from both station and ship. The *Dragon Queen*'s reactor gradually dropped into hibernation. Ziva unstrapped and launched herself back to her cabin, bouncing in long smooth arcs in the micro-gravity made by the hub's rotation; by the time she'd picked something to wear, the *Dragon Queen* was tucked safely away and the umbilicals from the Golden Gate were latched on. They'd bill her, of course, for the power and the fuel and the water and the air. No matter. She could afford it. She'd been able to afford it for years. Even without Newman she could have walked away from bounty hunting and kept the *Dragon Queen* to herself and taken En with her. She could have had the ship fitted out the way it had once been meant to be.

She looked at herself in the mirror, holding the dress up before her. There were reasons why she almost never wore a dress and micro-gravity was one of them. Blasted folds wandered all over the place doing their own thing and making you look like an idiot. She had no idea how she'd look up in the station's rim, whether the dress would appear the way it was supposed to or whether she *would* just look like an idiot. Probably that. But En liked her in a dress. En liked her to look feminine now and then; En would tell her she was beautiful, which always made her laugh because she wasn't, not in *that* way. En was the one with the classic elegance, with the curves and the arches and the long sensual fingers.

For a moment she thought of Khanguire again and quickly shook her away. If she looked like an idiot to everyone else, so what? This was for Enaya. She bagged the dress and put on a disposable jumpsuit. *The things we do for love* …

She left the *Dragon Queen* behind and took an elevator out from the hub, feeling the false gravity sink into her as she rose towards the rim. They had public changing rooms by the exits, discreet cubicles you could rent for ten cents every fifteen minutes, places where spacers from the hub turned into the elegant citizens of the rim and later turned back again. She stripped out of the jumpsuit and into the dress. Now that the folds and skirts and cuffs hung the way they were meant to, she supposed she looked good enough. Nothing special. A little awkward, perhaps, but not too bad. She tried putting on some make-up – another thing she hadn't done for almost a year – and discovered that yes, she still didn't really know how all that worked. Never had, probably never would. No matter – the cubicle had a bot which could do it for her and the only hard part after she'd scrubbed herself clean again was choosing from the hundreds of styles it had to offer. The new Independent look was tempting, but En wouldn't thank her and so she went for simple subtle classic Imperial. She let the bots do her hair as well. When they were finished, she hardly recognised herself. The scrawny sharp-edged bounty hunter Ziva was gone. She looked like what En would call a 'normal person'.

She tapped her earlobe, opening a link to the *Dragon Queen*. 'Where is she?'

'Go outside.'

Ziva opened the cubicle. En was standing right there, waiting for her.

'Ziv.' She was smiling. Ziva opened her mouth and then closed it again when no words came. There was a lump in her throat she hadn't been ready for and a wetness at the corner of her eyes.

'En,' she managed. 'En.'

'You're beautiful, Ziv.'

'You always say that.' Ziva laughed then. A relief. 'But not next to you I'm not.' She held out her hands and Enaya took them and squeezed them and then came closer still and wrapped Ziva in her arms.

'I'm so glad you came.'

There were things Ziva wanted to say. How she was going to come home, at least for a while. For a few months. Maybe as much as a year. See how it went. Get Aisha back on her feet. Forget the likes of Newman and Khanguire, that sort of thing, but they were all suddenly too big to fit her mouth. Her tongue felt awkward as though it belonged to someone else.

'I thought you'd prefer Wicca's World,' she said at last. Laughed. 'You and your retro Dreamwave shit.'

En laughed back. 'Oh come on! My "Dreamwave shit" is infinitely better than this month's k-cast sensation created especially in a sonic laboratory somewhere on Mars. Three songs, sell-out tours for a month or two and then they burn out and no one ever hears of them again? Do you remember that warbling pair of teenage boys who called themselves Jesus and Allah?'

'Barely.'

'Quite. A year ago they were everywhere. Where are they now? Gone, thank goodness. Iron Sky? Heroic Trio? Band of Brothers? Myq-L and the Bimblefunks?'

Ziva shrugged. 'The cult of celebrity. That's all anyone in the Federation cares about any more.'

'I only know them because I see the posters change in Ay's room.' Enaya leaned in to Ziva and lowered her voice. 'I think it's all the same three or four bands. They have a secret base on Mars and recycle them. They give them a whole body makeover, re-engineer them for the latest market trends and put them back out with a different name. That's why they all sound the same.'

Ziva wasn't really listening, distracted. 'I keep remembering the first time I saw you. Coming out of that club, the Quantum Tunnel. I was supposed to be watching out for this guy … shit, I can't even remember his name now. He was going to tell me where …' She shook her head. 'And so there I was, watching, and then you came out in your stupid sleeveless T-shirt and all that hair loose practically down to your fucking ankles and … Christ. I couldn't stop looking at you.'

'You stalked me.' En raised an eyebrow.

'I asked you where you were going next.'

'I said I didn't know.'

'You said you were going home! … You were so fucking tall!'

'An hour later you were trying to rent a room for us.'

'And they were all too expensive and so we ended up in Brotherhood Park. I think I spent the whole night kissing you.' Ziva's smile faded. She looked Enaya in the eye. 'I grew up believing in the Federation. In my culture, its values, in its potency. Now look at me.' She brushed her fingers down her sides. 'Forty years old and I look at the Empire and wonder, despite their slavery, if they had a point. I look at the Alliance and Turner and Argent and I don't wonder why they did it any more. It's the superficiality. The impermanence. How fucking shallow are we all? I don't want to be like that. I want something that lasts.'

'You look at the wrong things, Ziv.' Enaya stared back at her. 'You know what I look at? I look at you and I look at Ay. Just at the two of you.' She took Ziva's hand. 'Come on! I know what you're like. You've been sitting in that ship of yours for Allah knows how long, living off reconstituted nutrient soups of some sort. I'm sure your *Dragon Queen* looks after you very well in its own way, but now you're with me and I have a reservation for us at a very nice restaurant.'

'Aisha …?'

En put a finger to her lips and very slightly shook her head. 'Not tonight, Ziv. She's a grown girl. I can't stop her going wherever she wants. I can't ...' She blinked a few times and looked away. 'I can't tell her what to do any more.'

As Ziva and En walked together hand in hand, the *Dragon Queen* flashed a message to say that Newman was secure in the Golden Gate cells and that Harris had been handed over. He'd be on the k-cast news soon. He'd be asked for interviews, his life story. He'd have his five minutes of fame. He'd bubble back one more time when they sentenced him and then he'd vanish. If you had any sense, Ziva thought, you took your flash of glory and rode it for what you could and then quietly sank, content to have your obscurity back and pleased to have ridden the dragon, if only for a moment. There was nothing more pathetic than a low-talent loser who'd had their moment of lucky fortune, their flash of notoriety, and couldn't let it go. So many did that.

'You know,' said Enaya, who'd obviously caught her train of thought, 'there are rehab clinics on Wicca's World for those fifteen-minute wonders. Places to help you adjust to being normal again, to being not very interesting, to being not noticed. Special clinics for letting go. Next to them, they have clinics for people who haven't ever had their flash of fame but who can't let the idea of it go. They have speakers in those clinics who come from the first clinics, former fleeting k-cast faces telling suicidally attention-hungry wannabes what it was like to make it for a moment and then be forgotten again and how they were better off where they were; and yet in those talks they all get their fix of what they so desperately need. It's attention, that's all.' There was a bite behind the words.

Ziva tugged on Enaya's hand, spinning her round. 'Stop.'

'What?'

'Nothing. I just want to look at you. I could never stop looking at you.' Enaya stood still and Ziva drank her in. En was nearly a foot taller than Ziva, her long dark face framed by luscious black hair that shone all the way down to her waist. She had a perfect nose and huge dark brown eyes and a smile, when she let it out, that broke sorrow with hope. She wore a high-collared dress tonight, in embroidered white silk that flowed all the way down her to the ground and with a cream Roman chasuble over the top. There were designs woven in to the fabric of the chasuble, characters in old Arabic that Ziva couldn't read. She took the chasuble in her hands. 'This one's new. What do the words say?'

'Family. Honour. Loyalty. Friendship.' En was blushing now.

'You've always been too damn tall to kiss properly.' Ziva had something in her eye again. She blinked it away. 'I've missed you,' she said.

Enaya led her on to a quiet place on the edge of the rim – the Sungrazer, a name which made Ziva groan because it was obviously named after the quadruple platinum Jjagged Bbanner recording – hundred-year-old background muzak that everyone and his dog across the Federation must surely be sick of hearing by now; but En took her hand and pulled her in anyway. She tugged Ziva through a sprawl of discreet tables, each tucked away in its own nook. Plants and shrubs broke up the space, providing the illusion of a pleasant evening garden on the surface of some balmy world. The outside wall of the rim was transparent and through it Ziva could see out into space, to the stars, to the vast curve of New California a few hundred miles below. The sun was somewhere on the other side of the station and most of the planet below was

160

in daylight. Now and then bright lights flared as ships moved in and out of lower orbits.

'They say the gas giants of Alioth are beautiful,' said Ziva, looking out at the stars.

'That's why I came here. I'd like to see them.' Enaya reached across the table and took Ziva's hand.

'Do you remember the first time I met Aisha? We still hardly knew each other, you and I, but you'd told me where you lived and I came without telling you I was coming. She was at school. When she came back, you pretended so hard that nothing was going on. You were talking to her through that wall-hatch where she could only see you from the waist up. She couldn't see that I had my hand in your knickers. I always wondered if she knew. She had those holograms on her wall then. Do you remember? One was of the gas giants of Alioth.'

Enaya snorted. 'No! She had that later, and then only because you gave it to her.'

'What happened, En?'

Enaya let go of Ziva's hand and sat back. When she spoke, her words were measured. 'I didn't come here to talk about Aisha. I didn't come here to talk about us. I came here for me. To have something of my own. And, if you came too, to have some time the way we used to. Do you remember?'

Ziva took Enaya's hand again and squeezed hard. 'Aisha, En. Where did he take her?'

Enaya let out a little laugh. She didn't meet Ziva's eyes. She was fighting not to cry. 'They could be anywhere, Ziv.'

'Arcturus. Didn't she say once: "I want to breathe under the red light of a dying sun."?'

'She said …' En trailed off and let out a long heavy sigh. She started to laugh again. This time, the tears came as well.

'It's not your fault, En. It's him.'

'She's sixteen, Ziv. I have to let her go. She'll come back this time but one day she won't. So I've got a few days to find my strength and then perhaps two more years keeping it together for both of us and trying to make things right and teaching her how to be strong. After that she's gone and there's nothing more I can do.'

En was squeezing Ziva's hand so hard that Ziva felt her bones bend. 'You don't have to do it on your own,' she said.

'Yes, Ziv, I do.' Enaya drew slowly away. 'We'd better eat. Everyone says you should try the blandroot if you come to Alioth but I already did that and ...' she shuddered and made a face.

Ziva leaned across the table. 'No, you *don't*–'

En snatched back her hand with such force that Ziva lurched forward. The slap caught her across the cheekbone and it carried every ounce of Enaya's rage. 'Yes,' said En. 'I do.' She got up and ran from the table. When she came back, a few minutes later, she crouched beside Ziva and wrapped her arms around her and rested her head on Ziva's shoulder. 'I'm sorry,' she murmured. 'I didn't ... I've just heard so many promises before and they never meant anything. I deserve better from you.'

Ziva stroked En's hair. 'I never promised you anything,' she said.

'I know, Ziv. But you were going to.'

'You're right, En. You do deserve better. Never mind eating. I want to show you something.'

Three hours later, the *Dragon Queen* dropped into an orbit over the gas giant Bifrost with its rings and its pair of violet moons and its atmosphere awash with blues and greens. The Fer-de-Lance seemed to glide across the surface of the

162

rings to their inner edge. With the sun behind them, lighting them up, the curious mixture of ice and methane crystals refracted and scattered Alioth's light into sprays of colour: rainbows erupting through the rings that gave the gas giant its name. Bifrost itself hung overhead, filling half of space.

'Allah preserve me from such beauty as this,' whispered En.

Ziva let them drift a while, the *Dragon Queen* projecting holograms all around them, casting the illusion of floating in open space. En seemed to lose herself in it.

'I wanted to bring you out here to see this,' whispered Ziva. 'When we're done here, we're going to go and find Aisha.' She pushed herself out of the pilot's couch, unbuckled Enaya's straps and pulled her floating down the *Dragon Queen*'s upper spine to the airlock behind the cockpit. Once there, she pointed to a pair of armoured EVA suits. 'En, have you ever been outside?'

En looked at her as though she was mad. 'Outside? You mean in space?'

'Yes.'

'No!'

'Come on, then.'

'No!'

Ziva unclipped one of the suits. They were the heavy-duty armoured sort designed for working in a hostile environment with high radiation or EM interference or the danger of flying debris. She'd bought them for making external repairs before she'd discovered what a thoroughbred the Fer-de-Lance was. Cobras and even Vipers, if something broke you had a chance of jury-rigging a repair that would limp you to the nearest station. A Fer-de-Lance? Not a hope; but she'd already bought the suits by then. Now she opened one up and climbed inside.

163

'No.' En was waving her hands. 'No, no, no.'

'You came to Alioth to see the gas giants. You want to *really* see them, come outside.' Ziva took Enaya's hand and pulled her into the airlock. 'It's easy enough.'

'No, Ziv. I don't think ...' En looked hard at the suit. 'I don't ...'

'I'll be with you, En. This is my world and I want you to see it.'

En blinked a few times and took a deep breath. She climbed into the suit, legs and arms as Ziva showed her. 'I don't want to do this, Ziv.'

'Just keep breathing. Whenever you want to go back inside, you say the word. Seal the suit when you're ready. Like this.' Ziva pressed a stud and her own suit closed around her. The helmet came over her head and she heard the faintest hiss as the seals closed and the suit built up an over-pressure to test its integrity. Displays flickered across her visor. She watched as En did the same. 'En. You see a green light in the top right corner of your vision?'

'Yes.'

'That tells you everything's fine. I'm going to put you on a tether so you don't need to worry about anything at all. Just tell the ship if you want to go back and she'll reel you in, all the way back into the airlock.' Ziva turned Enaya so she was facing inward, tethered her, quietly de-pressurised the airlock and opened the door. Bifrost, thousands of miles below, filled her vision. The silver gleam of the rings stretched out between them, so close that the *Dragon Queen* might almost have been touching them. To Ziva they felt as though they were a solid thing, something she could step outside and walk on. She gave a tiny kick and drifted into the void. She loved this. The slow exit, hanging, supported by nothing but the abstract mathematics of gravity and mechanics, floating over something as immensely vast as Bifrost. The swirling blues and greens filled half her vision. If she looked one way, she saw the sharp curve of Bifrost's rainbow rings and a hundred billion waiting stars. The other way and the rings lost their colour before the bright giant of Alioth itself. The rings were close enough that she could see the elongated shadow of the *Dragon Queen* stretched across them.

She turned back to the Fer-de-Lance, inverted over the gas giant. En hadn't moved. 'You can turn around now, En. Slowly. Hold onto things.' She watched.

'Oh! Ohooooh! Oh no, no, no!' Enaya had turned enough to see the open airlock door and the vastness of the gas giant far beyond. 'Oh Ziv, I'm going to fall! Come back! Come back inside.'

'There's no gravity, En. You can't fall. Push away from the wall. Come towards me. I'll catch you.'

'Absolutely not! I'm going to fall. Ziva, come back inside and close the bloody door!'

'You're not going to fall, En. You can't. Close your eyes.'

'They're already closed.'

'Then let go. See. No falling. Just floating. I'm right here, En. You can see me, if you look. I'll catch you. Here.' She set up a command for the other suit. 'All you have to do is say go and the suit will do the rest.'

'No, no, no. No, Ziv.'

'Trust me, En.'

There was a long pause and then Enaya's suit gave a tiny burst and started to move forward to the mouth of the airlock. Ziva saw En clench her fists. 'Oh, I fucking hate you, Ziva Eschel, and may merciful Allah do many, many, extremely unpleasant things to you for—' As she drifted out into open space, the rest vanished into a terrified wail.

Seconds later, Ziva had a hold of her. She held En tight – not that you could tell under the armoured suits – and waited for her breathing and her heart-rate to come out of the red.

'Don't let me go don't let me go don't let me go I want to go back take me back!'

'I thought we might ride drones through the rings and surf Bifrost's stratosphere.'

'Take me back. I want to go back, Ziv. Don't let go. Get me inside – I'm going to be sick!' En's heart-rate wasn't shifting. She had both hands clamped onto Ziva's suit, her arms wrapped around her and clearly had no intention of letting go. She was getting worse, not better. En was falling into a panic attack.

Shit. She *was* going to puke in her suit …

Ziva pulled hard on the tether and jerked them both back into the airlock. She just about got the door closed, the airlock fast-pressurised and En's suit open in time for En to throw up. In the absence of any gravity, the effect was startlingly unpleasant.

'Oh En!' Ziva jabbed Enaya with a sedative and pulled her gently through the ship back to her cabin, then floated quietly beside her, stroking her hair and listening to her heartbeat. 'Sorry En. Space-walking wasn't such a good idea, was it?'

Enaya slowly shook her head. She was as pale as a ghost and shaking. 'No, Ziv.' Her voice already sounded slurred from the sedative. 'Was the most… scary … thing.' She clung to Ziva's arm, fingers still tight enough to leave marks. 'I was falling and it was so far and there was nothing and I was so scared. And then you caught me. I couldn't let go of you.'

'I'll always catch you, En.' Ziva stripped off her one-piece and started working on En's, both of them spattered with spots of vomit.

166

'How, Ziv?' Enaya's pupils were starting to dilate. 'You're never there.'

'I will be this time.' Ziva pushed En into the cabin's water-sphere. 'You ever shower without any gravity?'

Enaya twisted, trying to draw Ziva closer. The sedatives were blurring her. 'That would be nice,' she murmured. 'I'd like that. Isn't this how our lives should be, Ziv? Can't we be … *this* all the time?'

Ziva let out a heavy breath and looked away. 'I haven't really given you anything I said I would, have I?'

'No, Ziv.'

'I'll try, En.'

'Just stay with me until we find Ay, Ziv. Just that long. Then we'll see.'

'Have you ever thought about being a man?' asked En later. They floated naked, still damp, spooned together, Enaya wrapped around Ziva with one hand between Ziva's legs and the other tangled with Ziva's fingers, idly stroking each other. En was buzzing.

'What do you mean?'

'I mean a proper transformation.'

'Why would I?'

'Then you could fuck me like a man.'

Ziva tightened her thighs around En's hand. 'Is that what you want?'

'Sometimes. Sometimes I want to be ridden without mercy. Be beaten, hit, choked.' She paused. 'Does that frighten you? It frightens me.'

'You're not worthless, En.'

'I know. But it's still there.'

Ziva wriggled free and turned over to look Enaya in the eye. 'But I don't *want* to hurt you.'

167

'Which is why you could.' En stroked Ziva's cheek. A bruise was coming up from where En had hit her. 'I could let it all go with you.' She put a hand over Ziva's belly and splayed her fingers. 'You're older than I am and look at you – nothing sags. Everything still firm. I hate you.'

'I'm all hard edges. Always have been. There's a microgym on the *Dragon Queen*. I use it a lot. Also, no children.' She squeezed Enaya's breasts and grinned. 'Besides, you were always much fuller than I was. It was a long time before I stopped envying you for that.' Gently she pushed En around and straddled her, then lowered her face until their lips were almost touching. 'I don't want to be a man, En. I'd be stupidly short and everyone would laugh at me. But if you want to be ridden, I have some top line prosthetics.'

En sank her fingers into Ziva's hair and gripped her head. She didn't say anything, but her eyes were as wide as lanterns, full of eagerness.

'I'm going to stop,' Ziva said.

En gave a little shake of her head. 'No. Don't. Please.'

'The hunting, I mean. I'm going to stop the hunting. I've got the bounty I've been after for the last two months. We're going to find Aisha, you and I, and then I'm going to hand him over and then we're going to have some fun. Just the three of us. You don't have to do it on your own.'

Enaya was trembling. 'I don't believe you.'

'I know.'

Later, Enaya fell asleep in her arms. From where she floated, limbs wrapped around her lover, Ziva quietly piloted the *Dragon Queen* back to the Golden Gate to pick up Newman. She whispered to the ship to have her avatars in Delta Pavonis wake up. 'And then autopilot us to Arcturus,' she said. She already knew where Aisha was going. 'Send a drone to clean up the airlock, too.'

168

Once she had Newman securely in the hold again, Ziva curled up with Enaya. She closed her eyes and slept, letting the *Dragon Queen* find its own way.

Chapter Nine

Ravindra wanted to go back to bed. Knowing she still had a lot to do before she could rest made her want to take stims again. Working the mine in the Warren, she had needed them just to stay alive. She'd come out of the prison pretty strung out, a condition she didn't want to return to. So Ravindra settled for coffee. Between the bounty hunter and the Judas Syndicate she could feel herself running out of time – could almost see the red hourglass counting down for her and the rest of the crew. As it had already done for Harnack.

She bought the strongest, bitterest coffee available and made her way back to the *Song of Stone*. She found Jonty and Orla working on the ship. Both of them glanced at her when she entered. She couldn't quite read either of their expressions. Both seemed guarded, even suspicious.

Do they think I sold them out? she wondered.

What she couldn't work out was why someone had let the Syndicate into the ship in the first place, but not told them where the cargo was. And why had they taken Harnack's body?

'How's she doing?' Ravindra asked, reaching up to stroke the cutter's scarred hull. Then she stopped and pulled her hand back. Ji's words flooded her mind – *all you're thinking about is the ship, the crew and the next score.* Was that true?

'It's mostly ablative scoring. It's weakened the integrity of the armour. How long have we got?' Jonty asked.

170

'Not long,' Ravindra replied, unwilling to be precise. 'We could be facing off against an Anaconda with a fighter complement and a corvette. She needs to be as close to peak as possible.'

'Shame Jenny's not here,' Orla said from where she was perched on one of the ship's stubby nacelles. Ravindra looked up at the older woman, trying to read her expression. Orla held Ravindra's look but remained poker-faced. Ravindra turned and headed into the ship. She went into the cabin that few of them ever went into. Even after Marvin had been killed, Ravindra had chosen to keep her old berth on the ship and not move into the captain's cabin. She was pretty sure that Orla snuck in there sometimes.

Like the rest of the ship, the cabin had been well appointed. The Empire did not stint on luxuries. And like the rest of the ship's non-essential systems and areas it looked somewhat worn around the edges. There was little in the way of personal items in the cabin. None of them liked leaving evidence around on a working ship. Ravindra, however, still thought she could smell him in the cabin. A not entirely unpleasant mix of his deodorant, and sweat and oil from the various ship systems that he would work on with Jenny.

They had all wanted to pursue the shoot-in-the-back bounty hunter who had killed him. But none of them actually had done anything. Dane's Law had revenge down as one of the stupid things that got you caught or killed.

Now she was going to have to enact one of the less pleasant of Dane's Laws. She found the wooden case in the storage space under the bunk. She spun the ancient combination lock until it clicked open. It was empty. She stared at the worn, contoured, velvet interior where the item she was looking for was supposed to be. She opened a comms link to Jonty and Orla.

171

'Guys, could you meet me in the common room? Now?'

The common room was a communal rest area and mess. Again, like the rest of the non-essential areas of the ship, it had once been luxurious and was now a little tatty around the edges. The crew had eclectically and haphazardly decorated it. Mainly Jonty and Jenny, though the state of the art audio/holo system had been installed by Marvin and Harnack. Ravindra was leaning on the wooden table with the chessboard design on it. Marvin had insisted that they all learned the game in the Warren. He saw it as a firm grounding in the basics of strategy.

'What's that for?' Jonty asked pointing at the wooden case. He knew exactly what was supposed to be in the box. Ravindra ignored his question. When Orla walked in she glanced at the case and then back at Ravindra.

'Where is it?' Ravindra asked her first mate.

'With me,' Orla told her.

'What? Why?' Jonty demanded.

'Because one of you sold us out to the Judas Syndicate,' Orla said softly.

'And we know it wasn't you because …' Jonty demanded.

'You don't, I do,' Orla told him evenly. 'That's good enough for me. I can see why it wouldn't be enough for the two of you.'

Ravindra was watching her. Looking for a tell but keeping her own hands well away from the burst pistols at her side. She opened her mouth to say something, but Orla put a finger to her own lips. Ravindra groaned almost silently as Orla slid her fingers into a handheld, multi-spectrum scanner glove. Orla ran the scanner over Ravindra. The glove froze in place over Ravindra's hair. Orla reached for the bug – Ravindra guessed it was probably a tiny spybot

– but stopped when the pilot held up a hand. Ravindra tapped her comp ring and a small hologram keyboard was projected into the air. Ravindra typed a brief text message and sent it to Orla who took a moment to read the message in her lenses. Then Orla nodded and held up her hand before tapping her own ring and making its keyboard appear.

'Okay, I've spoofed it,' Orla finally said. 'It's playing random footage put together by an ongoing intelligent editing program. It'll beat casual observation but not a great deal of scrutiny. Sure you don't want to simply get rid of it?'

'Not just yet,' Ravindra said.

'You were bugged?' Jonty asked. 'By who? The Syndicate?'

'More likely the bounty hunter she's just had a drink with,' Orla muttered. 'Rookie error, Rav.'

The goldskin turned to look at Ravindra, eyebrow raised.

'Where were we?' Ravindra resumed.

'We were trying to work out who sold us out.'

'It could have been Jenny. A faked kidnapping makes good cover for an out,' Ravindra said. 'Could even have been Harnack.'

'It wasn't Harnack!' Jonty spat. 'He wouldn't do that. He wouldn't betray us,' he continued more calmly.

'No, and if it was Jenny, then why didn't she tell them where the cargo was? And why take Harnack's body? So that leaves you two, as I know I didn't do it,' said Orla.

'You'll excuse us if we don't remove you from the list immediately,' Jonty said.

'Sure,' Orla said, smiling wanly.

'So how do you want to do this?' Jonty asked. 'You going to kill both of us if you can't decide? That'd be convenient if *you* were the traitor.'

Ravindra was looking between the two of them.

'See, here's the thing,' Ravindra began. 'I don't think the person who did it thought it was a complete betrayal, otherwise why not just tell them where the cargo was and collect their thirty pieces of silver?'

'They were playing their own game,' Orla agreed.

Both the women turned to look at Jonty. He squeezed his eyes tightly shut. No tears leaked out, but his eyes were watery when he opened them.

'Lady Fates, you're going to kill me, aren't you?' He glanced down, unable to look either of them in the eye. Orla opened her mouth to answer.

'I don't think so. I think I see what happened here, but we need to *know*,' Ravindra said gently. Orla glared at her captain. Ravindra just shook her head.

'Look, I'm sorry.' Jonty said defensively. 'But it's the only chance that Harnack has.'

'Harnack's dead,' Orla said harshly. Ravindra felt her heart sink.

'Yes, but the Syndicate are backed by the Imperials, they have senatorial approval,' the goldskin said.

'So?' Orla demanded.

'The Empire has clone facilities,' Ravindra said sadly.

'You fool,' Orla groaned.

'There's been rumours that the Veils are all clones of this one guy, some thousand-year-old super-gangster. Look, I know it was bad, but that's why I didn't give them the cargo. They return Harnack and Jenny to us – both alive – and we give them the cargo.'

'But why did they take Jenny?' Orla screamed at him. He cringed away from the woman's anger.

'I didn't know they would do that. The deal was they just took Harnack and we'd swap him for the cargo when they ...'

'What?' Orla demanded. 'Brought him back?'

'Look, there's something that you don't know about Harnack and I,' Jonty told them. 'We were seeing each other.'

'Really?' Orla and Ravindra both asked, simultaneously and sarcastically.

'Oh.'

'But why did they take Jenny?' Orla asked.

'Added insurance, they told me. Look, I was furious with them. But we can still pull this off.'

'They took Jenny because they knew that when adults found out about this fairy tale they'd see the holes in your fantasy,' Orla told him.

'Wh-what are you talking about? The empire has entire armies of clones! They can manipulate genetic material. I mean, look at Ravindra. *She's been genetically engineered.*' Both women could hear the desperation in Jonty's voice. He had spent a long time convincing himself of this fantasy.

'It takes months to grow a clone to majority,' Ravindra told him sadly. 'Even then it's a blank slate. It wouldn't have Harnack's memories, his experience, his personality. It wouldn't be him, it would just look like him.'

Ravindra was surprised to see Jonty start to smile.

'I thought you might say that. Despite what you may think, I'm not a moron. They can use EM resonance with digital pulses of infrared and infrasound to map his mind and model it to regrow his mind as it was.'

'That technology's years away from practical application,' Orla said. 'And it's designed for storing minds electronically.'

'There's no way to take that raw data and imprint it onto a cloned brain. The problem's not the information itself, it's recreating the billions of neural connections that our mind makes as a matter of course,' Ravindra finished. If you grew up on New America then it was difficult not to have at least a passing interest in biotechnology. In Ravindra's case it was a matter of self-preservation, just in case the genetic tampering she had been subject to as a slave foetus ever went wrong.

'So why did they take Harnack?' Jonty asked. The desperation in his voice was back.

'Window dressing,' Orla said quietly. The anger had gone from her voice. 'To keep their inside man in line. But they knew we'd never fall for it – that's why they took Jenny; that's what the deal is now. Jenny for the cargo.'

'But you don't know,' Jonty whined. 'There could have been developments that you don't know about … secret labs …'

'That they're going to use to bring a pirate back to life?' Ravindra asked gently.

'Harnack's body probably got spaced the moment they left atmosphere,' Orla told him. It was enough. He started to weep. 'You want to cry, Jonty? Cry for Jenny. Fates know what she's going through right now.'

'I thought …' he mumbled.

'You want to make a play, then you speak to all of us,' Ravindra said. 'You know the rules on this ship.'

'You didn't speak to us because you knew we'd never buy in to your fantasy. You sold us out, you sold out Jenny, because you wanted to keep your hope alive a little bit more. That's pathetic.' Orla drew the Executioner from where it had been stuck through her waistband at the small of her back, concealed by her T-shirt. It was an ancient semi-automatic pistol. So old the rounds it fired still had shell casings. Marvin had been forced to machine the bullets himself. It was stainless steel with walnut grips and its name

176

was inscribed on the slide. Marvin had claimed that the pistol had been in his family for centuries and had belonged to a gun-fighting ancestor from Earth. The gun served only one purpose on the *Song of Stone*.

'But you said …' Jonty tailed off. 'I'm sorry.'

'Want me to …?' Ravindra offered.

'I've got this,' Orla said quietly. She pointed the ancient pistol at Jonty.

'Please …' he began again.

'You doing this here?' Ravindra asked, looking around the common room.

'Yes,' Orla said. Ravindra noticed that the gun was shaking slightly. Orla swallowed hard. Jonty was pleading with her now. 'Shut up!' Orla shouted at him. 'You know what the really sad thing is? If Harnack was here, he'd pull the trigger himself.'

Ravindra had a moment to appreciate the man's golden skin, one last time. He had always been as beautiful as he was exotic. He looked alien, or how she imagined a *deva* would look.

The report of the pistol in the enclosed common room was deafening. Jonty's body collapsed to the floor. The pistol wavered, dropping a little. There were tears in Orla's eyes. Then she stepped forwards and double-tapped Jonty, shooting him two more times in the head. Just like Harnack had taught them.

'You knew the law,' she said to the corpse through her tears.

Dane's Law: you killed traitors, no excuses, no mercy.

Ravindra took the Executioner from Orla's hand. She ejected the magazine and worked the slide, ejecting the round in the chamber. She put the ancient weapon down and then held her sobbing friend.

177

***

They were going to miss Jonty badly. They would have needed his skill as a gunner if they were going up against the Syndicate, particularly with Harnack dead and Jenny gone. His value as a gunner was, however, outweighed by the risk of having a traitor on board.

Orla was sat on the sofa in the common room. She had a bottle of whiskey dangling from one hand. She had promised Ravindra that she would take a Purge when she needed to. Jonty's body was gone. Ravindra had taken it down to the cold storage. They would eject it unceremoniously into space when they had the chance. The only trace of his passing was a red smear on the floor. Ravindra had also returned the Executioner to Marvin's old cabin.

Ravindra was leaning against the wall of the common room.

'When are you going to set the rendezvous?' Orla asked, her voice slurring slightly. Ravindra knew that she was probably going to have to go through this again with her later.

'Two days from now,' Ravindra said.

Orla's head swivelled around unsteadily to look at Ravindra. 'That leaves Jenny to the tender mercies of the Syndicate for a long time. The ship's not too badly banged up. We can be ready before then.'

'If they're going to hurt her, then they'll hurt her, regardless of how long we …'

'Don't be a cold bitch, Rav, not with me. I can see straight through you. If she's being hurt, then I want it to stop as soon as possible.'

'I genuinely don't think they'll do that. They'd gain nothing by it. The double-cross will come after they've got what they want. Then they're going to try to kill us.'

'So why the delay?' Orla asked.

'I think we're dead,' Ravindra said. She gave this a moment to settle in. Orla was looking more sober now. 'You, me and Jenny. I think that if we dumped the cargo, dumped the ship, ran now, found the shittiest stage one colony, on the most backward planet, in the most Podunk system, then maybe the Syndicate wouldn't find us. For a while.'

Orla took a long pull on the whiskey bottle.

'I don't want to live like that,' Orla said.

'Me neither.'

'So this is a suicide run?'

'Not very Dane's Law, huh?'

'So why the delay? Why are we leaving Jenny in a cage longer than necessary?'

'I need an out for Ji.'

Orla nodded.

'Can you get behind that?' Ravindra continued.

'Yeah,' Orla said after some moments of thought.

'Do you think Jenny could?'

'Yeah,' Orla finally said. 'I think she'd be okay with this. When we get her you can ask her. If she spends her last moments beating on you with a wrench, then we know that we were wrong. So where's it gonna be?'

Ravindra told her. A huge smile split Orla's face.

'I'm smiling because I'm drunk. That's madness.'

'And in two days time ...'

'It's going to be in a very interesting place,' Orla finished.

'Look, we both need some sleep, then we need to do what we can with the *Song* and I've got some things I need to—' The comms icon in Ravindra's lenses started flashing. It was a ship-to-ship link with a full holo avatar. She checked the caller ID. 'What does this arsehole want?' Ravindra

179

muttered. She piped the signal through the common room's holo-emitter, making sure its lens was turned away from the bloodstain on the floor. Merkel's bruised, broken-toothed, smiling visage appeared, flickering from the long-range nature of the transmission, in the common room.

'I'm afraid I can't recommend a plastic surgeon,' Ravindra told the image. Merkel's smile wavered slightly. Ravindra counted the delay. He was at least two light seconds out. That covered a whole lot of space.

'We're too pretty to need them,' a drunken Orla told him laconically.

'Big score, Khanguire? Seems you've got the Syndicate pretty pissed with you.'

'I'm busy, Merkel, what do you want?'

A pause. '*Captain* Merkel,' Merkel hissed.

'Bye,' Khanguire said and opened her mouth to give the order to break the transmission.

'I've got your son,' Merkel told her and grinned. Ravindra and Orla stared at the image. Orla reached into the knee pocket of her cargo trousers and took out a blister pack of Purge pills.

'Nothing to say now?' Merkel goaded. Ravindra couldn't talk through her cold fury. Orla popped several of the pills into her mouth and then stood up and headed for the bridge.

'See, everyone thinks you're a cold, hard bitch, don't they? But little Ji, he knows better. I've sussed this out over the last few months we've been hanging together. You really love that snivelling, fucking wretch, don't you?'

You've been looking for leverage to boost a score from me because you're too lazy and inept to pull a decent job yourself, Ravindra thought. Merkel was a stand-over pirate. The lowest form of scum.

180

'Well, bad news for you, your baby boy's fallen in with people just like you.'

'We're nothing like you,' Ravindra finally managed to say.

'Fuck you! Fuck you, you sanctimonious bitch! You've always looked down on me! Let me tell you something, you're not getting out of this alive. I'm not going to be looking over my shoulder for you, waiting to see the *Song* in my scanners. You're going to die, you're going to die suffering and messy. That and we get the cargo from your last score, the one that Ji told us got you into all that trouble.'

She hadn't told Ji anything about the score, but of course he'd known that they'd gone out on a job. She'd told Ji that she was in trouble. That was almost enough. *You fool, Ji,* Ravindra thought. The Syndicate connection, though, Merkel would have had to learn that from somewhere else. Someone in Harlan's organisation? Or Harlan himself? Maybe she'd become too much of a liability.

'Rendezvous point?' Ravindra's tone was calm.

'What? You think I'm going to face up to an Imperial cutter in a Cobra? Do you think I'm stupid?'

Yes. I'm not going to fire on a ship with my son on it.

'We meet on the station. I'm paid up. You try to move on me and Whit's gotta protect me. And I know what you're thinking, that you're paid up as well, but nothing's going to happen to you. Well, nothing on the station. That'll just be a simple exchange of goods and personnel – and in case you're thinking of trying anything, I'm going to have old Harlan and some of his people along, not to mention I've hired a few more people of my own.'

'When?' Ravindra asked.

'Two hours, my berth. Who's getting looked down on now, huh?'

181

'Still you,' Ravindra said and cut the comms link. There was a moment of self-pity, mostly brought on by fatigue, then she turned and marched to the bridge.

'Any luck?' Ravindra asked. Orla was seated at the scanner controls. She was covered in sweat and stank of whiskey from the Purge forcing the alcohol out of her body. She didn't look well.

'I managed to narrow it down but we're still looking at an awful lot of space. What're you going to do?'

'I'm going to go and see Harlan,' Ravindra said as she tapped her comp ring to make the holo-keyboard appear. She typed out the text message as she walked.

'You sold us out, you son-of-a-bitch!' Ravindra shouted. Harlan turned around away from the window in the station's Command and Control centre. He was leaning on his cane, backlit by Motherlode's planetary horizon. Almost everyone in the station's control centre stopped what they were doing and turned to look at Ravindra as she stalked up the steps from the door and onto the central gantry that ran above the workstations.

'How'd you get in here?' Harlan demanded. By either wall, the massive Harrelson and the whip-thin, vicious-looking Jonas kept pace with her as she strode towards Harlan. 'Keep those hands away from those pistols, girl, or my people will burn you down.'

'You let them take him!' Ravindra shouted as she came all but nose-to-nose with the station boss.

'He left here of his own free will. What happens out there isn't my concern, but if Merkel chooses to do business on this station, he's paid up, protected. You understand me? No trouble.'

'What about Ji? He's paid up.'

'I've got nothing to do with what happens off the station and he fell afoul of Merkel off-station. That's his look out. He's just contraband now. You should have looked after him better.'

Ravindra stepped back as if she'd been slapped. She stared at Harlan. She flexed her right hand, and felt, rather than saw, Jonas shift slightly in her periphery.

'Seems to me,' Harlan said – he was speaking low but his voice carried across the now deathly silent station control centre – 'that you're just causing me more and more trouble. I've spoken with Merkel, so me and some of my people are going to be at the exchange just to make sure everyone plays nice, and then you're finally off this station, understand me?'

Ravindra glared at him. 'If anything …'

Harlan placed a finger on her lips. Ravindra was so surprised that she went quiet. Harlan leaned in close to her ear.

'You threaten me,' he whispered loud enough for it to carry, 'and you die here and now.' In her periphery she was aware of Jonas smoothly drawing a weapon and letting it hang down by his side. Ravindra flinched away from Harlan, turned and stormed out of the control centre.

For Ravindra there had always been something comforting about the familiar, angular, wedge shape of the Cobra Mk. III. It was the ship that so many pilots had started flying, though her first ship had been one of the old Mk. IIs. In some ways they were reliable old workhorses, in other ways they were frustrating pieces of shit. Nearly every frontier pilot thought fondly of them, however. Except the *Magician*. Now, looking at the familiar lines of the Cobra, she couldn't stop wondering what had happened to her son on that ship.

Merkel had hired six gun-tramps from the station. Along with the captain himself, Alice and the other two crew – whose names Ravindra had never bothered to learn – that brought the count up to ten guns in the Cobra's shadow in the docking berth.

Ravindra was stood about halfway between the Cobra's ramp and the door to the docking berth, just under the tip of the Cobra's wing. Harlan was just to her right, leaning on his cane. The cube-shaped, coded and locked cargo box was on her right. Harrelson and Jonas were standing a little way back and to either side of Ravindra and Harlan. Harrelson had an automatic shotgun slung across her front. Jonas was looking bored and inspecting his nails.

Merkel stood halfway down the Cobra's ramp. Alice was next to him. The other two members of the *Magician*'s crew were at the base of the ramp. Two of the gun-tramps were walking towards Harlan and Ravindra. *Brave* Merkel, it seemed, was going to let them handle the exchange. The other four gun-tramps were in cover behind various crates, tool benches and the landing struts of the Cobra.

'Where's Ji?' Ravindra demanded.

'He's safe, inside. You can have him when we've got you and the cargo.' Merkel told her.

'I want to see him first.'

'So?' Merkel asked. Harlan sighed and looked down.

'What do you mean, "so"?' Ravindra asked. 'I'm not giving you a thing—'

'Shut up, you arrogant bitch!' Merkel screamed at her. 'You're not in control here, I am! You do what I say! What I want! Do you understand me?'

Ravindra was taken aback by the outburst. The thought of Ji being under this man's power sickened her.

184

'Can we get on with this?' Harlan asked. 'I've got an appointment with Al for a shave in less than half an hour and I don't like being late.' He held up a cheap comp ring. 'The decrypts for the locks are on here. Merkel, you owe me credits for this, understand?' Merkel glared at the station boss but acquiesced. The two gun-tramps came to a stop in front of the station boss. Harlan dropped the ring. 'Shit, sorry.' The closest gun-tramp leant down to pick it up. Harlan swiftly drew the rapier blade from his cane and rammed it through the neck of the other gun-tramp. At least a foot of the narrow blade burst from the other side of the man's neck. He started sinking to his knees, blood pulsing from the wound and bubbling from his mouth. Harlan let go of the sword-cane and took a step back, fast-drawing the ancient pearl-handled, nickel-plated, single-action revolver from his waistband as the gun-tramp who had reached down for the comp ring straightened up.

At the same time the explosive bolts on the mocked-up secure crate blew the top and front off. Orla emerged and straightened up. She was already throwing one EM carbine to Ravindra, and was bringing her own to her shoulder.

Harlan fanned the hammer on the ancient revolver. The pistol fired, the gun-tramp in front of him staggered back.

Ravindra caught the EM carbine and ran towards the *Magician*'s loading ramp.

Merkel and Alice turned and began running back into the *Magician* as the ramp started to rise.

Harrelson shouldered her automatic shotgun and was advancing, firing short bursts at two of the gun-tramps under the Cobra. Jonas had a laser pistol in each hand and was moving quickly to one side, looking for a shot.

Orla fired two short bursts from the EM carbine. Ravindra had been broadcasting lens footage to Orla the

185

entire time she'd been in the box. Orla had integrated the footage with her own lenses' targeting software. As soon as she had burst out of the crate she had known where to aim.

Harlan worked the hammer of the revolver with his thumb and all but shoved it into the gun-tramp's face. He pulled the trigger. The muzzle flash scorched the man's skin and the impact of the bullet made the man's face look as if it had just caved in on itself.

The two crewman at the base of the *Magician*'s ramp brought their weapons up as Ravindra sprinted towards them and the closing ramp. Orla's burst caught one of them in the chest. The needle-like hypersonic rounds punched straight through his armour and he stumbled back and fell to the ground. Seconds later she caught the other crewman in the head with her second burst. Little pinpricks of red perforated his face.

Harlan limped back as fast as he could as the two dead gun-tramps in front of him collapsed to the ground. Harrelson stalked past him. She was firing at two of the remaining gun-tramps. The shotgun's enormous barrel was twitching between both targets as she fired. The ball bearings from the weapon's combat load were tearing up cargo crates and workbenches as she suppressed both of them, forcing them to keep their heads down. They were only managing the occasional return shot. One of them tried to make a run for it. He was torn apart, the high velocity ball bearings making him dance a ragged red jig across the docking berth floor before he collapsed. The other one threw his gun down and put his hands up.

Jonas was being shot at. Much of the fire was inaccurate, panicked. The last two gun-tramps were rattled by the violence of the attack, at how quickly things had gone

186

wrong. Jonas kept moving. A few shots had tagged him, making him stagger, but he had invested a lot in his armour. He looked for the moment. He raised his laser pistols and fired one and then the other. The beams bathed the docking berth in a harsh red light. Both hit. Superheated armour exploded outwards and then cooked flesh did the same in plumes of red steam. The two gun-tramps hit the ground.

Ravindra threw herself at the closing ramp as the second crewman, shot by Orla, collapsed to the ground. She hit the ramp hard and scrambled into the interior of the airlock. The inner airlock door was just sliding shut. Ravindra threw herself through that as well, hitting the cargo bay floor just as hard. Alice was walking towards her bringing a shotgun to bear, a look of terror on her face. Ravindra fired a long, undisciplined, ragged burst at the girl. The rounds stitched a line in pinpricks of red across her target's torso. Alice staggered back. The shotgun discharged into the air as Alice fell to the ground.

Ravindra rolled to her feet. She started moving quickly through the cargo bay, checking all around her, heading towards the stairs that led up to the crew quarters. In front of her the door to the stairwell slid open and Ji stepped out. Merkel had hold of him. Using him for cover. He was hunkered down tight behind the boy, an EM pistol pressed against Ji's head. Ravindra brushed her fingers forward and switched the EM carbine to single shot.

'Now, here's what's going to hap—' Merkel started. Ravindra shot him in the centre of his forehead. Merkel stood still for a moment and then collapsed to the ground, almost dragging Ji to the floor with him.

'Mum!' Ji cried.

'Get away from him. Now!' Ravindra shouted. She switched the carbine back to full automatic and advanced quickly on Merkel as Ji tried to disentangle himself from the Cobra captain. Ravindra kicked the body onto its back, fired two bursts into Merkel's chest and a third into his head.

She glanced at Ji. There were tears rolling down his face. He looked beaten and bloody but he was on his feet.

'Mum, th—' he came forwards to hug her. Ravindra pushed him away.

'Is there anyone else on the ship?' she demanded.

'N-n-no. There was just Alice and Merkel, everyone else was outside,' Ji managed.

'Okay. You're going to hold onto my shoulder and we are going to back, quickly, towards the airlock, do you understand me?'

'Mum—'

'Do you understand me, Ji?' she demanded.

'Y-yes,' the terrified boy answered. He took hold of her shoulder and they backed up. Ravindra was still looking all around, the carbine at the ready. She heard Ji start to sob when he saw Alice's body.

'Two down in the cargo bay; I've got Ji,' Ravindra said over the comms link.

'Clear,' Harrelson replied.

'Clear,' Orla replied.

'Clear,' Harlan replied.

'Jonas?' Ravindra asked after a pause.

'Hell yeah, I'm clear,' Jonas answered.

'Two to come out,' Ravindra told them. 'Ji, open the airlock.' Ji did as he was told.

Orla was waiting for them at the bottom of the ramp, covering them as they backed out of the Cobra. Harlan was standing, favouring one leg, looking down at the two men he'd killed. The cocked revolver was still held in one hand, pointing down. Harrelson had the surviving gun-tramp down on his knees, hands clasped behind his head. The huge woman was covering the terrified prisoner with her automatic shotgun. Jonas was leaning against the wall of the docking berth rolling himself a cigarette.

Ravindra backed out from under the Cobra and pushed Ji to the ground behind some crates.

'Ask him how many of them there were,' Ravindra shouted to Harrelson. Harrelson gestured at the man with the barrel of the shotgun.

'Ten and the boy,' the frightened gun-tramp said. 'Merkel, three crew, and the six of us.'

'I'll check the ship,' Orla said. 'Doesn't hurt to make sure.'

'I'll go with you,' Harrelson said. 'Jonas, take over.'

Jonas rolled his eyes and pushed himself off the wall to walk over to the prisoner, lighting his cigarette as he did so. Harrelson and Orla headed into the Cobra, weapons at the ready. Ravindra knelt down close to Ji, carbine still sweeping the area, still keeping a look all around. A few moments later Harrelson and Orla gave the all clear. Ravindra sagged and slumped against the wall of the docking berth.

'Are you okay?' she asked Ji. He nodded numbly. She looked up at Harlan. He reached into his suit jacket and pulled out a silver hip flask. You had to know what to look for to realise that his hand was shaking.

'Boss?' Jonas motioned towards the prisoner. Harlan glanced down at the terrified gun-tramp. He nodded.

'Sorry, friend.' Jonas didn't sound very sorry at all. The beam turned the back of the man's head to steam.

Orla glanced at the executed gun-tramp as she and Harrelson emerged from the *Magician*. Ravindra pushed herself to her feet.

'Did you find them?' she asked Harlan.

'Did you trace the transmission?' Harlan asked over his comms link. Someone in the command centre had to have been helping Merkel. Someone had to have told the other captain about the Syndicate's connection to Ravindra's score. The confrontation in the control centre had been for their benefit. Ravindra had texted the plan to Harlan before she had gone there. They had hoped to flush them out and lull Merkel into a false sense of security when the traitor told Merkel that Ravindra and Harlan had fallen out. 'Okay, bring the son-of-a-bitch down to the main concourse. He'll get his publicly.'

Ravindra walked towards the station boss. She pointed at the ancient revolver he'd used.

'What was that about?' she demanded. Harlan held his hands up in mock surrender.

'I swear to the Lady Fate, girl, I am better with this old Peacemaker than I am with any modern gun.' It was all bullshit, of course. Just like that stuff about going for a shave. He was as shaken up as the rest of them were after the gunfight, with perhaps the exception of Jonas, but there was something wrong with Jonas. The swordcane, the revolver, it was all just part of the myth of Harlan Whit. A myth that made people less inclined to mess with him. Ravindra hugged him.

'Thank you,' she told him. She pulled away from Harlan and nodded at Harrelson and Jonas. Harrelson smiled, Jonas touched his hat. Ravindra walked over to Orla and embraced her.

'Well, sir,' Harlan addressed Ji. 'Ladies,' he said to Orla and Ravindra. 'If you'll excuse me, I have an appointment for a shave.' He took another long pull from the hipflask to steady his nerves, then turned and headed for the door.

Jonas and Harrelson fell in behind him. Harlan stopped as he passed Ji and glanced at him. 'You need to be a man now, son.' And he was gone. Only then did Ravindra turn back to Ji, haul him to his feet, and clasp him so fiercely that it hurt his already pained ribs. Only then did she let her tears flow.

Chapter Ten

The *Dragon Queen* quietly woke Ziva up in the middle of their artificial night. 'We have arrived,' it told her.

'Take us in-system and start looking for Aisha.' Ziva turned and tried to go back to sleep. When that didn't work, she looked intently at En, trying to lose herself in her lover; but for some reason she kept seeing Khanguire. In the end Ziva gave up and floated quietly out of the cabin, back to the cockpit. She started retrieving Khanguire's files from the *Dragon Queen*'s archives and then stopped herself.

'What are you doing?' she asked the air. 'What *are* you doing?'

She opened the *Dragon Queen*'s cockpit shields and let herself float up against the transparency in the ship's outer skin. She drifted there. Stars. There were so many. Out here, slightly off the axis of the galaxy where the interstellar dust clouds didn't obscure as much of the core as they did right on the galactic ecliptic, the Milky Way was dazzling. As bright as Earth's moon she thought; and then she realised that Aisha had never seen Earth's moon. The Federation, the Empire, the Alliance, they were all tiny drops in a vast ocean. Space could be magnificently beautiful. Sometimes it literally took her breath away. Riding the gas torrents of the contact binary Phi Persei had made her weep at the sheer grandeur of it. It had taken weeks to get out there, hundreds of light years from the Federation and the Empire, hundreds of light years from the nearest permanent stations.

The most spectacular piece of universe she'd ever seen and there was so much more waiting to be found. She could share all of that with En. With Aisha.

'Ziva Eschel, interstellar tourist guide,' she muttered with scorn, but there was a lump in her throat as she said it. It wasn't even as stupid as it sounded. The original Fer-de-Lance design had been a yacht. The pilot and the co-pilot were supposed to keep themselves to themselves – glorified chauffeurs – while the executives and tycoons lounged in their luxury cabins. Stupidly expensive for its size, though, and hardly anyone used a Fer-de-Lance as a yacht any more. It all came down to the power plant. The power plant in the Fer-de-Lance was insane – no other ship had one like it. You could juice a Fer-de-Lance with anti-hydrogen and quadruple its output for a while and it just said 'thank you very much' and asked for more. Even when you didn't juice it, size for size it was the best power plant ever built.

Except for that new Zyfon model …

Khanguire.

Ziva hadn't heard anything useful from the Sly-Spy she'd left behind. Everything that came back was garbage. She'd obviously been found and spoofed. Not that she was surprised. Khanguire wasn't the sort to make mistakes. She'd never fall for something so obvious. The *Dragon Queen* carried on monitoring the Sly-Spy anyway, but Ziva wasn't holding her breath for anything useful to come of it.

Let her go. Leave it be. Let her sweat not knowing what's happening, whether I'm out there, whether in some dark corner of some forgotten system a Fer-de-Lance will come shooting out of the sun spraying the space around her with minelets of anti-matter. That was the way to handle someone like Khanguire. With the patience of a spider …

She'd been telling herself the same things ever since she'd left Whit's Station. Trying to convince herself.

When a hand touched her shoulder, Ziva almost jumped out of her skin, but it was only En.

'Don't you bother to dress when you fly?' En asked. Dressed in a jumpsuit, En had that slightly distressed look she'd worn ever since they'd left the false gravity of the Golden Gate.

'I forgot I wasn't alone here,' Ziva laughed. 'You get used to there being no one about to watch you.' She paused and then frowned. 'I was thinking just now about the furthest I ever went. Hundreds of light years from the last settled moon. Just … jumping. Never too far to not be able to jump back if I couldn't skim fuel. I used to try to find places where no one had been before. Of course, you couldn't really know.' She laughed. 'But yes, I didn't used to bother much about getting dressed on those trips. Look …' She had the *Dragon Queen* start its series of micro-jumps further in towards Arcturus. 'Red giant stars have a cruel beauty to them, don't they? They glower. They're dying – and they know it. The big ones are the worst, the ones that go supernova and annihilate their own systems. Antares. That one. I always wanted to go to Antares.'

'Arcturus is too small to end like that,' said Enaya. 'See, I *do* know *some* things. Doomed to shrug off its outer layers and then fade as a white dwarf, she fills her system with a reddish-orange light that at sunset turns everything the brown colour of dried blood.'

Ziva chuckled. 'You've been reading the tourist guide.' And En laughed too.

'Yes.'

The *Dragon Queen* stopped its micro-jumps and lit up its engines, running them low, a fraction of a gravity as she burned in around the gas giant Kalliste. Its moon, Arcas, core-heated by the tidal effects of its two ill-matched parents, was apparently the place to go for sunsets.

'I still have that piece of human garbage in the hold,' muttered Ziva. 'I have to take him in after this. I can't keep dragging him from system to system. As it is, he'll bang on about human rights violations the moment I hand him over to a Federation court.' But that, thankfully, would be Darkwater's problem.

Enaya looked horrified. 'He's on the ship with us?'

'He's in the hold in a self-contained pod. He's locked inside it and he might as well be in a different ship.' Ziva squeezed Enaya's hand. 'This is more important. Are you all right?'

'I'm nervous. Angry. Frightened. What do I say to her, Ziv? Do we even know if she's here?'

'You tell her that she deserves better.' Ziva checked through her avatars. Delta Pavonis confirmed Aisha's passage out and that the shithead boyfriend, Odar Berkeley, was violating a non-transit order. 'Yes, she's here, some-where, and Arcas and Kalliste are where you come if what you want is a morose romantic tragedy of a sunset. You still fine with me breaking his kneecaps when we find them?'

'Actually, I'd rather you didn't. Don't get yourself in trouble over him, Ziv.'

'But I *want* to hurt him, En.'

'I just want him to go away. Ay's mine, Ziv, not yours. Leave her to me. Please?'

'Got them!' They weren't even trying to hide. They were out on their own in a backwater, in a cheap automated drone-run retreat, with a bottom-rust rental aerojet that probably hadn't seen a proper service for a decade. En shook her head. Right out into the middle of nowhere, as far as it was possible to go.

'You know Ay. No half-measures. She came here to drown herself in a dying star. If she had the money, she'd be on a cruise flirting with the edges of the chromosphere.'

'I'll take you both once we're done here. Strap yourself in.' Ziva dressed, dropped the *Dragon Queen* into a trajectory for atmospheric entry and then changed her mind and did one more low fast orbit of Arcas, this time scanning all the traffic she passed. Sure enough she caught that corvette, the one that had followed her from Whit's Station, just moving in at the edge of her sensor range. *Keep an eye on him*, she told the *Dragon Queen;* then she buckled up and dropped into the stratosphere and for a while they were blind, haloed by over-shocked plasma as the Fer-de-Lance smashed Arcas's atmosphere out of the way. As soon as she could, Ziva threw out avatars into the net, loaded them with hijack-ware and set them to infecting every camera she could find near Aisha, until neither she nor Odar would be able to so much as fart without Ziva knowing. Whatever this retreat was, they had the place to themselves. Not another sentient lifeform for a hundred miles at least. Almost made it too easy.

'What are you doing?' En asked. Ziva kept her talking through the ten rattling minutes it took the *Dragon Queen* to crash through Arcas's atmosphere and drop into subsonic flight. Talking about the good times, the things they'd done together, the days back at the start when Aisha had been eleven years old. Aisha, with all her questions about hunting bounties and her big dark wide eyes.

'I remember she wanted to be a hunter too. It lasted for a year and then boys were all that mattered.' En frowned. 'I never knew how to help her with that. What to say. How to guide her. Isn't that what mothers are supposed to do?

Puberty and periods and all that, yes. The emotions, the feelings … But not boys. I never understood boys and I never wanted to. And the emotions, they were different. She knows she doesn't have a real father, that she was conceived ex-utero, but I don't think she understands how completely lost I am there. I was far more confused than she ever was. Or you, for that matter.'

Ziva shrugged. 'You had a strange family, En. Pre-space dinosaurs. Nice enough, I suppose, as long as you didn't challenge their twelfth-century values.'

Enaya laughed. 'They were *not* helpful.'

'My problem was more that I never had any boundaries. Still is …' Ziva grinned. 'Speaking of which, if you *really* want to have some fun then we could space-walk again, except this time in the Arcturus chromosphere.'

En looked appalled.

'Sometimes I just want to go out there, En,' Ziva said. 'Did you know that starquakes can distort planetary magnetic fields from half a galaxy away? Fifty thousand light years. Thousands of jumps. Years of travel. To be so deep and so far and so alone …'

Enaya snorted. 'And halfway there you run out of toilet paper.'

'En!'

'Yes. Well. You talk about vanishing into space for years at a time but you can do that on your own, thank you very much. It's not safe out there. Wondrous, with treasures to sate desires both subtle and gross, but it's not for the timid. And that's what I am, Ziv. Timid. I don't *want* to go exploring. I want to stay at home with you and Ay and curl up in bed and eat chocolate and watch k-cast series about serial killers and pornographic re-imaginings of fairy tales.'

Ziva laughed. 'If that's what you want, En.'

'It is. But it's not what *you* want.'

The *Dragon Queen* smashed into the clouds. 'I've been thinking about what it would take to put back the old cabins and the lounge. Maybe I could get used to the idea of not being able to cross a hundred light years without refuelling. Then we could have both.' She connected with her avatars again as the *Dragon Queen* punched out the other side of the cloud and matched its flight to the terrain, looking for a place to land.

Ay and Odar Something were sitting up in bed, half clothed, sharing a mildly illegal Lavinia pipe. Ziva patched that through to the cockpit's screen so En could see too.

There was a flash and a bang. For a moment all the cameras went white. When they recovered, Ay and Odar weren't sitting on the bed any more.

'Ziv …' Enaya was sitting beside her. She'd gone as stiff as a board. The screens showed the same room now, only Ziva couldn't see Aisha. Odar was held, screaming, between two massive junkers. The camera stayed on Odar's face for two seconds and then someone shot him. The bullet went in just under his nose, caving in his teeth. A spray of red exploded from the back of his head. As Odar slumped, the picture zoomed in. Three more shots: face, throat and heart; and then the picture shifted sideways back to the bed, where two more junkers held Aisha.

'Ziv,' squeaked En, and then someone shot Aisha in the gut. Ziva felt her entire body turn suddenly numb.

The camera swivelled again, this time to a man wearing an immaculately tailored Imperial suit. He had a bowler hat and from under the hat flowed a white veil that obscured his features. In one hand he held an old-fashioned Tesla pistol. He gave Ziva a moment, maybe half a second, before he asked: 'Ziva Eschel. Do I have your attention?'

198

'Who the fuck—'

The Veil fired again. The camera turned to show Aisha sprawled across the bed now, blood all over her. In the cockpit beside Ziva, En was screaming.

'What you see here is a drone, Eschel,' said the Veil. 'A simple remote-controlled robot with a holographic projector. Cheap, expendable and yet very precise. I am elsewhere. Take a moment to check that for yourself if you wish.' He paused. 'This drone carries an anti-matter charge. You'll be perfectly safe in your ship. However, if you make any attempt to contact anyone, if you don't do exactly as I say, I will detonate the device. The girl here has thirty minutes before she dies if she doesn't receive trauma attention. The nearest emergency medical drone will take three minutes and six seconds to reach her. If you follow my instructions, I will allow the trauma drone to save her. Do you understand?'

The voice. She knew the voice. The voice that had spoken to her in the elevator as she'd been leaving the Black Mausoleum. A Syndicate Veil. Well, there was a thing.

'If you so much as …'

The man shot Ay in the chest this time. In the right lung. Then he cocked his head and waited. 'You have about nine minutes now before she dies,' he said eventually. 'Tell me, do you understand? Yes or no?'

'Yes.' Ziva spoke through gritted teeth. Enaya was still screaming.

'I paid a visit to a mutual friend not long ago. I had to tell her at length how unhappy it makes me to appear like this. Do I have to explain to you too?' The Veil glanced at Aisha.

'No.' Ziva shook her head.

'You understand how we work, bounty hunter,' said the Veil 'How I value my anonymity. What it means for me to

199

have to make a trek to this planet and orbit over your head. What all this hardware costs. I'm going to tell you what to do and you're going to do it.'

Ziva turned to Enaya and saw the tears rolling out of her eyes, the helpless desperation, the hopeless pleading. She nodded, slowly.

'If you open your mouth and utter a single word, I will kill your lover's daughter. If you try to bargain or negotiate, if you do anything except exactly what I tell you and exactly when I tell you to do it … When you're done, I'll simply leave. You can come after me then – if you like.' He frowned. 'Eight minutes. Do you understand? You may nod.'

Ziva nodded. The temptation to do almost anything else, to tell the *Dragon Queen* to chase this fucker right into the heart of a star if she had to, to send a message, to spit in his face, to have one of the avatars she had lurking nearby try to infiltrate his ship, anything … But she knew the Judas Syndicate well enough. Every bounty hunter came across them sooner or later. The ones that lived left them alone.

'We have no dispute with you, Eschel. You haven't ever hurt us enough. But sometimes this is the price of doing business. Are you armed, Eschel? You may nod.'

Ziva nodded.

'You have Newman on your ship. Yes or no?'

'Yes.'

'I want to see him. Show him to me. Seven minutes.'

Ziva took a deep breath but she must have taken too long about letting it out again. The Veil lifted the Tesla. Enaya wailed. Ziva jumped up before the Veil could fire. She hesitated an instant to see what he'd do. When the Veil hesitated too, Ziva nodded and ran for the hold.

'Six minutes,' said the Veil.

'Permission to speak?' asked Ziva as she ran.

'That depends on what you say.'

She opened the airlock seals to the cargo bay and then the second airlock into Newman's pod, a hovering camera drone buzzing at her shoulder. 'I've got him sedated. He can't talk.'

'Pull your camera back so I can see you both at once.'

The drone buzzed back a little way.

'I don't need him to speak, Eschel, I need him to die. Now draw your pistol and shoot him in the head. You have fifteen seconds before I kill this girl. The Syndicate will keep a recording of you murdering him. If you come after me, I'll use it. Ten seconds. Do as I say and do it now. Five seconds. Four. Three. Two …'

Ziva shot Newman in the head.

'Well done, Eschel. I'm sure that was hard. An emergency medical drone has been called. Stay where you are, Eschel. Bring your ship in if you like, but *you* will remain where you are, as will the camera. You will continue to show me Newman's corpse until it's too late for any reconstruction. The trauma drone will arrive shortly before you. Once you land you're free to do as you wish. I suggest you take the intervening time to consider your situation. Two weeks from now you will all be alive and well and this will simply be a bad memory. Consider the alternative paths we might have taken and then leave us alone, Eschel.'

The *Dragon Queen* had found the Veil's Anaconda now, already curling out of low orbit behind a hard fusion plume. The ship piped it directly to her Fresnels. The Anaconda had a name. The *Omerta*. And a partner – that mystery corvette. It had followed her all the way from Whit's Station. The Anaconda was so heavily militarised there was nothing much left of the original design except the shape. The cargo bay bulged oddly and the engines were putting out at least twice the thrust of a production model. A tiger dressed as a sheep.

'Khanguire,' she breathed.

The Anaconda micro-jumped and abruptly the link to the Veil was gone. The *Dragon Queen* was almost at the retreat. An emergency trauma drone was skimming in ahead of them from the west; for a moment, Ziva wondered if it was a missile tipped with anti-matter and almost had the *Dragon Queen* shoot it down. But she didn't. She didn't dare. Just stood there and waited to see what would happen until it landed in the motel courtyard in a swirling haze of dust thrown up by its rotors and detached a cadre of trauma bots.

The *Dragon Queen* touched down a minute later. 'Follow the Anaconda,' Ziva told it. 'Find out where he goes.' And then she ran with Enaya until they were safely far enough away for the Fer-de-Lance to engage its engines. It shot straight up.

The trauma drones wouldn't let her get close. By the time Ziva reached them, they had Aisha wrapped up in stasis gel and were busy settling her into a surgery tank. The junkers were all dead, neat round holes in their heads. Murdered by the drone Veil which had then wiped itself clean and quietly slagged its own circuits. Like he'd said, a cheap disposable bot. En stopped outside the room, her face in her hands, watching aghast, murmuring to herself.

'My baby, my baby ...'

Trauma bots didn't mess about. They'd fix Aisha up here and now, repair all the shredded tissue from the Veil's three bullets and then lock her down in a regeneration tank while they figured out who she was, who was going to pay and whether anyone had any rights over her. Until then they bustled even Enaya out of the way.

'En …' Ziva touched her arm. Enaya flinched away. 'En, she'll be okay … She'll be …'

Enaya rounded on her. 'She'll be *okay*?' She took a step away as Ziva came closer. '*Okay*? She'll be *okay*?'

'They'll fix her up. They do an …' She'd lost count of the number of people she'd seen patched up by trauma drones back when she wore a uniform. Far worse than this. 'They're excellent …'

Enaya kept backing away. The look on her face was terrible. Harrowed. 'You,' she hissed. '*You* did this. *You* brought this down on us. All because of *you*!'

Half a mile up in the sky the *Dragon Queen*'s fusion plume kicked in and she rocketed away into space. The dull boom of the ignition shook the flimsy walls. Across the horizon, the spectacular double sunset of Arcturus and Kalliste setting together lit the world with a brown like old blood.

Chapter Eleven

A lot of people shook after a gunfight. Ravindra didn't, usually. She did now as she held Ji and they both cried. Orla watched over them in the shadow of the *Magician*. The docking berth was full of dead bodies.

'Okay, this is no good,' Orla said finally. 'We need to go.'

They didn't talk then. Ravindra made sure that Ji was all right. They, mainly Merkel, had beaten on him a bit but not too much. He was mostly scared, and hurt by Alice's betrayal. It appeared that he really had fallen for the girl. Ravindra, on the other hand, was pleased she'd killed her.

Orla had looked after Ji's wounds in the *Song of Stone*'s common room. Ravindra had fallen asleep on the sofa. Orla had ended up putting them both to bed. She put Ji in Harnack's cabin and Ravindra in her own.

Ravindra opened her eyes. They felt sore and dry. She'd fallen asleep wearing her lenses. She checked the time display. She had slept for twelve hours. She barely slept half of that normally. It was time that she couldn't afford to waste. She still felt tired. She sat up on her bunk, her back against the cold bulkhead. It was the first time she had stopped in more than forty-eight hours. The first time she wasn't trying to think on her feet in crisis management mode. The first time she'd had to really think about the ramifications of her options.

She was a good pilot. The *Song* was a fine ship. She ran a hand down the bulkhead affectionately. She had no chance against an Anaconda and a corvette. The corvette was a comparable ship to the cutter, a little slower, a little less manoeuvrable, but also a little more heavily armed and armoured. The Anaconda, on the other hand, was a monster. Though it was fast and manoeuvrable for its size, she would still be able to fly rings around it. The problem was that it was a heavily armed, and armoured, behemoth. On top of that she was down two gunners and whether or not they could get their engineer back at all, let alone in a fit state to do her job, was as yet unknown.

Then there was Ji.

She sent a text to Harlan. As grateful as she was, for everything, she wasn't ready to speak to anyone just yet. He replied a few minutes later. She read and then re-read his reply. He had found her a cracksman. Then she took the lenses out and rubbed her eyes. She leant back against the bulkhead, grateful that she had done all the crying she was going to do for a while.

Ravindra stepped out of her cabin. She could hear voices – Orla and Ji. She could smell coffee brewing and eggs and pancakes cooking. Mostly on the ship they ate meals prepared from food cartridges, like every other ship's crew. She'd insisted on the coffee machine and real coffee. Orla had a portable stove/grill combination and when she had time to track down real ingredients, actual food, as Orla called it, she would treat the rest of the crew.

There was an incongruity about the cutter that Ravindra had never quite come to terms with. The *Song of Stone* was a thing of beauty and grace. Inside the ship there was often a warm, comforting atmosphere. It was home. Yet it was a warship, a tool of destruction that she personally had used to kill. Many, if not most, of those she'd killed had been either innocents or people just trying to do their job.

Ravindra walked into the common room. The conversation stopped. Orla looked up, spatula in hand. Ji looked up and then looked away, guilt written all over his face.

'Want some breakfast?' Orla asked. Ravindra nodded and sat down. 'You okay?' her first mate continued.

'Tired,' Ravindra told her. 'But I'm good. You get any sleep?' Orla shook her head. 'You stimmed?'

'A little,' Orla said flipping one pancake and adding another to an already large stack. 'Now you're up I'll crash.'

Ravindra felt like crap that she'd put Orla into the position of having to do stims. Then ... she didn't so much hear or feel as *sense* something outside the hull of the ship. She froze.

'What's going on?' she demanded.

'See?' Orla turned to Ji as she stopped ladling scrambled eggs into a bowl. 'Creepy, isn't it?'

Ji smiled.

'I've had a crew working on the ship,' Orla said.

Alarm bells started going off in Ravindra's head. They had always done the work on the ship themselves. Nobody touched the *Song* but them.

'Who?' she demanded.

'Some of Harlan's people. And the crew of the *Scalpel*, would you believe?'

'McCauley's crew?' Ravindra asked, surprised. Orla nodded. 'Part of me thinks that we're more popular than we thought we were, the other part of me thinks that everybody just hated Merkel on account of having talked to him, but mostly I think they wanted the chance to see under a cutter's hood.'

'And we—' Ravindra started.

'No, we don't trust anyone. I've been overseeing them. I only came in to make breakfast when the *Song* told me that you were awake. I'll check the work once they've gone but, frankly, if we want the *Song* operating as close to peak as possible then we didn't have much choice.'

Ravindra nodded. At this late stage in the game there was only so much difference it was going to make anyway. She would have to thank McCauley, his people and Harlan. Harlan had done so much for them, gone above and beyond what he'd been paid for.

'How're we looking?'

'How much longer we got?'

'There's a couple of things that I need to sort. Thirty-six hours and it will all be in place.'

'In thirty-six hours she'll be ready to sing.'

They lapsed into silence and ate their breakfasts.

Orla had discreetly left the common room and left Ravindra with Ji, who still wouldn't meet her eyes.

'Hey?' Ravindra said, gently. 'Look at me. It's okay.'

Slowly Ji turned to her.

'I'm sorry,' Ravindra went on.

Tears started to fill his eyes. 'What are you sorry for, mum? I caused this. I …'

'No. Who I am, what I am, where I brought you, put you in harm's way. I wanted us to get clear of all this, but I was never quite satisfied that we had enough so I kept working. Always said that after the next job I'd quit, we'd leave. I almost did when Danc died, but this is me. I can't get away from that. If I'm honest, I like it – but I was never going to let you into this life. That's why Merkel took you, because inadvertently I let him. We've got money, we should be a long way from here.' She reached over and ran her hands through his hair. Suddenly his tear-stained face, his vulnerability, made him look even younger than his seventeen years.

'Mum, it's all right …' Ji was struggling for words.

'You're a pain in the arse but you're intelligent, you can be thoughtful – though you wouldn't know it these last few days – you're sensitive. You can do anything you want to, but this isn't the place for you.'

'You're sending me away, aren't you?' he asked. Ravindra reached up to wipe her own eyes with the back of her hand as she nodded.

'I'm sorry I was so harsh on you, so distant. I thought I had to be, to protect you, but I was being selfish because I'd put you in harm's way in the first place.'

Ji took her by the hand. 'Mum, please don't. I won't be like this anymore, I'll do what I'm—'

Ravindra was shaking her head as tears rolled down her cheek. 'I've really done it this time, Ji. I've really fucked up, and there's no way to walk away from it. We've … I've pissed off some very bad people and they're just not going to stop.'

Ji threw himself into his mother's arms.

'Please,' he said between the sobs.

'You're going to have to go in the other direction,' she whispered to him as she held him.

'You okay?' Orla asked.

'I'm really not,' Ravindra said. They were both stood in the docking berth looking up at the *Song of Stone*. The station's repair team had already left, and McCauley and the three-man crew of the *Scalpel* had just finished packing up their tools and were heading out of the docking berth.

'Hey,' Ravindra said. McCauley and his people stopped. Ravindra walked over to them. As she did, she noticed Ji come to the top of the *Song*'s loading ramp.

'Thanks,' Ravindra told McCauley. She held out her hand. The craggy-faced pirate took it. Orla was chatting with the rest of the *Scalpel*'s crew.

'Nice to see under her hood,' McCauley said, glancing back at the *Song*. 'She's a beauty. When you die, can I have her?'

Ravindra grinned. 'When I die I don't think there's going to be anything left of her.'

McCauley nodded. 'You need anything else?' he asked seriously. Ravindra looked past him. McCauley glanced back at Ji. 'Anywhere in particular?'

'Somewhere that I don't know about.'

McCauley nodded.

'Good luck.' He turned to walk away.

'Captain McCauley?' Ravindra said. McCauley turned back to look at her. 'Why're you helping us?'

'I remember when I first saw her,' he nodded at the *Song*. 'She was a holy terror. She'd taken out Gipps's Fer-de-Lance, the two Vultures that the Hammond sisters flew. Then I saw some young ex-con execute a fifteen gee turn, in a Mk. II Cobra no less, and hit the cutter's engines with a laser so fast that the laser overheated and blew the front of the Cobra off, damaging it so badly she had to eject. I nearly killed myself in simulators trying to replicate that turn.' McCauley pointed at her. 'You've got some Simpson Town genes in you, haven't you?'

Ravindra nodded. 'I was still pretty much a bruise for a month, and I burst just about every blood vessel in my eyes.'

McCauley nodded. 'I'll get your boy away,' he said after a moment.

209

'Thank you.'

McCauley turned and headed for the door, his crew falling in behind them.

'What's the other reason?' Ravindra called to his back.

'I spent ten years in the Warren,' he said, not stopping or looking behind him.

Ravindra watched McCauley leave before turning to Orla. 'Look, we don't both have to …'

'I will slap you,' Orla said and walked off.

There was only so much they could do. The *Song* was as ready as she was ever going to be. But they couldn't act yet. The cracksman that Harlan had found them had to do his work, and they must wait for the alignment of stellar bodies on which their plan depended. Ravindra spent the time with Ji. Helped him pack. Gave him access to some untraceable accounts set up in different systems under different aliases. Then they talked. Both of them shed many tears. After a while she started to realise, too late, that it was probably the best time she had spent with him since he was a small boy. She learned a lot about her son's life. Some of it she didn't want to know. Alice had been his first.

She remembered how frightened she had been going out on jobs with her little boy at home back on the station. How much she had wanted to be with him. How frightened she'd been that she might not come back, and he would be left on his own. She wondered when that had changed and she had started craving the scores more.

He asked to come with her. She said no. There had been an argument, but she wasn't going to get her only son killed. Ji said that they should meet up once she had done what she needed to do. Ravindra had not allowed him any false hope.

Ji didn't have much by the way of real friends it seemed, but she couldn't let him make his farewells to those he did have. She took him to the ship to say goodbye to Orla. Then they took the elevator up to see Harlan. Anywhere they went, Harrelson and Jonas accompanied them. They had been looking after Ji ever since they had helped get him back.

'Got a good memory, kid?' Harlan asked. Ji nodded. Harlan reached over his desk and touched his comp ring to Ji's. 'That's not just a false identity, that's who you are now. You don't just need to learn it. You need to forget this life, all of us, and become that person. You need to convince yourself that that's who you are, understand me?' Ji nodded. Part of Ravindra was proud that he didn't get upset. It was easy to scoff, but effectively the boy had just been told to annihilate his own identity and past. That was what it was going to take. The other part of her was depressed that she could see Ji toughening up in front of her. 'Will you give me some time with your ma, please?' Harlan asked. Ji stood up and left the room.

Harlan went over and poured Ravindra a brandy and himself a generous bourbon over ice.

'My cracksman do the business?' he asked, handing her the glass of brandy.

'Yeah, he came through. Don't know how, that was some pretty hardcore security …'

Harlan nodded towards the door. 'That's hard,' he said, meaning Ji

'Yeah,' she agreed bitterly.

'We'll look after him. McCauley's a cold bastard, but he'll do what he says he will. I've set up a meeting for Ji with a fence I trust, then he needs to be gone. He is a ghost.' Ravindra, feeling numb, indicated she understood. Harlan watched her.

211

'Thank—' Ravindra started.

'Let's just enjoy our drink,' Harlan said, looking down.

Ravindra felt totally wrung out by the time she finally got back to the *Song*. She found Orla down in the small engineering workshop. She was removing the warhead from one of the medium range missiles' nose cones.

'How many?' Ravindra asked.

'Two at the most. Wish we had the time to get hold of another E-bomb.'

'How're we going to detonate?'

Orla held up a comp ring. 'It's got to be a timer, because of the delivery.'

'Wish we'd had time to find a replacement E-bomb,' Orla repeated. Ravindra's face indicated her agreement.

The statue of Ganesh was glued to a small shelf against the bulkhead at the rear of the *Song*'s bridge. Ravindra knelt before it and pushed her hands together and bowed to the elephant-headed god's statue. She took some joss sticks and lit the end of them with the utility torch from her tool kit and placed the sticks into the putty stuck on the shelf in front of the statue.

'You think that helps?' Orla asked. Orla had grown up in a gnostolic anti-religious mining community.

'I don't think it hurts,' Ravindra said. She climbed to her feet and both of them strapped themselves into their respective seats. 'Drop the spoofing to the bounty hunter's Sly-Spy.'

'You sure?' Orla asked.

'They'll attack anyone else who turns up and there's no way Eschel can get there before us.'

'We can't know that.'

'They want that cargo so bad, and we're going to the one place where you can get away with murder. The moment she shows, they'll hit her. It might not put her on our side, but she won't be on theirs. She'll have to defend herself and she won't want to pick a fight with us. We lay off her and she's a pain in their arse, and that's a good ship, and she can fly it,' Ravindra said. Orla was looking at her sceptically. Ravindra turned in her chair to face her first mate. 'We need every edge we can get. If you've got a better idea.'

'What if she gets there before the Syndicate?'

'We hide, negotiate or fight, do anything we can to stall her.'

'It's a big risk.'

Ravindra actually laughed and turned to look at Orla sceptically. 'All we do is take risks.' She left it unsaid that they were almost certainly dead anyway.

'Calculated risks.'

'We're a little beyond Dane's Law now. I need everyone, the bounty hunter included, looking at us, not at Ji.'

Orla thought about it for a moment, then nodded. 'Dropping the spoofing and opening a secure sub-space link to the Black Mausoleum,' Orla said, her fingers tracing patterns in hologramatic light to make it happen. Ravindra waited until the crackling, interference-heavy FTL comms link was connected.

'Can you hear me?' Ravindra asked.

'Yes,' the Veil answered, his voice distorted by the static.

'The Cave, Jackson's Lighthouse.'

'When?' If there was trepidation at the location of the rendezvous, Ravindra couldn't pick it up across subspace.

'As soon as you can get there.' She cut the link.

'He must know it's a trap,' Orla said.

213

'I think he really wants his cargo,' Ravindra responded. She pushed her fingers into the scan glove and ran it over her hair until she found the tiny Sly-Spy and picked it out. 'What about you?' she asked the tiny wriggling bot and then crushed it between her fingers.

Ravindra took the *Song of Stone* out of the docking berth for what was almost certainly the last time. She spun the ship through a hundred and eighty degrees as it rose, turning it to face the station, reversing thrust to push it out and away from mushroom head of the huge aerostat. She circled the station until she found the window to the Command and Control centre. Harlan and Ji were stood at the window. Ravindra brought the *Song* in close enough for Orla to have to switch off the proximity alarm manually and for them to get automated complaints from the station.

She was less than ten feet away from Harlan and her son. Separated by two feet of transparent hull and Motherlode's thin, toxic upper atmosphere. She wasn't looking at Harlan, she was just looking at Ji. She held the *Song* steady there, making incremental corrections to hold it in place. She didn't think she had been a good mother, but there was only so much guilt to go around. She had done what she knew how to do. She was sure that he knew that she loved him. She hoped that was enough.

Chapter Twelve

'My name is Ziva Eschel,' Ziva said to the empty air. 'I've murdered a man and this is my confession.' Murder without cause. Executing a prisoner. There wasn't any way to paint that except that she'd crossed the line at last. The shocking part was how easy it had been. How she hadn't even hesitated.

She paced the empty landscape around the retreat. Everything was cheap. Old plastic that had started to go brittle with age and no one to care for it but the drones. Even the aerojets in the landing field were drones. Drones to service the drones that looked after the drones that looked after the now-and-then people who came here.

Drones. She was looking at her life.

Aisha and Odar had chosen this place because of how abandoned it was. Perhaps they thought no one would find them. Was that what she'd been doing for the last twenty years?

Ziva closed her eyes and saw Newman again, saw his head jerk back as she shot him. There was no getting away from that.

A police aerojet was on its way. The trauma drones had reported back. They had Aisha and were flying to wherever was the nearest outpost of civilisation. The drones had let Enaya fly with her. Family. Ziva wasn't family and so she'd been left behind. En didn't want her anyway. *You did this. You brought this down on us.*

Yes, Ziva thought. It was her fault. She *had* brought this down on them, simply because of what she was. She'd turn herself in, stand up and be judged for what she'd done and when they let her out of prison, she'd spend the rest of her life hunting Veils.

Probably a very short life, then. She deleted the recording she'd been making and started again. 'My name is Ziva Eschel …'

A tone rang in her ear. The *Dragon Queen*, back in low orbit over Arcas.

'Did you follow them? Where did they go?'

'They left Arcturus. Their jump trails indicate their destination was Beta Hydri.'

The Black Mausoleum. 'And then?'

'Captain, standing orders dictate—'

'Yes, yes.' Never to jump without her. Those were her instructions and of course the *Dragon Queen* obeyed because the *Dragon Queen*, beneath her persona, was nothing more than a complex interaction of linear expert systems that had no choice. The immutable rules of algorithms. The *Dragon Queen* would have let Aisha die because it wouldn't have seen any other way. The Veil would have known his threats were pointless and so would never have made them. Humans, on the other hand, were fallible.

'I have picked up a k-cast for you from the Sly-Spy in Whit's Station. The spoofing has been removed.'

Khanguire, gloating? Whatever this was, Khanguire wanted her to hear.

Can you hear me? The k-cast was audio only, but there was no mistaking Khanguire's voice.

'Yes, you fucking—' But the k-cast was going on.

Yes. A male voice. So this was a recording then.

The Cave, Jackson's Lighthouse.

216

When? Christ, was that the Veil? It just might have been. *As soon as you can get there.*

A pause. Then a different voice. *He must know it's a trap. I think he really wants his cargo.* Khanguire again. The next words she spoke seemed directed to the bot, to Ziva. *What about you?*

The k-cast ended as the Sly-Spy duly reported its own destruction and died. For few seconds Ziva simply stood where she was, too dazed to think.

'When did that come in?'

'Twelve minutes ago.' Not that there was any way to tell how long the k-cast arrays had spent trying to find the *Dragon Queen* to pass it on. Not long, though. She tried to do the math in her head. Khanguire must have had that conversation before the Veil's ship had jumped to Beta Hydri but he'd gone there anyway.

Which gave her a chance.

Sometimes a decision came and made itself without being asked. In Ziva's experience, those ones were often the best. 'Come and get me,' she snapped. 'Run the male voice against the man who shot Aisha. Dump every bit of weight we don't absolutely need. Prime the anti-matter injectors for the core.' She could already see the bright spark of a fusion plume in the sky far overhead. 'Get a jump ready to take us out to Jackson's Lighthouse. Overcharge the shield generators and shut down everything electronic that isn't military-hardened.' Not that it would help much, but it would help some. 'When you've picked me up and we're clear of Arcas, set two attack drones for survey and telemetry, three for decoys and weapons-ready everything else.'

The *Dragon Queen* acknowledged. After a little pause it asked: 'Do you wish to arm the energy bomb?'

Ziva watched the spark as it grew brighter. 'Yes. I *especially* want you to arm the E-bomb.'

The Cave. She almost laughed. Of all the fucked-up places in the galaxy, Khanguire had gone for the Cave.

So here was the trick. You jumped into Jackson's Lighthouse and hopped as close as you could to the dark side of the Cave, wherever it was in its erratic orbit around the Lighthouse. After that, you came in fast and you didn't hang around because the moment you appeared anywhere near the Cave, your ship got savaged by bursts of X-rays and gamma-rays strong enough to flay your shield; and once *that* went down then the strength of the Lighthouse's magnetic field began to destabilise the core containment of your reactor. The radiation was bad enough with the Cave acting as a shield. In the direct beam of the pulsar it was much, much worse.

It was a rite of passage; something that young punk pilots did to prove themselves. You got it wrong and it was a race to see whether or not you got fried by gamma radiation when your shields failed or whether your core destabilised and destroyed your ship. You rarely had the time to jump back out of the Lighthouse before the harsh environment degraded your systems. It was a dumb thing to do and a dumb place to go. Ravindra had done it twice. Once because she was young and stupid and the second time had been to hide some very hot cargo for another crew to pick up. The second time had badly damaged the *Song of Stone*. The first time had nearly killed her.

She came out of jump space and everything went to shit. The *Song* had already shut down every non-hardened system and even then several others immediately failed. Warning data appeared in her lenses as shields and core containment

218

started to degrade. Whenever the pulsar's beam swept anywhere close the scanners were all but useless, due to interference on nearly all spectrums.

'Sorry, baby,' Ravindra whispered to the ship. She was looking around hoping to physically see the Cave, very much aware of the distant glow of the pulsar. So far away it seemed an innocuous, even pretty, white light. What got her each time was that the pulsar was so *small*, a pinprick with two faint bluish lines stretching out from it marking the X-ray beams that lanced out from the magnetic poles. That and how fast they spun through space. 'What've you got for me?' she asked Orla.

'Multiple screens of static and interference,' Orla muttered.

'That's not very helpful,' Ravindra said. She didn't like feeling helpless, just waiting to be cooked by hard radiation. They had downloaded the orbital data on the Cave from the observation station two light-minutes away, whose only job was to observe the pulsar. The station had been set up in 2673 after the stellar collision of the two dwarf stars in the binary system had created the pulsar. Some time later a passing nickel-iron planetoid had been pulled into an erratic orbit around the Lighthouse; and since it was constantly being dragged closer by the pulsar's magnetic field, the whereabouts of the Cave were only ever a very educated guess. So when you made the last micro-jump in, you needed to jump in close to have a chance of finding the Cave in the first place, but you also had to make sure you didn't get caught in the pulsar's beams. They would rip shields apart faster than the sustained fire of a Majestic-class Interdictor. They called it being in the eye of the Lighthouse. She had waited for two days, left Jenny to the tender mercies of the Judas Syndicate for two days, just so

219

she could be sure that the Cave would be in the path of the pulsar's beam.

'Okay, I have a gravitational anomaly that loosely fits the shape and size of the Cave,' Orla said.

'Loosely?' Ravindra asked. The coordinates appeared in her lenses. It was roughly five thousand kilometres away, starward. Ravindra watched the spinning beam of the Lighthouse. The trick was to make the dash from well outside the worst of the danger zone into the shadow of the Cave quickly enough to keep your shields intact while keeping as far as possible from the very heart of the spinning beam.

'What do you want from me?' Orla asked, an unfamiliar hint of desperation in her voice. 'And remember when you accelerate that I'm still hu—'

Orla was thrown back into the gel padding of her acceleration couch by seven gravities of thrust. Ravindra looked at the beams. It wasn't enough. She had sunk into the gel of the couch. She could feel the force against her body, pulling at her skin and battering her musculature. Her flight suit was doing the best it could to compensate by injecting gel into pads over certain areas of her body, like the joints. She was looking at the countdown. They weren't going to get there in time. Ten gravities. Orla had passed out. Ravindra could see a black dot ahead of her, more an absence of stars than anything else, though she wondered how much was wishful thinking. Her vision was red with warnings from the ship as system after system went down. She was convinced that the distant light was brighter now. Modified genes or not, she couldn't keep this up. Yes, she'd pulled a turn at fifteen gravities once, but that had been for a brief moment in a deadly combat. Not sustained like this. She looked at the distance remaining to what she hoped was the Cave, compared it to the time before the next burst ratio. She didn't like what she saw. Twelve gravities. She would have screamed if she could. She would have been worried about breaking something in Orla's body if she'd been able to think about anything other than pain and keeping the *Song* on track.

Through blurred vision she was sure that she could see the dark shape of the Cave, seeming to hang still in the blackness. She shifted course incrementally, putting yet more stress on her skeleton, putting the distant but brightening light of the Lighthouse into eclipse.

At the last moment she reversed thrust. Her body screamed at her. She struggled to retain consciousness. She had a moment to take in the scarred and pitted canyons of the surface of the current dark side of the Cave before everything was thrown into shadow and light filled her vision all around the Cave. She had a moment to think. She saw a cave big enough to fit the *Song* in and she angled the ship towards it. Her lenses were full of red warning icons.

Then she passed out.

She awoke when the acceleration couch had administered a stimulant. The Cave was riddled with a network of huge caverns and tunnel networks formed as massive induced eddy currents from the pulsar heated it up and now and then vaporised parts of it. The same forces drew the planetoid closer with every orbit and would eventually destroy it, but not for a few hundred years.

They were in the eye of the Lighthouse. Light shone through the induction-gouged holes in the rock from the far side of the planetoid. The ship had automatically moved itself to a dark part of the massive cavern. Shielding itself from the worst of the Lighthouse's radiation excesses.

221

From head to toe, Ravindra ached. She accepted an injection of painkillers from the acceleration couch and then another stim to avoid the loss in coordination that the powerful painkillers would cause. She glanced over at Orla. The other woman was unconscious, but nothing looked broken. The medical telemetry she was receiving from Orla's couch seemed to confirm that. She ordered the couch to inject the other woman with a painkiller and a stim as well.

They were in Jackson's Hole, the largest and most prominent of the caverns on the current dark side of the Cave. It was where she intended to meet the Syndicate. Prep would involve checking the area, looking for an escape route. Normally they'd seed the space with missiles, but here they wouldn't even be able to reliably send the signal to engage them; their own automated guidance systems weren't hardened to the same level as a ship and they wouldn't be able to track targets. Even dumb proximity-fused warheads were going to be unreliable. Loitering inside the Cave gave some shelter from the pulsar's magnetic field, but it was still strong enough to wreak havoc on anything without a shield. Missiles became expensive aim-by-sight rockets. Smart-mines became obstacles to everyone. The only real advantages they had were Ravindra's modified genes and the fact that they would, hopefully, have time to update the last map of the inside of the planetoid.

She would pilot and work the various beam weapons. Orla would watch the scanners – for all the good they would do in this environment – run the missile batteries, *and* manage engineering, unless they were able to get Jenny back.

They waited and waited. They had mapped as much as they could using optical systems and an expert system to interpret the data and turn it into a three-dimensional representation of the inside of the Cave. Even then they had to deal with a near-constant degradation of the *Song*'s systems. Ravindra felt like the ship was rotting about her.

They had situated the ship less than three kilometres from the mouth of Jackson's Hole, and the position gave them visuals on the entrance to the mouth of the cave via the transparent hull that surrounded the bridge. They trained the long-range optical systems on the cave mouth as well, but the images were grainy and intermittent.

They were in about the third most obvious hiding place. If the Anaconda and the corvette came in hot, wanting to take out the *Song* and then take their chances using fuel scoops to sift through the wreckage for the cargo, then the *Song*'s hiding place might give them a few more seconds of life.

Orla and Ravindra had their lenses on high magnification and were straining, looking for any sign of movement in the cave mouth. Conceivably the Veil could come into Jackson's Hole through any of the tunnel networks that were large enough to fit their craft, but it seemed unlikely they would have time to find another cave mouth that they could be sure would get them where they wanted to go.

They were in the eye again. They could see the glare of the light from outside the cavern and beams of white light shining through the holes in the planetoid. Their systems went even more haywire. As the beam passed, the *Omerta* came in hard all of its manoeuvring engines burning bright as it tried to check its momentum.

'That was at least seven gees,' Ravindra muttered. There would be a lot of pain on the other ship at the moment. If it hadn't been for Jenny, this would have been the perfect moment to strike. Instead, Ravindra moved the *Song* further back into the nook in the wall.

The *Omerta* managed to halt just before it hit the rounded cave wall opposite the mouth of the enormous cavern. Ravindra was impressed despite herself. The Anaconda was a big ship, but the mil-spec upgrades to the weapons and shields had clearly extended to the engines as well and the pilot knew how to handle it. The *Omerta*'s manoeuvring engines burned again as she banked hard, avoiding the harsh light, into an area of 'shade' big enough to hold the Anaconda. Then lights stabbed out from the big ship. The beams of powerful searchlights. They started sweeping the area.

'They're using lidar as well, which will only be partially effective. I'm also receiving badly garbled comms.'

'We'll be able to communicate with them, right?' Ravindra asked, though she knew the answer.

Orla laughed humourlessly. 'Through close range tight beam, yes, though even that's going to have background interference. I'll be hitting them with a signal not far from the power of a pulse laser. You want to talk to them?'

'No. I want to know where the corvette is.' She still couldn't see the smaller, faster ship, but refused to believe it had not come too.

As they came out of the glare of the eye the Anaconda moved away from its holding position and started moving around the giant cave. It was searching for the *Song* visually, its massive searchlights illuminating the darkness of the cavern. Ravindra checked all the weapons and flight systems again, and was sickened by their ongoing degradation.

The Anaconda didn't so much remind her of its serpent namesake as an ocean-going predator searching for bottom feeders. Ravindra felt sweat run down her skin.

'What happens if it finds us?' Orla asked.

'Hopefully we start negotiations. The problem is, we start

negotiations without knowing where the corvette is, then it gets to blindside us.'

'The bounty hunter?'

'Perhaps she's too smart to come here.'

'There,' Orla said, and pointed through the transparent hull towards the curving cavern wall nearly opposite them. The nose of the corvette was just about visible sticking out of the exit of one of the tunnel networks, protruding just enough to allow its optics and bridge crew to see into the cavern. This was not good. This meant that the corvette's pilot had managed to find an external cave network in between pulses. They were *good*. Ravindra suspected another military slave pilot with Simpson Town genes.

'Ready?' Ravindra asked. Orla answered by unstrapping herself from the acceleration couch and pulling herself out of the bridge towards the closest airlock, where the cargo waited.

Ravindra slowly moved out of their hiding place and started moving across the cavern. The *Omerta* finally noticed the movement and turned two of its searchlights on the *Song*. The light was bright enough for the *Song*'s transparent hull to polarise.

'Now that's just obnoxious,' Ravindra muttered as she moved the ship to the other side of Jackson's Hole. She was now above the corvette and obscured from its view. The corvette moved out of its hiding place. The Anaconda started moving towards the *Song*, while the corvette rose within the cavern, attempting to find an overwatch position. Ravindra kept the *Song* moving, trying to deny the smaller ship a strong position over her cutter.

'It's done,' Orla said. Even the internal comms were crackling with interference. 'Three minutes.'

'This is the *Song of Stone*, to the *Omerta*,' Ravindra said over the tight beam link. 'Drop Jenny and once we have her onboard and have ascertained that she's okay, then we'll drop the cargo.'

'Let's not waste each other's time.' Even through the static, Ravindra could tell that the voice belonged to the Veil. 'In precisely thirty seconds you will drop my cargo and we will drop your engineer. You try to pick up your engineer faster than we pick up our cargo, and then we try to kill each other.'

Well, at least he isn't pretending, Ravindra conceded.

'Understood,' she told him. The *Song*'s targeting systems were slaved to her lenses. The crosshair would appear wherever she looked. She was looking between the Anaconda and the corvette right now. Windows were appearing in her vision as, with a word, she tasked the laser batteries to cover the two ships.

She continued to jockey for position in the cavern as Orla pulled herself back into the bridge and strapped herself into her couch.

'Remember what I said about acceleration earlier, before you accelerated so hard that I passed out?' Orla asked.

Ravindra glanced at the timer counting down from thirty, and then the other countdown for the Cave's next intersection with the pulsar bursts. They were going to be close. Ironically, Jenny would be better shielded in a lifepod than they were on the *Song*. The countdown ran down to zero. Orla opened the airlock. The evacuating air forced the crate to tumble out into space. The *Song*'s optics picked up a plume of gas from one of the Anaconda's airlocks. That wasn't right ... Orla magnified the image. They saw a small figure in a cheap spacesuit tumble away from the massive ship.

'Bastards!' Orla shouted. Jenny, assuming that she was

in the spacesuit, had until the next sweep from the Lighthouse to live, if the existing radiation hadn't already cooked her and her suit's systems were still working. It also meant that although they could pick her up with the fuel scoop they wouldn't be able to accelerate until she was safely secured, or they would break every bone in her body.

Ravindra was moving the ship, the manoeuvre engines burning brightly. She glanced at the third countdown. They passed close to the *Omerta*. Ravindra was worried that the huge ship would open fire. It didn't, presumably equally worried that the *Song* would destroy the cargo crate in retaliation. What she did get was a close-in view of the Anaconda's bristling weapons systems, close enough to see the ball-mounted beam and missile batteries track the *Song*. A window showing fuzzy imagery from one of the rear lenses allowed Ravindra to see the external hatches to the converted cargo bay opening. She could just about make out the fighter bays inside. She'd momentarily lost sight of the corvette.

'Orla, where's the corvette?' Ravindra asked. Orla was looking all around.

'I've lost it!'

The *Dragon Queen* winked into existence on the outskirts of Jackson's Lighthouse and started micro-jumps towards the Cave. Ziva pulled up the Federation survey data for the system, not that there was much to look at. From the edge of the system there was nothing to see. There was gravity but no apparent star – at least, not unless you came at it from the right angle. Look at the right point in space and put on enough magnification and you'd see a tiny faint dot. Try looking at other parts of the spectrum and maybe you'd see a bit more clearly, although you'd start to wonder what sort of tiny star could be so bright in X-rays and gamma-rays and yet be so dim in the visible spectrum. Then maybe, as you started to come in closer, you'd notice something wasn't quite right with the magnetic fields in the system. Maybe you'd start to realise how strong they were, but then again maybe not. Who the hell ever measured a system's magnetic field when they'd just jumped into the Kuiper belt?

Or, if you got it wrong, you got hit by the pulsar beam, an unexpected deluge of X-rays and gamma-rays, and simply died. Jackson's Lighthouse: a magnetar system, a spinning neutron star X-ray pulsar flinging out more hard radiation every second than anything short of a blue supergiant, and all of it tightly focused into two narrow spinning beams, one out from each magnetic pole. Add to that the magnetic field itself – about three orders of magnitude higher than any star ought to have – and you had a shipkiller of a star.

'And the Hole is *how* close to that?' muttered Ziva.

'Its orbit is erratic. Currently less than a million kilometres.'

'Marvellous.'

'It could get worse,' observed the Fer-de-Lance. 'A few thousand miles from the surface of the magnetar and the gravitational tidal forces would rip us apart. The magnetic fields that close in are strong enough to support a whole new science of chemical molecular bonding.'

'Let's not get that close, then. Can you see the Cave yet?'

'No.'

Ziva gritted her teeth. 'Closer, then.' The *Dragon Queen*'s more sensitive instruments were starting to play up in the magnetic fields, even muted as they were through the ship's shields. 'We're here for a fight. What happens if we lose our shields out here?'

'Uncertain. The Cave will act – to an extent – as a Faraday cage shield against the magnetic fields and a physical barrier to the magnetar X-ray beam. Inside it *may* be possible to survive. Outside, at that distance from the star, the beam will strip our shields and the magnetic field will disrupt most systems. Failures are likely to be widespread and catastrophic.'

Another micro-jump took them as close to the Cave's orbit as the jump drive could manage. Still a few million klicks out. Still comfortable to loiter, provided she kept out of the pulsar beam, but the last dash for the shelter of the Cave was going to get interesting. Ziva dropped to silent running, as black and quiet as the Fer-de-Lance could get, and launched a reconnaissance drone. She watched for a few seconds as the sensor telemetry broke up. The drone reported a steadily worsening series of faults and then died.

'That's a bit fucking crap. Is that going to happen to all of them?'

'A few hundred miles from the neutron star's surface and the magnetic field will simply dismantle us on an atomic scale,' observed the *Dragon Queen*.

'And you're telling me this …?' Ziva wasn't sure whether the Fer-de-Lance was trying to cheer her up and take her mind off En and Aisha or whether it was trying to persuade her not to do this. It wasn't really supposed to be able to do either.

Decision time. She didn't have long out here in open space, not this close in to Jackson. The magnetic field was already fraying her shields. She needed the protection of the Cave or she needed to leave. Although if she went for the Cave, it was going to get a whole shit-storm worse before she reached it.

'Found it.' Right in the sweep of the pulsar beam. The *Dragon Queen*'s long-range optics started scanning the planetoid but from this far out there wasn't much to see. Jackson himself, the one and only madman who'd been crazy enough to explore this place, had never made a map of it; or if he had, he'd kept it to himself. Either way, Khanguire knew the maze of tunnels in there better and going after her here was just plain stupid. The dark side of the Cave was going to be bad enough and Khanguire had set her rendezvous in the full sweeping glare of Jackson's beam where it hit the planetoid smack in the face every twelve and a half seconds. Caught in that, the *Dragon Queen* would be as good as blind and would fry in less than a minute. *But I don't actually have to go in. I can have a look. If I don't like it, I can always leave, right? Simple as that. Just fly away.* Although she already didn't like it and yet she was still here. Every thought of backing out threw up the sight of Aisha, lying on that bed, bleeding out.

The *Dragon Queen* presented a full systems diagnostic report. Ziva hadn't asked for it but the ship had done it anyway. Even through the ship's shields, she was getting mild interference on the magnetic containment in the reactor core and the fusion drives. Every sensor on the ship was registering some sort of disruption and they hadn't even been hit by the pulsar beam. *Well played, Khanguire. Well played.*

'This supposed to be some sort of a hint, is it?' Ziva muttered acidly.

She ought to bail out. Khanguire had chosen the terrain, had given herself the time to set up whatever ambush she liked; and when it came down to it, she had the stronger ship.

Again Ziva saw Aisha in that motel. Blood everywhere. The Veil.

230

'Plot a course out of here,' she said. 'We're not here for Khanguire. If the Veil doesn't—'

She froze.

Another ship had entered the system. Maybe it had been there a while and she hadn't seen it, but she saw it now because it was burning hydrogen hard, a mile-long streak of fusion light heading straight in for the Cave.

Khanguire?

But the plume was too big for the *Song of Stone*. 'Mass estimate?' she asked and the *Dragon Queen* came back with a number based on the plume size and apparent acceleration. Not the *Song*. But a heavily modified Anaconda – that would about do it …

The *Omerta*. So he *had* come.

She waited, watching the Anaconda flip on its tail and burn the other way, slowing down. A second fusion plume lit up a few seconds behind it. The corvette. She watched Jackson's beam slice through the space between them, then waited until they both vanished into the glare of light that surrounded the Cave.

'Take us in,' she said. There was so much murder in her voice that she barely recognised it as her own. 'Get the decoy drones racked and ready. Load the rest for hunting bear.'

'You have a k-cast incoming from Enaya.'

'Not now. Take a message.'

One more micro-jump as the *Dragon Queen* dosed her up with adrenaline and nanites for a hard burn into the planetoid and then the g-force ripped her back into her cocoon. The Cave appeared ahead of her and all hell broke loose as Jackson's Lighthouse lit her up.

Chapter Thirteen

It was the moment before a fight. Everything seemed to slow. Everything was taking too long. A few spoken commands and the fuel scoop was reprogrammed to a gentler setting for handling human cargo. Ravindra had slowed the *Song* right down. They were currently facing the mouth of the cavern. She could not see the corvette, but she was searching the feed from the rear optics. The corvette would want to be positioned behind and below the *Song*, the optimal vantage point for a dogfight.

'We've got Jenny,' Orla said. They had managed to get into position a lot quicker than the *Omerta*. 'The suit's badly malfunctioning … I've got life signs. Some irregularities.'

'Orla? Rav?' Jenny's voice at that moment was the best thing either of them could hope for, even if it was full of pain.

'Jenny, can you get yourself out of the suit? Quickly?' Orla asked.

'Doing it.' There had only been a moment's pause.

'They're at the crate, scoops deployed.'

Where's the bloody corvette? It was a silent scream. Then, more rationally: *If it's not where you think it should be …* Ravindra ran all the optics through expert analysis programs. There were too many of them to run as windows on her lenses. She put the *Song* in a lazy spin through its horizontal axis, heading towards the mouth of the cavern as she looked all around through the transparent section of hull that surrounded the bridge.

'They've got the cargo,' Orla said. Ravindra could hear the tension in her first mate's voice.

In his berth on the *Scalpel*, Ji reached into his rucksack and took the object out. Even considering its origin, it was still difficult to imagine all the death and suffering that was connected to it. In a few days they would be on the other side of human occupied space. There he could sell it, disappear and become someone else.

Harlan's cracksman had finally broken the security of the crate the cargo had come in. It hadn't been easy, but he had done it and been well paid for it. Now to find out if it had been worth it. Ravindra glanced at the countdown. It reached zero. The two missile warheads they had put in the crate, replacing the cargo, should have gone off by now. If they had, she couldn't see any external sign of it. There was a chance that the explosion could have been contained by the *Omerta*'s heavily armoured hull. She let herself imagine the effects of two warheads going off inside the ship.

Jenny pulled herself into the cockpit. Ravindra couldn't help but take a glance at her. The younger woman looked badly burned. The engineer ordered her acceleration couch to inject a painkiller/stim cocktail similar to the ones the others had taken, along with a battery of anti-radiation compounds.

The expert systems had flagged a number of the screens. Ravindra opened the windows for them in her lenses. *There!* The corvette was hiding amongst long, sharp, teeth-like protrusions of hard rock, each one about the size of an apartment block. The induction effect had long since removed the more metallic rock from around them. The

Song told Ravindra that Jenny was secured in her couch. She used the manoeuvre engines to tip the *Song* forty-five degrees on its horizontal axis and then bank hard from a nearly standing start.

The corvette shot out of its hiding place, burning hard to block the *Song*'s attempt to reach the cave mouth. The *Omerta* started rising from the pickup point, again towards the mouth of the cave. The dark space was bathed in red light from a multitude of lasers fired by both vessels. The corvette and the Anaconda launched a spread of rockets, a tactic as much about denying area as actually trying to hit the *Song*.

Ravindra slaved the pulse and beam laser batteries to the targeting system and the optics, effectively turning them into space's most ineffective automated point defence system. The batteries drew lines of red light from the *Song* to the missiles-come-rockets as Ravindra triggered a hard burn towards the cavern mouth among the silent blossoming explosions from the missiles' warheads. The *Song* shed ablative and reflective chaff and clouds of particulate matter in a bid to refract the incoming laser fire from the *Omerta* and the corvette. They tried to leave a clear path for Ravindra to fire the military laser again and again at the corvette. The laser scored a black line down the other craft's ablative armour, beating the corvette's weakened shield, but the corvette pilot was good. A series of chaotic, counterintuitive manoeuvres resulted in Ravindra missing the corvette more than she was hitting.

Orla rained missiles on the *Omerta*. Their contrails lit the cavern up, many of them dying in a hail of point defence fire. The missiles fired from the *Song* passed missiles fired from the *Omerta* rising in flight and then blossoming into submunitions. The *Omerta*'s point defences became strobic as they attempted to keep up with the incoming warheads fired by the *Song*. The few warheads that made it through exploded against the hull, and from this distance the damage they did to the heavily-armoured ship looked like exploding puffs of dust.

Ravindra was banking hard through violent light and exploding submunitions, racing for the mouth in a constantly renewing cloud of chaff and countermeasures. The *Song* was handling much better with Jenny compensating for the constant system degradation, but frankly Ravindra had other things to worry about. The *Omerta* launched a pair of Sidewinder fighters from its hangar bay. It would soon be over. They could have fought the corvette, or maybe the Anaconda, but not both – and definitely not with a fighter escort. The *Song* ran for the cavern mouth.

'Er, Rav?' Orla said nervously. Ravindra checked the time until the pulsar bathed the Cave in hard radiation. The corvette was on an intercept course. Ravindra could just about make it out through the wall of exploding warheads as their point defences intercepted incoming missiles. The corvette's own military laser was burning a hole through their countermeasures and working through their ablative armour. Ravindra memorised the corvette's trajectory.

'Rav!'

The light of the pulsar came again. Everything went white. Ravindra closed her eyes. Her sight was still bathed in red as warning icon after warning icon appeared on her lenses as system after system dropped out. Blind, she turned the *Song* over, changing trajectory away from the mouth. Then, with the aid of a hastily assembled navcomp simulation, she fired the military laser again and again, at where she knew the Corvette was supposed to be.

They made 'shade'. Ravindra could hear Jenny swearing constantly as she attempted to bring a number of systems back on line and compensate for those she couldn't fix. Ravindra cut the fusion torch, keeping momentum, just using the manoeuvring engines now – not even bothering to fire – as she made for the canyons of tooth-like, building-sized, jagged hard rock. The other ships would take a moment to find the *Song* again.

Ravindra caught a glimpse of a shadow in the pulsar's light, a ghost ship existing only in silhouette.

There was an art to a good ambush. Ziva came in from the light side of the Cave riding a sweep of the pulsar's beam, power plant juiced with anti-matter and every Watt of energy thrown at holding up the aft shields. The pulsar was shredding her anyway, but no one would be expecting her to come in like this because no one in their right mind ever would.

The Anaconda was heading across the cavern. The hangar doors to the converted cargo bay were open and the first pair of Sidewinders had already emerged. She was firing and launching ordnance at something Ziva couldn't see. There were at least two other ships out there somewhere but the *Dragon Queen* couldn't get any sort of fix on them before the pulsar's beam swept over the cave again and all her imaging processors shut down. By the time they powered up again, Ziva was coming in.

She had enough time for a momentary glimpse before it happened again. It was like watching the world through a slow strobe.

No matter. She wasn't here for Khanguire, not this time. She had three salvoes of drones in the air and a fourth ready to go when the *Omerta* finally saw her coming. Ziva lit her fusion torch and lit the drones at the same time, their plasma plumes offering some protection, at last, against the sweep of the pulsar beam. They burned hard for a second and then bloomed, each one becoming a cluster of thousands of submunitions, some real and tipped with anti-matter, many nothing more than a scatter of infra-red lamps and corner reflectors. Two decoy drones ran ahead of her with their signatures set to match her own, both jamming hard – for all the difference it would make with so much radiation already burning into the cavern. If she'd done it right, the very first impression the Anaconda would have was of three Fer-de-Lances bearing down on it from point-blank range amid a salvo of enough ordnance to vaporise a battlecruiser, while all the Anaconda's sensors and warheads would have to look straight into the pulsar beam with no plasma plume to screen them.

Then again, with the way the Jackson pulsar was buggering her own sensors, maybe they wouldn't see anything at all.

A slew of diagnostics came back from the drones. Hundreds of malfunctions. Sensor failures, comms failures, half of them were flying blind … no, nearly *all* of them were flying blind. It came down to manoeuvring by eye.

The first Sidewinders out of the fighter bays had already lit their torches and were powering deeper into the Cave. Ziva let them go. She had the *Dragon Queen*'s targeting servos slaved to her Fresnels and lined up on the next Sidewinder as it came out. Half a dozen rapid-fire pulse lasers opened up from the *Omerta* in point defence. At the same time it launched a dozen small drones that immediatcly fragmented into hundreds of micro-interceptors. Countermeasure dispensers threw out clouds of particulates, anti-laser aerosol and microscopic reflectors. For a moment, Ziva blinked at what was coming back at her, as the *Dragon Queen*'s targeting systems jumped from not having much to do straight to overload. There was simply no possible way to know exactly what the *Omerta* had just thrown back at her and how much of it would get through.

The pulsar beam swept across the Cave and her entire sensor suite went down again. Ziva swore loudly. The displays returned almost at once but the whole targeting system had reset. Fucking thoroughbred over-sensitive Fer-de-Lance design, that was. Ziva shuddered and whispered a quick prayer that the *Omerta* was having it just as bad. Even so, what should have been a delicate calculated tactical battle was turning into two blind men blasting at each other with sawn-off shotguns. *Christ!* Maybe turning backside on to ram the fucker with her fusion plume turned full blast wasn't such a bad idea.

The *Dragon Queen*'s own point defence pulse lasers were already on full-automatic, although it was a mystery how they knew where to shoot. Ziva took a gamble and kept the main lasers for herself, targeting them by eye on the next Sidewinder. The *Omerta* could throw up as much jamming and as many countermeasures as it liked: she'd still caught it with its pants down and it wasn't going to get away.

'Keep our eyes on the Anaconda and feed targeting solutions to the drones,' Ziva snapped to the *Dragon Queen*. Assuming there were any drones left whose comms hadn't failed.

A Sidewinder flared as a fist of coherent X-rays from the Fer-de-Lance punched through its shield and its thin skin of armour and ripped its insides to vapour. The Sidewinder exploded so close to the *Omerta* that it had to have hurt the Anaconda as well. The *Dragon Queen*'s canopy

238

darkened to protect her from the plasma flash. Through the chaos of thousands of submunitions flying at each other, Ziva steered the Fer-de-Lance's laser across to the hangar door where another Sidewinder was coming out. She caught one wingtip as it tried to dart behind the bulk of the *Omerta* and then lost sight of it. She couldn't tell whether she'd crippled it or whether it had escaped.

The two waves of blind, dumb drones and countermeasures came together in a crash of hard light and high-end radiation. Tiny anti-matter warheads smaller than pinheads detonated around one another, converting into a brilliant quantum flurry of exotic particles and energetic photons. The *Dragon Queen*'s canopy blackened while the ship threw up a hopelessly inaccurate simulated rendering of the colliding warhead swarms. For a few seconds, Ziva lost sight of the *Omerta*. The point defence pulse lasers started up as some of the *Omerta*'s return fire began to leak through, then stopped for a moment as the pulsar beam swept past. Ziva caught a glimpse of what might have been another Sidewinder bolting out of the *Omerta* and turned the *Dragon Queen*'s main laser on it, firing steadily until the power circuits started to overheat. Something flashed bright as a nova, enough to see even through the wall of fire erupting between them.

'Arm the next salvo.' The *Dragon Queen* crashed through the remnants of the *Omerta*'s return fire. Radiation was battering at her shields. Something exploded close by, an anti-hydrogen warhead set off by the pulse lasers just before it hit. Ziva felt the *Dragon Queen* shudder. She had shield warnings all over the place.

Change of tactic. This had turned into a case of getting up close, throwing as many rocks as hard and fast as you could and then getting out again, fast. Ziva could see the

239

Omerta now. There were half a dozen Sidewinders out and the Anaconda was manoeuvring. The hangar bay doors were a mangled mess and a great scar ran down half the Anaconda's length. She'd hurt it.

'Drones away. Target their engines.' Oh, what was the point? 'Just scatter the fuckers as soon as they're loose and point them in about the right direction if you can.' The Sidewinders already out would have to wait. Ziva blew another one to bits as it tried to escape. She'd lost both decoys now. Brilliant light flared around the back of the Anaconda as warheads randomly broke through the defensive fire of the *Omerta*'s pulse laser. Yes, she'd hurt it, but not enough. Another two seconds and she'd be right on top of it.

Warnings flashed. She was being lased now – hard, military grade X-rays with as much punch as her own. She put the *Dragon Queen* into a corkscrew roll to spread the damage as best she could and lit her own fusion torch. Christ, the *Omerta* was already burning through her shields and vaporising her ablative armour.

'Out! Fast! Strafe as we pass her!' She felt the acceleration crushing her back into the pilot couch and the needles biting her skin as the *Dragon Queen* pumped her with another dose of nanites and adrenaline to keep her alive while the engines ripped up to twelve gravities of acceleration. 'Particle. Canister,' she grunted. The *Dragon Queen* shot past the Anaconda, the two ships spraying laser fire and micro-missiles at each other. Another bright flash came from the Anaconda's stern, a last few lucky submunitions hitting home. The Fer-de-Lance sprayed the space between them with smoke and gamma-absorbent aerosols. The *Omerta* was doing the same; the ships passed only a few hundred yards apart and yet they could hardly see each other.

240

Ziva had open space in front of her and what amounted to a violently furious light cruiser behind her. 'Cut engines.' The sudden lack of acceleration felt as if it almost catapulted her out of the pilot couch. 'Turn and face!' The *Omerta* was still hitting her with laser fire and a deluge of jamming and the *Dragon Queen*'s targeting system was picking up missile launches, a hell of a lot of them. And there were still god-knows how many Sidewinders out there somewhere. 'Throw out a membrane, countermeasures across every spectrum and then find me a way out of here …'

The pulsar beam swept over the Cave. All the *Dragon Queen*'s systems crashed and then came back up. She spotted a Sidewinder out in the open, momentarily exposed. The *Dragon Queen* flipped sideways, lurching her in the couch. Ziva tracked it by eye and brought her main laser to bear. The Sidewinder vanished in fusion fire.

'Membrane! Now! Countermeasures!'

The *Omerta*'s lasers were all over her, flaying what was left of her shields. Damn thing was packing a punch far beyond its size. The *Dragon Queen* returned fire, lighting up the *Omerta*'s bows and raking its side and then the membrane went off and six tiny rockets shot out in a spiral, throwing an opaque, micron-thick, semi-rigid screen between the two ships. The space behind it filled up with the *Dragon Queen*'s countermeasures: aerosols, gamma-absorbing smoke and corner reflectors with a smattering of microscopic nuggets of metallic anti-hydrogen. None of which would stop the *Omerta*'s lasers for a second but that wasn't the point – what the *Omerta* couldn't see, she couldn't shoot and Ziva had already put the *Dragon Queen* into a random erratic corkscrew, the best manoeuvre pattern she knew to throw off a targeting system. She dropped another pair of decoys. Next thing was finding a way out, a place to hide. Then damage assessment and then …

The *Song of Stone* was right there, barely half a click away, duking it out with what looked like a Federation corvette. In the chaos of ten thousand other targets flying about the place, she'd lost the *Song*'s track and forgotten about it. *Forgotten*, for fuck's sake. Khanguire had her cold. That was how you got killed. Just as well the *Song* had that corvette to keep her busy …

The same corvette that had followed her from Whit's Station? It seemed a good bet. Ziva's finger flicked the safety-cap from over the energy bomb release. Right here, in the state she was in, in a confined space like this with no way obvious exit, she'd blow herself to pieces too. They'd all go down together.

The *Dragon Queen* started setting targeting solutions and hit the *Song* with a hard narrow-beam scan. The missiles already primed to go after the *Omerta* switched targets and turned active and locked up on the cutter. Not that it was going to help. If the *Song of Stone* decided to ignore the corvette and opened up on her with a full salvo right now, the best thing Ziva could do was eject …

No. She had the *Dragon Queen* drop weapons lock. Whatever the hell Khanguire was doing, she could keep on doing it for now. The Anaconda was already more than she could handle and Khanguire looked to be conveniently busy.

The Anaconda's lasers were shredding her membrane. Any moment now and the first missiles would punch through and start hunting for her. Or flying randomly and blind, whatever the case was. She flipped the safety back over the E-bomb release and guided the *Dragon Queen* towards the nearest tunnel out of the cavern. As the membrane finally failed and the *Omerta* picked her up and its missiles turned to give chase, Ziva kicked in the Fer-de-Lance's fusion torch and bolted.

Like a rabbit running for its hole. The thought pissed her off, but that was the way it was. The *Omerta* should have been dead but only a tiny fraction of her drones had actually functioned properly and only a tiny fraction of *them* had actually hit.

They'd had a word for this sort of thing back in the twenty-first century. Clusterfuck. That was it.

The canyons of tooth-like rock protruding from the cavern wall were at a roughly ninety-degree angle to the mouth of Jackson's Hole. Ravindra was aware of a battle being fought above her but didn't have much time to pay a great deal of attention to it. It looked like Eschel had taken the bait and now, for some reason, the *Dragon Queen* was taking on the *Omerta*. A Fer-de-Lance against an Anaconda converted to a light cruiser. That wasn't a fair fight either, but she wasn't going to complain.

The corvette had found the *Song of Stone* again. The corvette was right behind the cutter, which was bad. Unguided missiles were a waste of time amongst the canyons as they were banking and turning too quickly. This was good. Ravindra was still using just the existing momentum and the manoeuvring engines. She was triggering the fusion torch only incrementally whenever the manoeuvring engines caused the *Song* to lose inertia, for a sudden burst of speed, or to light up the corvette's world when it got too close. The *Omerta*, despite its Fer-de-Lance shaped troubles, was still finding the time to launch missile after missile at the *Song*. Bad. That blind strafing pass on the corvette must have done some damage, because the pilot was flying like he was angry. He wanted the *Song* too badly. Good.

Rock loomed up against the transparent hull at the front of the bridge. The *Song* veered hard left. More rock, slightly further away, then close again. She banked hard right as they veered in and out between the rock protrusions. The *Song*'s pulse lasers fired up again and again, taking out incoming missiles from the *Omerta*. The beam lasers were expensive, energy-hungry flashlights refracting against the chaff and countermeasures that were constantly being discharged from both vessels. Only the military lasers on both ships were punching through. Ravindra was concentrating on flying. She seconded control of the military laser to Orla who was hitting more than she missed. Jenny was running damage control. You couldn't dodge a laser – the secret was being where the laser hadn't been aimed. Inevitably, this meant a degree of erratic flying. And there was only so much counter-intuitive flying you could do when you didn't want to slam into a rock at velocity. The pilot in the corvette had definitely been gene-altered, Ravindra decided.

The missile fire stopped. Ravindra spent a moment checking the windows showing feed from the upwards-pointing lenses. The *Omerta* had disappeared.

'Incoming! Eleven o'clock!' Orla shouted. There was a series of staggered explosions amongst the rock teeth, submunitions warheads detonating in quick succession as someone tried to walk missiles in on their position. Ravindra slaved the beam laser to point defence along with the pulse. She rolled the *Song*, and the laser batteries reached out to touch the incoming spread of submunitions. Multiple waves of force from the explosions battered the *Song*. Orla fired a spread of missiles along the incoming trajectory, the submunitions programmed for a wide spread. She was using the missiles like a shotgun and was rewarded with an explosion. Ravindra wasn't even sure who had shot at them and what Orla had just killed. She had a moment to register debris raining down into the teeth and then she had passed it.

'What was that?' Ravindra asked.

'Sidewinder,' Orla answered. 'There's two more left. That I can see.'

They must have come from the Omerta, Ravindra decided. They were playing cat and mouse now. All the corvette needed was a clear shot and some distance to use its energy bomb and it was all over, probably for the other ship as well. Ravindra wondered just how insane the corvette pilot was.

They started taking beam laser fire from above. The two wedge-shaped fighters were staying out of the canyons and just firing down on them. The fire was inaccurate but, like the misses from the corvette's military laser, each time the beam hit the cavern wall it caused a molten plume of superheated rock. It was like flying through a firework display. The *Song* had been hit more than once. The rock did more damage than a pulse laser and the countermeasures were no good whatsoever.

'I have the laser,' Ravindra said. She hit full burn on the manoeuvring engines, angling them down so the *Song* shot out of the canyons, firing as they rose. Orla fired a spread of missiles at the fighters coming in, skimming the tops of the rock teeth. Ravindra flipped the *Song* until they were upside down and travelling backwards over the teeth. The military laser was still firing. The beam and pulse laser batteries were targeting incoming missiles fired from the two Sidewinders, missiles that had just blossomed into submunitions. Ravindra triggered the fusion torch. About a mile of space lit up. It turned the top of one of the hard-rock teeth into so much molten slag and halted, then reversed the *Song*'s momentum. Now they were going in the opposite direction, though still upside down. The two Sidewinders realised what was happening too late. Both started a sharp bank. One of them made it. Ravindra's military laser fire lacerated the other one and then it all but flew into Orla's hail of missile-borne submunitions.

The corvette rose out of the canyons firing at the *Song*. Ravindra triggered a hard burn and banked back down into the canyons. Slower this time, still weaving in and out of the spires. It would take the corvette a moment to find and then catch up with the *Song*, but Ravindra kept the *Song's* speed down. She saw the mouth of the tunnel complex ahead. She used the manoeuvring engines to curve in on it so she could enter in a shallow arc that wouldn't take her above the points of the teeth.

The *Dragon Queen* rocketed through a twisting, winding tunnel. She had three Sidewinders on her tail – too many of the damn things for an Anaconda so maybe the corvette had brought a couple too – and more micro-missiles than she could count and the *Omerta* was also powering after her. None of them knew where they were going, all of them were flying half-blind, and they were already moving fast enough that the *Dragon Queen's* collision sensors were permanently screaming at her. Long spires of almost molten stone speared the tunnel, their surfaces glassy. Long ago, this would have been a vein, heavy in iron, running through the planetoid's heart. The currents induced by Jackson's overwhelming magnetic field had melted and vaporised parts of the Cave and made these tunnels; other parts of the planetoid were still molten under the skin, oozing and pulled into odd shapes by the tidal effects of the pulsar's gravity. Ziva flew around the spires, nipping to either side. The *Omerta* was too big for that. She blew the spires apart with her lasers, filling the tunnel with super-heated vapour, or else simply crashed through them, barging them aside

246

with her shields and her massive armoured nose. The stone didn't so much shatter as burst, its semi-liquid insides scattering in globules from under a thin hard crust. The Sidewinders stayed close to Ziva, nipping at her heels. Her defensive pulse lasers were firing almost constantly now, keeping them back and picking off any of the drones that got too close; and if the lasers weren't enough and a warhead looked like it might be about to get through, a brief burst of the main fusion drive soon put an end to that. Only trouble was that it meant she was going faster and faster and didn't have a clue where the tunnel was leading.

She dropped the *Dragon Queen* tight to the tunnel surface and powered through a narrowing too small for the *Omerta*. Three missiles chasing after her hit the tunnel wall, exploding in a cloud of debris and vapour and light. The Sidewinders followed, frantically shooting pieces of spinning debris as they curved away; and then behind them all came the *Omerta*. She fired a salvo of missiles into the tunnel wall, blowing great chunks out to make it wider and then smashed head-on through the debris, firing her lasers all the time.

The tunnel widened into a maze of columns bridging a narrow space between the roof and ceiling, while to either side the walls fell away. Ziva wove between them, darting this way and that, flipping sideways to use the main engines for each sudden change of direction, pulling the *Omerta's* missiles into detonating on the columns behind her. This deep inside the Cave she was starting to get her sensors back, even if they hazed with static every time the pulsar beam swept past. Pieces of debris tumbled across her path. She shot the columns as she wove between them, leaving an impossible maze for the Anaconda behind her, and turned her own fusion drive up to a full gravity, accelerating away. The *Omerta* lit its own engine too, blasting its way through her wake, vaporising pieces of half-molten stone as they tumbled across its path, ramming through the cavern columns with sheer brute force. She was taking a hammering though, more and more debris crashing into her shields.

Come on, come on! The more Ziva drove the Anaconda to keep up, the more damage it would take. A Fer-de-Lance was as nimble as the Sidewinders chasing after her. An Anaconda handled more in the manner of a brick.

The *Omerta* slowly fell back as Ziva guided the *Dragon Queen* into one of the winding tunnels at the far end of the cavern. She had no idea where it went, but she was starting to get an idea of how deep they must be from how badly her displays speckled with each sweep of the pulsar outsi—

Without warning *Dragon Queen* flipped over, pointing her back the way she'd come, and what felt like fifty gravities slammed into her back. The wail of the collision warnings turned to a howl. The needles came again. Ziva felt them as she lost consciousness for a moment and then was jolted back by the hard rush of noradrenaline injected straight into her heart. Safety warnings flashed everywhere and the Fer-de-Lance's engines were on maximum burn. She could see the three Sidewinders suddenly racing towards her. She wanted to shoot at them but she couldn't even think, never mind move.

The Sidewinders had turned back and were on full burn too, trying to stop, spraying plasma all over the remnants of her shields. It would have been the easiest thing, if she could have moved, to have shot them.

She passed out for a second time. When she came back, the acceleration was down to a bearable five gravities and one of the Sidewinders was behind her again.

'What the hell was—?'

248

An explosion a little further down the tunnel answered her question as the Sidewinder behind her, still decelerating furiously, hit the dead-end wall of the tunnel and disintegrated in a flare of plasma.

With the *Omerta* still coming, somewhere ahead of her now. They'd passed other tunnels, hadn't they?

Shit.

The first of the two surviving Sidewinders reminded her it was there by being stupid enough to shoot at her. She lit it up with the *Dragon Queen*'s main laser and it disintegrated. The second Sidewinder was already tearing back the way it had come. Ziva let it go. She wasn't in any great hurry to come nose to nose with the *Omerta*.

'Find me another way out,' she said. 'And give me a damage assessment on the Anaconda.'

The *Dragon Queen* offered a sequence of blurry images taken as the two ships had passed one another. The aft quarter of the *Omerta* looked like it had taken multiple hits hard enough to burn through its armour and hurt whatever was underneath, hopefully the engines. The mouth of the hangar bay was a ruin and the ship's hull beneath had been split open. She must have hit one of the Sidewinders before it got out, or else a warhead had detonated inside, scoured the hangar and ripped the Anaconda right open. A deep wound – but they were tough bastards.

For a moment she almost passed out again. She'd no idea why. They weren't even accelerating. Just a shimmer and a roaring in her head. Then she looked at what the *Dragon Queen* had pumped into her to keep her alive and conscious through that last deceleration.

'You can't keep doing that, you know,' she whispered.

* * *

249

Twelve gravity turn in a tight cavern. Before Jenny had passed out, she'd told Ravindra that they were about to run out of countermeasures. Thirteen gravity turn in a tight, induction-formed rock tunnel. Before Orla had passed out, she had slaved all the weapons systems to Ravindra. The beam and pulse lasers were just point defence weapons now. The missiles fired on her voice command. Between the rear of her ship and the front of the corvette was an ongoing storm of explosions as each ship fired and their point defences subsequently destroyed the missiles from the other ship, but only one needed to get through to cause real damage. Each explosion triggered sprays of molten rock and iron ore. The military lasers punched through the explosive storm, time and time again, though Ravindra could see that their laser was close to over-heating. The corvette was getting the worst of it. They were moving at speeds that had it flying through the ongoing explosions and molten sprays, but it was more heavily armoured than the *Song* and it just kept emerging out of the violence, spinning to spread out the damage. Meanwhile, its military laser was cutting up the rear of the *Song*. The tunnels were so tight that the only real evasive manoeuvre Ravindra had was to spin her ship also. Ravindra was pretty sure that the remaining Sidewinder was behind the corvette, which at least meant that it couldn't fire on her. The main advantage she had was that she'd had time to map the area.

The walls of the tunnel fell away and they were in a wide but low cavern interspersed with floor-to-ceiling columns of rock. The Sidewinder spun out from behind the cutter and launched missiles and started firing its beam laser. Without any more countermeasures, even the beam laser would start to do significant damage. More missiles meant more work for the already close-to-overheating pulse and beam laser batteries. They were nearly overwhelmed.

A right-hand gentle bank took them out across the flat cavern floor. Light shone through holes in the cavern like moonlight through gaps in thick tree canopy, playing across the stone as the planetoid slowly tumbled. The *Song* was so close to the cavern floor that Ravindra felt like she was piloting a ground-effect vehicle.

Here the size of the Sidewinder worked in the fighter's favour. A burn from its fusion torch lit up the cavern. It could almost fit sideways between the floor and the ceiling as it banked hard one way and then the other, weaving in and out between the columns. The corvette was acting as point defence support for the smaller craft as the Sidewinder closed, taking out the missiles that the *Song* fired from its rapidly diminishing supply.

Waves of force from multiple warhead explosions buffeted the *Song*. Ravindra's heart lurched when she felt her control of the ship drop out for a moment. Then an impact. It took her a moment to realise that she had scraped the roof. She instructed the *Song* to inject the battered bodies of Orla and Jenny with yet another stim. She hoped they didn't have a heart attack before they had time to die in the dogfight.

'Wha—?' Jenny asked. 'Did you crash the ship?'

Ravindra fed data from their earlier mapping expedition to the autopilot and the navcomp. She told the *Song* her plan. The *Song* objected in the most strenuous way a complex expert system had, short of shutting down. Unguided warheads exploded ahead of them. They flew through a shower of molten metal and rock. Ravindra ignored the new warning icons that appeared in her vision. That was all Jenny's problem now.

'What the fuck?!' Orla had a moment to scream. Perhaps it had been cruel to wake them just then.

The fusion torch, at full burn, was close to two miles long. Too late, the Sidewinder pilot realised what was happening and started to veer out of the way. The fusion torch just clipped the edge of the fighter. It was enough to turn it into a spinning pile of debris flying through the cavern, ricocheting off floor, ceiling and columns. The corvette banked as hard as it could in the tight cavern, as stone was turned to liquid in the torch's wake. The pilot must have thought that the *Song* had just committed suicide.

It wasn't as simple as just turning all the manoeuvring engines forward and burning hard to stop their inertia. The surroundings were too tight and they were moving too fast even for Simpson Town genes to pilot through the columns. Ravindra had slaved a glitching autopilot to a glitching navcomp and provided it with the unreliable topographical model of the cavern they'd made during their earlier reconnaissance. The autopilot did its best to steer them one way and the other whilst at the same time trying to slow forwards momentum. It almost managed.

One of the nacelles just bumped one of the columns. The column and much of the nacelle ceased to exist. The *Song of Stone* bounced away from the stone in a flat spin.

Ziva drove the *Dragon Queen* hard back up the tunnel and then waited by the first exit while she sent a reconnaissance drone ahead. The drone died on her after a few seconds when the pulsar beam swept over the Cave but the glimpse she saw looked promising. More of a fissure than a tunnel, narrow but very deep; and a little light coming in a few miles away suggested an exit to the surface. More columns and pillars of stone bridged the fissure, glassy smooth where they'd once melted in the heat.

Close to the surface suited her better than it suited the *Omerta*. It was more seat-of-the-pants flying and the Fer-de-Lance was made to fly like a fighter.

The Anaconda, when it came, was moving slowly and at a slight angle. It drifted steadily, changing its attitude now and then, still blasting aside any obstacles in the tunnel. Ziva opened up with the *Dragon Queen*'s main laser as soon as she saw the *Omerta* nosing around the corner. She gave it a second of sustained fire, enough to scorch off its armoured nose, and then darted for the fissure before the *Omerta* could fire back. Sniping like this, maybe she could take the behemoth after all. On the off-chance it would make a difference, she left a scattering of contact mines drifting around the fissure entrance and powered away.

The Anaconda came slow and careful. It disappeared from view behind twists and turns until the fissure opened up and the Anaconda nosed out after her. The mines hadn't killed it. *Too obvious, Eschel. Anyone could have seen that coming.* The last Sidewinder flitted about her, keeping on the edges of visual contact while the *Omerta* moved steadily to a position between Ziva and the surface. The sensor disruption was bad again here. Even sheltered inside the cave, the pulses every twelve and a half seconds kept resetting half her systems. The Anaconda didn't seem to be in any hurry now. Both ships took pot-shots at each other. Ziva didn't dare get close: when it came to lasers, the *Omerta* out-gunned her three to one. The Anaconda seemed content to stay up near the surface even though that meant its shields and sensors got more of a hammering with every sweep of the magnetar's X-ray beam. Ziva, carefully out of sight, couldn't work out the shift in tactics. They were putting themselves at a disadvantage up there.

Something detaching from the *Omerta* and the small plume of a rocket flared towards her. It seemed odd. *Easily dodged*, she thought.

The Sidewinder turned away and his engine flared up to full thrust, the sort of acceleration that would practically kill its pilot.

And that was when Ziva understood what the *Omerta* had launched.

E-bomb.

G-force held her in place. The *Song of Stone*, her poor, battered, wounded ship, fed data direct to her lenses. Ravindra moved her fingers a tiny little bit. She triggered the remaining manoeuvring engines, one after the other, each burn slowing their spin a tiny bit. She expected to feel the *Song* impact into rock at any moment, but it never happened. She controlled the spin, but the *Song* was almost at a complete stop, all inertia gone, half her manoeuvring engine on the ship's port side destroyed. Ravindra had never much liked the seafaring terms adopted for space combat, but dead in the water was a good way of describing their position. The corvette was on the other side of the cavern. The corvette's pilot had them dead. Launching their E-bomb to finish off the *Song* was just a formality now.

'Jenny, it would be really nice to be able to manoeuvre soon,' Ravindra said.

'Don't fly the ship into rock then!' a terrified Jenny screamed at her.

'Please don't ever do that again,' Orla told Ravindra.

There's not going to be an again, Ravindra thought.

'And we're out of missiles.'

Then the corvette fired its E-bomb.

Ravindra did it again. The heat of the fusion torch

turned most of the metal and rock in the cavern wall directly behind them into liquid. This time Ravindra didn't bother with the glitching autopilot, though admittedly it was a much less complicated route, almost a straight burn, just a few nudges with the manoeuvring engines. Pretty much the same trajectory as the E-bomb, only in reverse.

The acceleration crushed her throat. She couldn't breathe. Not that she *needed* to breathe. The *Dragon Queen* was keeping her alive. The acceleration had everything redlining. They shot towards the *Omerta*. She could see what the Anaconda was doing – it was flushing her out. And the *Dragon Queen* couldn't get out of the blast area – too late for that – but maybe she could ride the blast wave, and that meant getting up speed.

There was a hole in the planetoid's crust past the *Omerta*.

Fire the lasers, she wanted to say, but she couldn't speak. Under so much acceleration the weight of her own jaw kept it firmly shut.

Not that there was any point.

The Anaconda's own lasers were finding her. Stripping away the last of her shields, starting to bite into her ablative armour again.

The *Dragon Queen* aimed itself for the hole out into space. Out towards the bright white light of Jackson's pulsar. No shields left. The beam, when it crossed the Cave again, would scramble everything; but she was screaming towards the *Omerta* and wasn't going to get that far. The last of the Fer-de-Lance's shields failed. The *Omerta*'s lasers flayed her hull. Ziva could see the metal turning to vapour, the outer wrap of ceramic foam armour ablating away.

For an instant the crippling acceleration stopped and the *Dragon Queen* flipped around. Ziva had a half-second. It was enough to thumb the safety cap off her own energy bomb and then she was staring back down into the fissure. The Anaconda was almost directly astern, the *Dragon Queen*'s fusion plume stretched out between them. At least the plume blocked those fucking lasers. The spark of the *Omerta*'s E-bomb was dead ahead of her now.

The bomb flashed. Blinding white. Ziva felt the engines kick in again, slamming into her back, trying to slow her down as her ship hurtled backwards towards the Anaconda and the hole in the cavern roof. The *Dragon Queen*'s canopy turned black but she could still see the light of the E-bomb as it went off. She tried to speak. How close was the *Omerta* now? Close. Must be.

She let her finger fall and dropped her own bomb.

It was a gamble. Ravindra was vaguely aware of Orla firing the lasers at the corvette. They couldn't trust a proximity detonation from the E-bomb, so that left impact or timed. Ravindra was aware of – rather than saw – the corvette's E-bomb flashing by. She knew she was going to be caught in the blast radius, but the crew of the corvette wouldn't expect her to fly into the explosion. The question was, how much distance could she put between it and the *Song*?

She saw the corvette turn and run as Orla hit it with shot after shot from the laser. She was aware that the planetoid was shaking. Light, energy and heat was leaking through from somewhere else. She didn't understand that – the corvette's E-bomb hadn't even detonated yet …

The cave filled with lightning. Energy connected matter. Everything turned to light and force. The *Song of Stone* was engulfed.

The *Dragon Queen* shot past the *Omerta* and out of the hole in the surface. It burst into the empty space between the

256

Cave and Jackson's pulsar, a long fusion tail streaming ahead of it. Alarms went off everywhere. They were out in the raw strength of the magnetar's field now, unshielded by the metal-rich planetoid. Containment failure warnings flew up. The magnetics of the power plant and the drives, holding back all that fusion-heated plasma, were being warped to breaking point from a million miles away.

The pulsar's beam swept across the *Dragon Queen* and everything went dead for an instant. The acceleration didn't stop and she was still alive. That was all she knew.

The planetoid surface below erupted. Two E-bombs. Two anti-matter charges as big as a man's fist. Through the *Dragon Queen*'s blacked-out canopy, through her closed eyes, the light still overloaded her Fresnels. For a moment she was blind. The radiation blast would kill her more slowly, not that it was any worse than the pulsar's beam. Without her ship's shields it *would* kill her. Was just going to take a little time that was all.

Abruptly the acceleration stopped. She was adrift in open space, still floating away from the Cave.

'The plasma containment is about to fail.' The *Dragon Queen* sounded almost apologetic. 'The core is shutting down.'

'No. Inject the anti-hydrogen.'

'Captain, the safety requirements for the use of …'

'Override the fucking protocols.' She was a mess. She'd probably pass out from sheer pain as soon as the *Dragon Queen* stopped flooding her system with endorphins and repair nanites. 'Inject the bloody anti-hydrogen. Keep the engines running until we get back into the Cave. Or until we explode.' There was a monstrous hole in the Cave now where the fissure had been. No sign of the *Omerta*. But the ship couldn't have survived that, not in a confined space. Nothing could have survived that. Nothing.

She felt acceleration kick in, much more gentle this time. Erratic. The eking out of a last few minutes of the power plant's life.

'Hey, En,' she whispered to nothing. 'I'm sorry.'

The pulsar's beam swept over her yet again, crashing all her displays. She turned her head to look at it, at the pale white light of it.

White light. Heaven?

Battered upwards, move fingers slightly, manoeuvring engines force the ship downwards. Buffeted downwards, do the opposite. Repeat. There was more room to manoeuvre now there was significantly less rock. Of course, that didn't really do justice to the fact that the force of the buffeting was threatening to tear apart a spacecraft whose hull was now mostly liquid with lightning playing over it. Nor that lightning was playing all across the controls in the bridge blowing one system after another. Another explosion shook the *Song* as the military laser died. Somehow the damage seemed reasonable to Ravindra. They had flown into an E-bomb. They had gotten off lightly.

They came out of the explosion pulling clouds of energised gases with them. They were in a glowing, flowing, molten cave, racing the explosion. Even if the navcomp had been working, their map wouldn't have helped them. The terrain was significantly changed now.

There was one way out. The corvette was taking it. Ravindra followed as the stone behind her was turned to gas.

No sensors. Life support was down. Optics were down. Ravindra was flying by sight alone. Damage control was down. The bridge was filling with smoke. Orla was screaming. The panel in front of Orla was on fire but her acceleration couch was holding her in place so she had to sit there and burn. What Ravindra had was engines – and *some* manoeuvrability.

She caught sight of the corvette and fired. Nothing happened. Then she remembered the military laser was gone. The corvette disappeared around a bend in the stone tunnel. Ravindra moved her fingers, she found the manoeuvring engine she wanted wasn't working and attempted to compensate. She scraped the ship off the wall.

Jenny somehow managed to get the bridge damage control to work. The extinguishers put out the fire currently cooking Orla's legs.

Ravindra saw the corvette again. Its still-working military laser started punching hole after hole in the *Song*'s armour. Ravindra triggered the beam laser. Nothing happened.

Orla slumped in her seat. Her couch was working enough to inject her with massive amounts of painkiller and sedative.

Hit after hit into the front of the *Song*. It was just a matter time now. The military laser would take them apart. Ravindra tried firing the pulse laser. A red light reached out to hit the back of the corvette just before it disappeared around another bend in the tunnel.

Ravindra smiled. She was in a ship with no sensors, limited handling and only a pulse laser. It reminded her of her old Cobra Mk. II.

'We've had it?' Jenny asked.

'Yes.' Ravindra manoeuvred around the bend. She saw the corvette's forward manoeuvring engines burn as the other ship tried to bleed off inertia, slowing down so it didn't lose the *Song*. They traded laser fire, their stocks of missiles and countermeasures exhausted.

There's no shame in this, Ravindra thought. They'd fought a good fight, won more than they should have. They were moments away from being spinning wreckage in the narrow, bending tunnel.

Except there was Dane's most important law. *Never give up.*

Ravindra started rolling the *Song* in the narrow confines of the twisting tunnel. Some of the laser fire from the corvette missed, and the rest of the hits were distributed across the ship. She hit the corvette time and time again with the underpowered pulse laser. Ahead, she knew that the tunnel split. One tunnel led to a cavern, smaller than Jackson's Hole, but it led out of the Cave. The other took you deeper into the tunnel complex. She would take that, hide, and see what they could do with the ship before they were found.

The corvette took the branch that led to the cavern and out of the Cave. Ahead of them there was light. Ravindra couldn't understand this. And then thousands of tonnes of molten rock and metal flowed into the tunnel that the corvette had taken, engulfing that ship. It flowed into the main tunnel. Ravindra pulled up hard. The *Song* shuddered as her belly just brushed the molten rock and then she took the other tunnel deeper into the Cave.

Ziva was staring at the pulsar, dazed by its eerie beauty, the arcs and coronas of light flickering in shapes and patterns defined by the crushing power of its gravity and magnetism and the brilliance of its beam, spinning with impossible speed, raking the distant stars and then coming back to murder her little by little. And then she was staring into darkness, the dim glow of molten orange stone. She must have passed out again. The *Dragon Queen* had given her that respite. Too little chance of survival. Yet here they were. In shelter again.

'System test,' she whispered. She wasn't going to like the answer.

'All primary systems functional,' answered the *Dragon Queen*. 'Life support is green. Hull integrity is amber. There is loss of pressure. The cockpit is sealed. Power is red. Emergency power is operational. Drives all green. Shields are red ...' The list went on but it didn't matter. It didn't matter if everything across the whole ship still worked if she had no power. They were running on batteries. Enough to keep the life support systems running for a month, that was mandatory, but not enough to run the magnetics she'd need to get the main drive back on line, not enough to jump. Barely enough to fire the X-ray lasers.

'K-cast?' she asked. 'Long-range comms?'

'Non-operational.'

Dead in the water. And fuck-all chance of anyone picking up her distress beacon, nestled up this close to a pulsar. 'How long have I got to live?' she asked.

'Unknown. There has been extensive radiation damage. Between two and three days. Reversible provided we reach a competent medical facility within forty hours.'

'And our chances of doing that?'

'Manual repair of the plasma containment chamber is required.'

Ziva tried not to laugh. 'Manual repair. On a Fer-de-Lance? You want me to get out there in a space suit and fix it?'

The *Dragon Queen* didn't answer.

The *Omerta* was gone. With it the Veil who'd shot Aisha and so casually torn her life to pieces. Maybe Khanguire was still out there, maybe not. Maybe the corvette had got her. The *Dragon Queen* had killed a Veil, though. So that was something. The biggest bounty there was.

261

Ziva shunted what power she had to the laser and slaved it to her Fresnels. She could always shunt it back out again if she needed it for something else. 'Did En leave a message when she called?' She wished she'd taken it now. One last goodbye.

'Yes.'

'Play it.'

The video was broken up beyond hope. The sound popped and crackled. 'I suppose you're busy like you always are.' En sounded horribly distant. 'Ay's going to be fine. I thought you'd want to know. They've got her in regeneration for a few days.' A pause. 'I love you, Ziv. But I think it's best if you stay away a while. Take care of yourself.'

The *Dragon Queen* was down to its last salvo of drones. She had them rotated into place and ran system tests. To her amazement they still worked.

She continued to drift.

'What state are we in?' Ravindra asked.

'I don't know,' Jenny said sarcastically. 'Because this,' she knocked on her control panel, 'is pretty much an inert piece of moulded composites, ceramics, hardened plastic and metal. That said, if I was forced to guess, I'd say the ship's fucked.'

Orla was still sedated.

'Yeah, that's pretty much what I thought. We've got power and drive and that's only because the Imperials keep things so heavily shielded.'

'Can we jump?' Jenny asked. 'Everything's all right if we can jump.'

'Yes, we can jump. What we can't do is navigate.'

Ravindra turned in her couch to look at Jenny.

'Those burns look bad.'

'They're not fun, but let's sort out Orla first.'

'Whatever happens, I'm glad we got you back.'

Jenny nodded, smiling.

'Why'd we fight?'

'I needed to distract them from going after Ji, and give him time to get away. I discussed it with Orla and she agreed. I'm sorry. I damned you.'

Jenny gave this some thought.

'None of us had any illusions.'

The *Song* risked a shade-side external hop across the surface of the Cave. The glowing cavern acted as a beacon. As they sank into the cavern they saw rock and iron flowing like liquid. The already-hot rock of the inductively-unstable planetoid prevented the cold vacuum from hardening the molten rock quickly. It was like sinking into the basin of a huge waterfall of lava. In places harder rock had cooled enough to solidify.

It was only then that Ravindra worked out what had happened. Someone had dropped two E-bombs. The first had melted everything. The second had created a blast wave that flushed the molten rock through the tunnel systems and caught the corvette. The *Song*, and its crew, had been very lucky.

Orla was still out cold.

The Fer-de-Lance was a point of darkness against the backdrop of glowing lava. She was drifting. Ravindra couldn't tell whether it was dead or not but it looked mostly intact. Ravindra triggered the manoeuvring engines and slowly moved towards the bounty hunter's ship. It looked like it had been through hell. Most of its armour had been stripped, and laser scars and other more extensive energy burning had blackened most of the ship's hull.

Ravindra dropped the unreliable crosshairs over the Fer-de-Lance. Her finger poised in the hologramatic control glove. A twitch would fire the pulse laser. She was impressed despite herself. Cutter versus corvette was a reasonably fair fight. Anaconda modified to light cruiser spec versus a Fer-de-Lance wasn't. She could make out light coming from the other ship's bridge. She moved the *Song* around until they were nose to nose. Less than ten feet apart. Closer than she had been to her son the last time she had seen him.

The *Song of Stone*. And there was Khanguire – close enough that Ziva could actually see her face and know it was her. The *Song* was maybe even more mangled than the *Dragon Queen*, but she'd survived. In the end that was probably all that mattered to Khanguire. She still had power too. *Lucky bitch.*

The adrenaline and the endorphins were wearing off. Everything ached. Ziva peered to look Khanguire in the eye. Her finger moved to the trigger for the *Dragon Queen*'s lasers. She had one shot left. By the looks of things, that might be enough.

The finger hovered there, waiting.

The bounty hunter was still alive on the *Dragon Queen*'s bridge. Eschel was looking at her, but Ravindra couldn't read her expression. She stared back. She could hear Jenny shift behind her, though the engineer said nothing.

The pulse laser twitched, its targeting system glitching, but from this range it really couldn't miss.

'I am never going back,' Ravindra said quietly to herself.

ACKNOWLEDGEMENTS

First of all, thanks to David Braben and Michael Brookes at Frontier who made this possible and to Marcus Gipps at Gollancz who had the vision and who edited this. Thanks also to Olivia Wood for her work rearranging our words into coherent sentences and everyone else who worked behind the scenes. Thanks also to David Braben (again) and Ian Bell for destroying literally weeks of our lives with the original Elite until we learned how to dock without a docking computer.

Steve Deas would like to thank Gavin 'What acknowledgements section?' Smith, who was managing perfectly well as an SF author without some fantasy writer showing up and throwing the laws of physics and occasional urban fantasy books at him. We learned a lot about how not to do collaborative writing and we're still talking. If anything is wrong with the magnetar physics, it's entirely Steve's fault. The Ziva half of this story was largely written to a soundtrack of Fragile off the album Promises by The Boxer Rebellion.

Thanks to you, the reader for getting this far. If you liked this book, please say so. Loudly and to lots of people.

Gavin would like to thank all of the above as well, so he's effectively copying Stephen's homework. He'd also like to thank the workingman's Ming the Merciless, Stephen Deas, for proving that physics gets in the way of science fiction (though I maintain that lasers are colourless in a vacuum), and repeatedly picking up the slack whilst I went off gallivanting around the world. I'd also like to thank Michaela Deas as well for their hospitality whilst working on Wanted.

I would not, however, like to thank the bastard who designed the little plastic lenses that you had to use to decipher the security code to gain access to the original game. In fact I'd like to sharpen one of those lenses and stab him with it. Without you I'd probably play a lot more computer games today!